T0247959

RUTHLESS

Also available by Anne Mette Hancock

The Kaldan and Schäfer Mysteries

The Collector
The Corpse Flower

RUTHLESS

A KALDAN AND SCHÄFER MYSTERY

ANNE METTE HANCOCK

NEW YORK

Copyright © 2023 by Anne Mette Hancock
By Arrangement with Nordin Agency APS, Copenhagen

Published in the United States by Crooked Lane Books, an imprint of The Quick Brown Fox & Company LLC.

Crooked Lane Books and its logo are trademarks of The Quick Brown Fox & Company LLC.

Library of Congress Catalog-in-Publication data available upon request.

ISBN (hardcover): 978-1-63910-489-5
ISBN (ebook): 978-1-63910-490-1

Cover design by Kara Klontz
Translation by Melissa Lucas

Printed in the United States.

www.crookedlanebooks.com

Crooked Lane Books
34 West 27th St., 10th Floor
New York, NY 10001

First Edition: October 2023

10 9 8 7 6 5 4 3 2 1

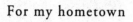

For my hometown

Let sleeping dogs lie.

SUNDAY JULY 14TH

Prologue

"I s this the first time you've seen a corpse dug up?"
Homicide investigator Erik Schäfer stuck a cigarette in his mouth and looked over at the crane.

The hoist creaked and screamed as the rusty red behemoth maneuvered a clay-caked coffin out of the hole in front of them.

Heloise Kaldan fanned a fly away from her face and nodded.

"It's no joke, I'll tell you that."

"It's limited what we can find here, though. Right?" Heloise said, turning her attention to the tombstone, a black-flecked marble block that the authorities had removed before they started digging. The stone lay face down on the yellow, sunbaked grass.

Schäfer tilted his head, nodding in a way that said both yes and no.

"That depends," he said. "For the most part, bodies in coffins are surprisingly well preserved."

Heloise gave him a skeptical look. "Even after so many years?"

He formed a hollow with a hand the size of a baseball glove and lit the cigarette. Smoke poured out of his mouth and nostrils as he spoke.

"Corpses that lie freely out in nature decompose quickly. They are reduced to bones in a matter of no time. Months, sometimes weeks, if the weather is like now."

Schäfer surveyed Flensburg Fjord. The sun's rays seethed on the surface of the water, and white sails stuck up everywhere.

He turned his attention back to the crane.

"In a coffin, you are kept in good condition for many years. Don't get me wrong: it's not a pretty sight, but you can safely assume that there's something resembling a human being inside that." He pointed his chin at the coffin which, at that very instant, was lifted out of the hole.

The salty fjord air and the smell of barbecue coals from the campsite down by the beach were suddenly mixed with deep notes of rot, and the smell made Heloise take a step away.

"Now what?" she asked.

"Now we have the coffin transported over to the forensic scientists and then they look at the contents."

There was a bump as the coffin was set down on the metal stretcher in front of the refrigerated transport.

"Is it going to Aabenraa or Sønderborg?" asked a uniformed officer standing with the driver.

"No, no," Schäfer said, waving an index finger at them. "Devil's Island, folks."

He walked up to the men, and Heloise could hear him explaining that the coffin was to be transported to Copenhagen. She watched him fish the warrant out of his back pocket and show it to the police officer.

She felt her phone vibrate. It was connected to a German cell-phone network because they were close to the border, and no number appeared on the screen.

"Hello?"

"Hello, am I speaking with Heloise Kaldan?" asked a soft-spoken, almost whispered voice.

"Yes, that's me."

"My name is Markus Senger, I work for the Vigil. I'm calling regarding Jan Fischhof."

Heloise's heart sank, and she let her head fall forward.

"Is he dead?" she asked, running her hand around her neck.

"No, but it won't be long now. He's in a lot of pain and constantly drifts in and out of consciousness, so . . . We think it's a matter of hours."

"But I talked with one of the caregivers last evening, and he seemed to be doing pretty well then."

"Yes, but he started feeling very bad late last night. He asked for you several times. That's why I'm calling."

Heloise nodded and looked over at the German coastline on the opposite side of the fjord.

"I'm not in Copenhagen right now, but I . . ." She looked at her watch. It was just over two hours until the next departing flight. "I can be there in the late afternoon."

"Thank you very much. Then we'll keep our fingers crossed that you arrive in time."

"Is there anyone with him now?"

"Yes, we have people at the house, but he doesn't want us to come into the bedroom. He only wants to see you."

"Okay," Heloise nodded. "Tell him I'm on my way."

"Thank you, I'll tell him."

"And Markus— was that your name?"

"Yes."

"Tell him . . ." Heloise looked up into the cloudless nothingness above her, searching for the right words. "Tell him not to be afraid . . . and . . ." She swallowed a few times. "Tell him to wait for me."

Heloise finished the call and met Schäfer's gaze. He had appeared at her side and was looking at her with furrowed brows.

"Fischhof?" he asked.

She nodded and put the phone away.

"I have to go home. They expect him to die sometime today."

Schäfer took a long pull on his cigarette as he watched her.

"All right," he nodded, peeling a shred of tobacco from his lower lip. "But don't let it take up too much space, okay?"

"What do you mean?"

"Just remember, we're not talking about a family member here. He's not your father, so . . . maintain some perspective, Kaldan."

Heloise held his gaze for several seconds. "He's dying. Do you understand that? He's dying and he's all alone."

Schäfer nodded. "Yes, I know, but people are dying every single day. You can't hold everyone's hand."

Heloise shook her head. She was too tired to get worked up.

"I don't plan on holding everyone's hand. I'm talking about *one* person. One person I can be something for. Now. Today! Isn't that the whole idea of the Vigil?"

"Yes, and it's a very nice gesture," he said, nodding. "But you have to have the right mentality for it."

"Right. What's your point?"

Schäfer shrugged.

"You seem pretty affected by the whole situation."

Heloise's gaze drifted from Schäfer's black eye, over to the coffin, and back to Schäfer again.

"Of course I'm affected," she said. "I don't know if you've noticed, but it's been a pretty intense couple of days. Now Fischhof is about to die, and I promised him I would be there. I promised to free him of all this shit." She pointed to the coffin.

"Oh hell, Heloise . . ." Schäfer shook his head with an overbearing look. "You damn well know better than to . . ."

"I'm going home!" Heloise turned her back on him and started walking over toward the car. "I've made a promise."

Schäfer threw the cigarette away and stepped on it.

"You shouldn't have done that," he muttered.

WEDNESDAY JULY 10

Four days earlier

1

Heloise unlocked the door with the key she had been given by the Red Cross and stepped into the dim hallway. Since the first meeting three months ago, the time between her visits to the small half-timbered house in Dragør had become shorter, and today she stopped by for the third time in a single week.

She hung her shoulder bag on the hook in the hallway and went into the kitchen to announce her arrival to one of the night nurses she heard moving around.

"Hi Ruth," she said to the back of the small, compact lady who was wiping off the kitchen table. The woman's movements were pointed; she did not raise her gaze, but continued her work with her head hunched over. Her hair was short like a man's, and Heloise could see white streaks in the folds of her neck where the sun had found no way to reach in.

Heloise peered down the hall toward the bedroom, where the door was ajar.

"Is he asleep?"

"No, I don't think so," Ruth said. "I brought him out into the garden so he could get some fresh air." She gave the dishcloth a hard twist and laid it over the faucet. "It's so dark and sad in here, and he's been hanging his head all day, so I thought he needed to get out a little bit. But of course he's not too thrilled about it, the old grumbler. He acted like he'd been told his leg would be amputated."

Heloise smiled. She could just hear Jan Fischhof puffing himself up over something as harmless as a bit of sunshine.

She spotted the plate on the kitchen table, where a slice of meatloaf and a few potatoes from Meals on Wheels looked untouched.

"Didn't he want to eat anything today either?"

"Not a bite." Ruth wiped her hands on her apron. "I told him he couldn't have a beer unless he ate a little, but he couldn't be pushed or persuaded."

"But I guess he's got his beer now, hasn't he?"

"Has he eaten his food?" Ruth's face was expressionless as she pulled a piece of plastic wrap over the lunch plate.

"Aw, come on, Ruth," Heloise said, tilting her head. "If the man's dying wish is to have his last meal served in a bottle, shouldn't we grant it?"

Ruth pursed her lips tightly.

"Maybe that's the headline you're going for in your article? 'Death By Drink'?"

The words fell hard, and Heloise got the feeling that they had been lining up to get out. She raised her eyebrows and smiled in surprise.

"Do you have a problem with me being here, Ruth?"

"Yes, I do." Ruth turned and met Heloise's gaze with her forehead raised and her arms crossed. A deep blush spread up her thick neck. "An old man dying isn't supposed to be entertainment in a newspaper. This is serious, what's going on here."

"Yes, I'm well aware of that."

"It is the Vigil's job to show care and presence during the last, difficult time. We listen and comfort and do what we can to ease the great sadness of saying goodbye to life here on Earth."

"Yes, that's exactly what I'm here for." Heloise shook her head uncomprehendingly. "Don't you think Jan seems to enjoy my visits?"

Ruth hesitated for a moment before answering. "I think your presence is stretching out the agony."

Heloise wrinkled her brows.

"What do you mean?" she asked.

But Ruth didn't need to say more. Heloise already knew the answer. When she had first visited Jan Fischhof, the Hospice Vigil had said that he would die before the week's end. That was almost three months ago. Now they thought it was Heloise's visits that had made the difference; that Fischhof had been given something to live for, and it obligated Heloise in a way she had not experienced before. She felt like she had the man's life in her hands, though she knew that was a lot of nonsense. He would die no matter what. But she still couldn't bring herself to walk away from him.

"He's in a lot of pain, Heloise, and half the time he has no idea who he is or what planet he's on," Ruth said, referring to Fischhof's incipient dementia. "His brain is turning to mush, and his body . . . well, you know what he looks like!" She threw out her arms. "Why do you keep coming here? For the sake *of a newspaper article*?" She practically spat out the words. "Let him have peace now, Heloise. Do you understand? Let him have peace!"

Heloise put her hands on Ruth's shoulders so that they were facing each other.

"I get that you worry, but you should know that even though it started as a job for me, it's become something else. I'm no longer here just as a reporter. I'm here because I *want* to be here and because Jan and I, we . . . we have bonded with each other. Do you understand?"

Ruth regarded Heloise with silent skepticism.

"It's not about my job anymore," Heloise continued.

Ruth nodded grudgingly. "So you're not going to write about him after all?"

Heloise bit her lower lip for a moment as she selected her words.

"Not just now, in any case, and not in the way you are imagining. I promise."

The ripples around Ruth's mouth signaled that she accepted the statement. She gave Heloise a few conciliatory pats on the cheek with a moist hand. Then she put the lunch plate in the fridge and pulled off her apron with a swish.

"Well then . . . if you're going to sit with him for a bit, I think I'll go for today."

"Yes, you do that," Heloise nodded. "I'll take good care of him."

Ruth left the kitchen, and when Heloise heard the front door shut behind her in the hallway, she walked to the open patio door in the living room and looked out into the garden. She spotted Jan Fischhof sitting in his wheelchair under a large, chartreuse parasol. The poison-green fabric reflected on his face, making his complexion look even sicker than usual. His head was bald, his teeth large in the bony face, and there were no brows or lashes around his sunken eyes. The man was no more than sixty-seven years old, but in a short time the lung cancer had made him look like someone fast approaching ninety. He sat in his wheelchair with the oxygen tank at his side. His eyes were closed, his mouth open and limp, and his rough hands rested with palms facing up in his lap.

He looked like he was already dead, Heloise thought.

"Jan?" she called.

Jan Fischhof opened his eyes slightly, and his gaze drifted over her without focusing.

"Well, you *are* awake," she smiled.

He closed his eyes again.

With her hand, Heloise shielded her eyes from the sun as she walked toward him. It was searing hot for the third week in a row. The beaches across the entire East Coast had begun to stink of rotten seaweed, the fields were dry as cotton wool, and the prophets of doom, in keeping with tradition, heralded the end of the world.

Jan Fischhof also struggled with the high temperatures. His blood vessels swelled under his paper-thin skin, and his shirt was blotched with sweat on his collar and chest. The closer Heloise got to him, the louder the wracked, raspy breathing sounded.

"You look like you're hot," she said, crouching down in front of him. She put a hand on one of his legs and gave it a squeeze. "Don't you need something to drink?"

His eyelids slid open, and this time he looked more alert. He nodded slowly.

"Yeah, thanks," he nodded. "A beer would be nice."

Heloise smiled. "I'll be right back."

She got up and disappeared through the patio door. Inside the small house, it was cool and dim, and Heloise's gaze slid over the furniture in the living room. The room seemed to have been decorated by a woman. The large-flowered sofa was equipped with embroidered decorative pillows, and on the dusty bookcases stood crystal vases and porcelain figurines of polar bears and little girls with their hands folded in prayer. There was a bouquet of heather in a wavy Aalto vase on the desk at the back of the room. The flowers had long since lost their color, and Heloise wondered whether it was Fischhof's late wife, Alice, who had tied the bouquet a long time ago. Maybe that's why he hadn't had the heart to get rid of it?

Her gaze ran over the many framed family photos standing on the table next to the bouquet. Some of them were sepia colored and pointed far back in time; others looked more recent. Heloise lingered over one of them, a photo of Fischhof's wife and daughter that looked like it was taken by a provincial photographer. The girl, whose name Heloise could not remember, was wearing a caramel-colored suede jacket and a pair of stone-washed jeans, and the lenses of her tortoise-shell glasses' frames filled half her face. Alice stood at her daughter's side in a bright, screaming-green shirt from Marc O'Polo with huge shoulder pads and was one big jumble of permed curls. The look could hardly be more dated, Heloise thought with a smile, and walked on into the kitchen.

She opened the refrigerator, where the middle shelf was filled with medicine bottles of various sizes and colors. Meds that all aimed to postpone the inevitable by days, hours—minutes. Fischhof had stopped taking his pills three weeks ago. All life-prolonging measures were accompanied by a sea of side effects, and he had now reached the point where he turned down anything other than a cold beer.

Heloise grabbed a Carlsberg from the shelf in the refrigerator door and went back out into the garden. She set the bottle on the table in front of Fischhof and sat down in the wicker chair next to him.

He grimaced nervously, but otherwise didn't react.

"Jan, it's me." She drummed her fingers on the table to get his attention. "Heloise."

"Heloise," he repeated softly. He began to nod, slowly at first, then with increased speed, and the rubber hose from the oxygen apparatus bobbed in and out of his large nostrils.

He turned his head and focused on her.

"Heloise?" he said in amazement, as if it had been a long time since they had last seen each other.

She smiled at him and nodded. "How are you today?"

The old man's face contracted. "Thoughts, thoughts," he muttered, waving her question away.

Heloise put an elbow on the tabletop and propped her chin in the palm of her hand as she watched him.

"What are you thinking about?" she asked.

"This and that and death. This and that and death," he repeated, as if it were a stanza from an old nursery rhyme he had just remembered. He continued to hum the syllables. The prominent jaws kept time with a clacking sound.

Heloise pushed the bottle closer to him.

"Here, have something to drink! It's hot today and it's important to stay hydrated."

Jan Fischhof reached out for the beer, put a finger in the bottle neck and quickly flicked it back up again, causing a wet plop. He put the bottle to his mouth and took a sip.

Heloise leaned back in her seat so that the braided backrest creaked, and looked around. On the other side of the white picket fence that surrounded the garden was Von Ostens Gade, a winding little cobblestoned street where lupins and peonies grew alongside the old thatched houses. At the end of the road, she could see Øresund Strait, the sound lying between Denmark and Sweden. The old quarter of Dragør was so idyllic that it almost seemed like a caricature, and for many of its inhabitants, the neighborhood was the center of the world.

For Jan Fischhof, it was even more than that. It was the place he had chosen to die in.

"Ruth told me you feel down today," Heloise said, watching him with gentle eyes. "Is there anything you want? Something that can help your mood?"

He lowered his gaze, lifted the bottle again, and hesitated for a moment as it hit his pursed lips. Then he shook his head and took another sip.

"How about if we play cards? Your doctor says it's good to exercise your brain." She put her hands on the armrest, intending to go and get the cards.

Jan looked down toward the strait. He was silent for a moment.

"I once knew a girl who lived over on the other side of the water," he said. "Claudia was her name."

Heloise smiled and settled back down. "Were you sweet on a Swede?"

"No, I told you, she was from Glücksburg. She was a German!" He pointed down toward the water. "She worked over here one summer until something . . . yes, it was probably a summer party of some kind they'd arranged for us when I worked at Benniksgaard."

"But we are in Dragør now, Jan. And on the other side of the water is Sweden. Not Germany."

The old man narrowed his eyes and focused on Heloise as if he were about to lash out at her. Then a cloud slid across his face and his gaze dropped.

He nodded slowly. "Oh, yes. That's right. Sweden."

"Yes, I know that you were born and raised in southern Jutland, but you live in Dragør now and have for many years."

Heloise could see that he was on the verge of diving down into the dementia swamp again.

"Can you tell me a little about Rinkenæs?" she asked in order to get him to stay afloat. "When did you move away, you and Alice?"

Something indefinable flickered across Jan Fischhof's face, and he met Heloise's gaze.

"What about your daughter?" she asked. "What's her name again?"

With a force that caught Heloise by surprise, Jan Fischhof reached across the table and grabbed one of her wrists. His eyes were suddenly wide with fear.

"Do you believe in God?" he whispered.

"God," Heloise repeated in a calm tone of voice. She carefully freed herself from his grip and tried to calm him down by stroking a thumb over the back of his veined hand. "That's a big question."

Heloise had gone to the Marble Church since she was a child, and it had always been her special place, her refuge. She never attended regular services, but she visited the church several times a month, and her feet always found their way up the narrow spiral staircase that led up the tower. It was safe and familiar up there, and there were lots of existential questions pressing in when she was there.

But God?

"I guess I believe in something. There must be more between heaven and earth. A meaning to it all," she said, shrugging. "What about you? Do you believe in God?"

The old man lifted his chin and took a deep, painful breath. He squeezed his eyes tightly together, but no answer came.

"I think we'll end up somewhere when our time here is up," Heloise said. "Call it heaven, or whatever you want, and I think that . . ."

"What about . . . hell?"

Heloise tilted her head and smiled affectionately at him.

"You don't have to worry about that, Jan. You can be a grumpy old fart sometimes, but you're all right. When you knock on the gates up there, they'll let you in."

"But they say that you . . ." His voice dropped, and the skin around his eyes contracted as pain gnawed through his body, ". . . that you'll be held accountable."

The face of Heloise's father materialized before her mind's eye and an uneasiness began to quiver in her chest.

"Are you worried about that?" she asked, instinctively pulling away from Fischhof without letting go of his hand.

He nodded, looking like a child who feared his father's wrath.

Heloise frowned. "Why? What do you think you have to answer for?"

The old man turned his face up to the sky and breathed in quick, shallow jerks. As he spoke, the words fell in guttural thrusts, as if they came from somewhere deep within him and hurt to say.

"Mads . . . Orek."

Heloise leaned forward in her chair to hear him better.

"Are you saying Mads Orek? Who is that?"

Jan Fischhof shook his head. "No, *Mads* Orek . . . *Mads* Orek."

His eyes widened, as if he saw something in his mind's eye that terrified him, and the lines on his face seemed to smooth out for a moment. He held up a warning index finger in front of Heloise.

"It is written in Deuteronomy 24:20."

Heloise shook her head. "I have no idea what that mea—"

"Eye for an eye, Heloise. Tooth for a tooth. The same injury he causes another must be added to himself."

The words crackled in the air between them.

"Jan, you have to explain to me what you . . ."

"The blood!" He held up a hand in front of his mouth and whispered through the cracks between his fingers. "So much blood, Heloise, and I . . . I can't . . ."

"What are you talking about? Where was there blood?"

"On my hands . . . On my clothes . . . Everywhere!" Tears welled up in his eyes. "I thought it was over, but . . . it goes on! You must do something, I . . . I can't trust the others. They're watching me, and I'm scared, Heloise. You have to help me. Will you please help me?"

"I'm right here, Jan," Heloise said. "Breathe calmly, then try to explain to me what you're afraid of."

"The gates you were talking about . . ." He pointed up to the sky. "Up there!"

A cloud drifted over the sun, and it felt like the temperature dropped a couple of degrees.

"I'm not sure they'll let me in."

CHAPTER

2

HELOISE PARKED IN front of Detective Sergeant Erik Schäfer's small red-brick house in Valby and walked up the overgrown garden path to the front door. She put a finger on the bell and waited for the sound of his steps in the hallway, but all she could hear was the engine ticking away under the hood of the car out on the street. She pressed the doorbell again and knocked on the door a few times. Then she frowned and looked at her phone.

She had sent a message twenty minutes ago asking if she could stop by, and Schäfer had answered succinctly with a single, thumbs-up emoji.

Heloise first made sure his car was in the carport. Then she started moving around the property, peering through every window of the house, before finally finding him in the backyard. He was sitting sunning himself in a garden chair made of sand-colored, woven plastic and wearing nothing but a pair of red swim shorts and a cap. His stomach was large and hairy, legs slightly spread apart.

He hadn't heard her coming, so Heloise cleared her throat to draw attention to herself.

Schäfer turned his head in the direction of the sound.

"Hey, Kaldan!" he said.

"Hi, sorry about sneaking up on you like this, but I guess the bell doesn't work." She pointed toward the street entrance. "I tried knocking, but . . ."

"No worries. Come on in!" Schäfer waved her over and pointed to one of the other chairs. "Have a seat!"

Heloise sat across from him and spotted a thin gold chain glinting around his neck. She had always thought he looked like the patriarch of a New Jersey Mafia family rather than a homicide investigator from the Copenhagen Police Department, and today he had turned up the volume on his inner Tony Soprano.

"Coffee?" Schäfer squinted and pointed to the pot on the garden table. "Or maybe you'd rather have a glass of white wine? We've probably got a bottle inside somewhere, but I'll be damned if I know whether it's on ice . . ."

"No thanks, I don't need anything." Heloise ran her eyes over his body and met his gaze with a suppressed smile.

Schäfer raised an eyebrow. "What?"

"Nothing."

"You've never seen a little pork before, is that it?" He slapped his stomach.

Heloise stuck her tongue in her cheek. "No, I . . . I'm just used to seeing you in your work clothes, and now all of a sudden you're sitting here in swimming trunks looking all gangster-like." She drew a square in the air around him with her finger. "We just need a stripper and a cigar to complete the picture."

Just then, Schäfer's wife came up the basement stairs with a laundry basket in her arms. Her hair was thick and curly, and she was dressed in a black nylon swimsuit that blended in with her dark skin. The cleft between her breasts was deep, and she had tied a pink scarf around her waist like a skirt.

Schäfer smiled contentedly at the sight of his wife. He turned his gaze to Heloise and raised an eyebrow.

"Did you say you have a cigar, too?"

Connie bared her white teeth with excitement when she caught sight of Heloise. She set the laundry basket down in the grass.

"Heloise!" she exclaimed in surprise. "Erik didn't tell me that you would come over today."

Connie's Danish vocabulary was close to complete, but the pronunciation was broken, and she "sang" exotically.

Heloise stood up and hugged her.

"It was just an impulse," she said. "I have a few things I need to talk to your husband about."

"Won't you stay for dinner? Erik has bought ribeye steaks and corn for the grill."

Heloise looked at Schäfer, who nodded in agreement.

"Aren't you going to work?" she asked. "Don't you usually have an evening shift on Wednesdays?"

He shook his head. "Not anymore."

"Well, in that case . . ." Heloise looked at her wristwatch. It was approaching six o'clock, and she had no other plans. "If it's not a bother?"

Connie let out a laugh as if that were the craziest thing she'd ever heard, and before Heloise could count to ten, she was holding a glass of Chardonnay in her hand, watching as Schäfer turned steaks on the grill. He had replaced his swim shorts with a pair of dark-blue jeans, a gray T-shirt, and an apron across his stomach that read FBI's MOST WANTED accompanied by nine photos of gruff-looking men and women. The picture in the upper-left-hand corner depicted Osama bin Laden.

"I think that's an old list, that one," Heloise said, tapping Schäfer in the stomach with an index finger.

"Yeah, this one?" He looked down at himself and stroked a hand over the apron. "I won it once at some employee Christmas bingo event at headquarters a hundred years ago. I assume they are all dead and gone now. The terrorists, that is. Not the employees."

"How's it going in there?" she asked, taking a sip of her wine. "At HQ?"

He twisted the corners of his mouth downward and shrugged.

"Fine, I guess. Augustine has moved over to a new task force dealing with gang-related matters," he said, referring to his former partner. "So I don't see much of her, but otherwise everything is more or less business as usual."

"And what about the cases? Do you have anything special going on at the moment?"

"What constitutes 'special' these days?" Schäfer met Heloise's gaze. "The boundaries of what is twisted sure have shifted a lot in recent years. But, no, it's actually weirdly quiet in the homicide department right now."

"Well, that's a good thing, right? Fewer cases, fewer killings?"

"Sure, that's one way of looking at it, but I have this unsettling calm-before-the-storm feeling. Hell, it's always when you think the statistics look oh-so-nice that something sinister crawls out of the shadows." He turned down the heat on the gas grill a bit.

Connie came out onto the patio and began to set up at the table.

"What's the ETA on those steaks, baby?" she asked.

"Heloise prefers her meat cremated, so it just needs a few more minutes, but our ribs are done," he said, and handed her a dish of the tinfoil-packed steaks.

He took the corn on the cob off the grill and left the last ribeye, pressing it with the tongs so that it sizzled and sputtered on the hot grating. Then he turned his gaze to Heloise.

"By the way, what was it you wanted to talk to me about?"

"It's probably nothing," she said, swirling the wine around in her glass. "But I . . . how did you phrase it? I also have a feeling that something sinister is about to crawl out of the shadows."

3

"How's Jan Fischhof doing?" asked Connie, pushing the salad bowl over to Heloise. "You're still visiting him, right?"

Connie had a sixth sense for this kind of thing, Heloise thought. It was almost as if she instinctively sensed that this was why Heloise had come. Or perhaps she had just been with Schäfer for so many years that his ability to read people had rubbed off on her.

"Yes, I still visit him," Heloise said. "But I'm honestly starting to regret that I involved the newspaper in it."

"Oh? Why is that?"

"I just really don't want to write about him after all. It feels too private."

"Well, I'm sorry to hear that." A vertical wrinkle appeared between Connie's eyebrows, and she sounded disappointed. "Then I shouldn't have encouraged you to . . ."

"No, that was a good idea Connie. It's still a good idea to write about the Vigil. People ought to know more about what it is. But I just can't write about Jan. I simply don't want to."

"Who are we talking about?" asked Schäfer.

"Jan Fischhof," Connie said.

"Who?"

"This guy!" Heloise took her cell phone out of her pocket. She pulled out a selfie that she and Jan had taken together the week before and held the phone up in front of Schäfer.

"He's the one Connie hooked me up with," she said.

Schäfer glanced at the picture and nodded aloofly.

"It's important to remember to keep these kinds of relationships at arm's length," he said, driving the steak knife through the meat on the plate in front of him. "I always tell Connie that too."

"Get close, but not too close," Connie nodded.

For the past twelve years, she had worked as a volunteer at the Vigil. She had held the hands of more dying people than she could count, and she was the one who had told Heloise that more and more Danes were leaving this world totally alone—without family around, without a single friend. She had encouraged Heloise to join as a volunteer with the purpose of writing about the experience and, in this way, create awareness about the Vigil.

If more people signed up, fewer would die alone.

Heloise poked at her steak. It was still too red for her taste, and the yellow-white fatty edge, which Schäfer shoveled into his mouth with great pleasure, led her to think of soap production and liposuction.

"Arm's length or not, I think it's incredible that you've been able to handle it for so many years," Heloise said, looking over at Connie. "You know, you get attached to those you watch over."

Connie shook her head. "You only have that perception because you and Jan have something special together. It takes two to tango."

"What do you mean?"

"A lot of the old folks are tight-lipped with me. You should see them when I first walk through the door." Connie widened her eyes so that the whites of her eyes shone in her face like car headlights. "Good God—a *Negro!*"

Schäfer shook his head. "There will always be someone who's out of educational reach, darling. You know that."

"Yes, but I'm still amazed every time. Because we are talking about people who are on the verge of dying. They are lonely and scared, and they need someone to sit by their side. But a black woman? No, that's where they draw the line. So I give them some time to get used to it, and most people end up appreciating that I'm there. Death disarms everyone— that's how it is. But we don't bond in that deep way you're talking about, Heloise. That, we do not."

Heloise put her silverware down hard.

"I'm sorry, but why the hell do you bother helping such assholes?"

Connie smiled slightly and shrugged. "Because . . . they can't help it."

Heloise leaned back in her chair, flabbergasted at Connie's indulgence.

"You're a better woman than I."

"Nonsense!"

"You are! I would let them die alone, those motherfuckers. Am I right?" Heloise turned her eyes on Schäfer.

"I don't disagree," he said.

"But Jan Fischhof is also a pretty challenging acquaintance," Connie said. "Still, you keep on visiting him, so maybe you're more broad-minded than you think."

"No, because Jan is not like the people you describe. He's a little reserved and defiant, and God knows not all the caretakers are equally fond of him, but when you get to know him, he's . . ."

"Yes, I know," Connie nodded. "He seems nice. I was one of the first to come visit him, and he was very polite, but he wouldn't talk to me. Not really, at least. It wasn't my skin color that bothered him, though. I'm sure of that."

"Then what was it?"

Connie shrugged and poured butter sauce over her corn cob.

"He just seemed so . . . what is the word? Measured. Guarded! As if he was afraid to let anyone in. I think it was very difficult for him when his wife died, and since then he hasn't really had anyone who . . ."

"What about his daughter, do you know anything about her?" asked Heloise, and continued, "he lost it today when I asked about her and started saying all sorts of strange things. He seemed scared."

"In what way?"

"He said a lot of incoherent things about biblical sanctions and blood and other spooky stuff."

"Blood?" Schäfer pricked up his ears.

"Yes, it was actually kinda scary," Heloise said. She told them what Fischhof had said, and by the time she had finished, the plates on the table were empty. Only Heloise's steak lay there, uneaten.

"Was he talking about a crime, do you think?" It was Schäfer who asked. He fished a cigarette out of the breast pocket of his T-shirt.

"I don't know," said Heloise. "But he has certainly been involved in something that he's afraid of being punished for. He referred to lines from Leviticus. The ones that are about . . . well, what are they really about? Karma? What goes around, comes around—that kinda thing?"

"An eye for an eye," Connie nodded, topping up the wine in Heloise's glass. "The punishment for a crime has to match the crime, but that's an Old Testament thing. Remind him that there is an updated version where you are told to turn the other cheek."

Schäfer lit the cigarette and leaned back in his chair as he listened.

"His breakdown seemed to come out of the blue, but I think it was because I mentioned his daughter," Heloise said. "We've never really talked about her, and the times I've tried to ask about her, he's just kinda slid off the subject. But today I hit a nerve. The cup simply overflowed."

"I do remember the daughter," Connie nodded, staring into midair as she tried to recall the details. "I met her briefly when I was out there the first time, and I believe she lives in Stockholm or something like that. That's why no one visits him besides us and why she contacted the Vigil so Jan wouldn't be alone at the end. She's married to a Swede and has one of those ABBA names, as far as I remember."

"Agneta?" asked Heloise. "Or Anni-Frid?"

"No, I'm talking about the last name. Her married name is the same as one of the ones from ABBA. Something with a *U*?"

"Ulvaeus," Schäfer said. "Björn Ulvaeus."

"Yes, exactly." Connie pointed at him. "Ulvaeus!"

"And you don't remember her first name?" asked Heloise.

"Isn't it in the papers you received from the Vigil?"

Heloise shook her head.

"Well, I can try asking some of the other caretakers if they know," offered Connie.

"Yes, please. I would appreciate that very much," said Heloise, turning her gaze to Schäfer. "I can't talk you into doing me a favor, too, can I?"

He lifted his chin, already on guard. "What?"

"The name Fischhof mentioned: Mads Orek. Can you do a search on it?"

Schäfer took a drag on his cigarette. He watched Heloise as he slowly blew out the smoke.

"Well, now, you said yourself that he's demented, so chances are that these are just ramblings. You understand that, right?"

"I'm also just asking you to do a quick search. Just to see if anything shows up on the radar. For his peace of mind."

"*His* peace of mind, or yours?"

Heloise nodded.

"Mine too. After what happened with my father back in his day . . ." She gave Schäfer a long look. "If I'm going to be the one who's there until the end, I need to know that I'm holding the hand of a decent person. Right now, an uncertainty that I can't shake has crept in, and you know how I feel about surprises. I need to find out what skeletons he has in his closet."

Schäfer pursed his lips and nodded.

"I know that you prefer full disclosure, and I get that." he said. "But I can't just go into the system and look someone up when I don't have an investigative cause for taking an interest in them. Or, well, I *could*, but I'm not allowed to."

"Why not?"

"Because those are the rules. Otherwise, people would constantly go in and search for their neighbors and their ex-wife's new boyfriend and things like that. It's an invasion of privacy, and it's *verboten*."

Heloise cocked her head and raised an eyebrow. "Are you telling me you've never bent those kinds of rules?"

"In the past, sure. But back then people weren't so anal about that kind of thing. When you do a search today, you leave an electronic trail, and if someone comes along and asks questions about what you're doing and you can't come up with a good explanation, you risk disciplinary action."

"But just how likely is it that someone would ask about that?"

Schäfer did not respond. Instead, he rubbed a flat hand over his stubble, making a loud scratching noise.

He and Heloise stared at each other as if trying to challenge the other to blink first.

Heloise capitulated and leaned back in her chair.

"Come on, Schäfer. For the sake of old friendship?"

"Whose friendship?" he asked dryly, snuffing the cigarette on his plate. "Yours and that old grumpy guy's? Or yours and mine?"

Heloise smiled. "What's the difference?"

THURSDAY JULY 11

CHAPTER

4

SCHÄFER FOLLOWED THE helicopter with his eyes as he drove. It was an AS 550 Fennec from the Copenhagen Police, and it was flying low over the residential area somewhere behind the rooftop billboards on the Sortedam Embankment. After a few peaceful months, the gang war had flared up again, and the night had offered three shooting deaths. There were no civilians among the victims—they were all criminal assholes, so it wasn't something Schäfer really got his pulse up over. But his former partner was on the task force investigating the cases, and he knew she was up there in the iron bird. He could just picture her: black battle suit over sinewy muscles with sweatbands around her hair, Rambo style. Lisa Fucking Augustine.

Schäfer smiled at the thought, and for a second there he almost missed her.

"Do we know who they're looking for?" he asked, nodding up at the sky. "Do they have a suspect?"

Homicide investigator Nils Petter Bertelsen, who was sitting in the passenger seat, raised his eyes and looked out through the windshield.

"Some drug dealer who killed off a few of the competitors at a pizzeria last night. A Dimitri . . . something or another." Bertelsen snapped his fingers as he tried to think of the last name. Then he turned his gaze to Schäfer and raised his eyebrows. "It's time for lunch, isn't it?"

Schäfer looked at the clock on the dashboard. "It's a quarter past ten."

"Yeah, but I was up at five thirty, and I'm starving. There's a kebab place down on Dronningens Tværgade, so if you drive that way, I can run in and pick up a few for us."

"I have a lunch scheduled with Michala Friis in an hour and a half, so I'll skip the kebabs," Schäfer said.

The appointment he was talking about had been on his calendar for a week and a half; a lunch appointment with profiling expert and former police psychologist Michala Friis. They had to go through the details of a murder case they were both called to testify in. He as an investigator in the case, she as an expert witness for the prosecution.

"Oh?" Bertelsen looked at Schäfer with his eyes half closed as he waggled his brows up and down. "I bet she's looking forward to it."

Schäfer wrinkled his forehead and looked at Nils Petter Bertelsen.

"What are you talking about?"

"The investigator's intuition, Schäfer." Bertelsen drummed his index finger on his nose. "Don't try to tell me you can't smell which way the wind is blowing."

Schäfer stopped at a red light and stared expressionlessly at Bertelsen until it changed to green and a black Tesla honked behind them.

He shook his head. "I don't get it."

"Shut up . . ." Bertelsen chuckled. "If you don't know what I'm talking about, then you've lost your touch, old man. For real."

"Old man, my ass!" snorted Schäfer. He stepped on the accelerator and turned left onto Dronningens Tværgade. "I'm not . . ."

"That's why Michala left the police. Didn't you know that? Have you never noticed that she—hey, slow down, it's right here!" Bertelsen pointed through the windshield. "Do you see the sign that says Bazaar? If you stop there, I'll run in and get some food."

Schäfer stopped at the curb and looked at the storefront. Bazaar was not a small, dingy kebab shop with a naked bulb in the the ceiling, as he had imagined, but a neat establishment with designer furniture, floor-to-ceiling windows, and room for just over a hundred people. Its door was wide open, but the lights in the restaurant were off, and Schäfer could see the bar stools upside down on the bar counter.

"It doesn't look like it's open yet," he said.

"It's not, but the chefs are already in full swing in there, and they usually take the trouble to make me a quick takeout. I'll be back in ten!"

Bertelsen jumped out of the car, slamming the door behind him.

Schäfer saw him walk into the restaurant, where he was greeted by a young, tattooed hipster type. They greeted each other as if they were old friends, then disappeared into the darkness together.

Schäfer turned on the radio and flipped back and forth between stations in search for something sensible to listen to, but there was nothing but teenage noise, gangster rap, and radio hosts laughing at their own jokes. He turned it off again and sat in silence, looking out at the traffic as he thought about what Bertelsen had said.

That he had lost his touch.

Schäfer didn't like that idea. If there was one thing he counted on it was his gut instinct. The investigator's intuition.

He pulled the note out from his inner pocket and smoothed it with his fingers. It was the pink Post-it note that Heloise had written the name on before she'd left the night before. He had crumpled it up the second she'd closed the door behind her, but had woken up from a feverish sleep at three AM and lain there listening to Connie's breathing in the darkness while thinking about Heloise, and Jan Fischhof's cryptic confessions.

By half past four he had gotten up and slipped down the stairs to the kitchen, where he had fished the note out of the trash.

Something about what Heloise had said had taken hold and was now gnawing at his thoughts.

Eye for an eye . . . Tooth for a tooth . . . What you send out will come back again.

What was it that Jan Fischhof had been trying to say?

Connie regularly brought home stories from her time at the Vigil: confessions from people who, on their deathbeds, needed to confess to everything from adultery to social security fraud. Mothers and fathers who had mourned lost time with children who, for one reason or another, had dropped them. People who, in the last hours of life, had told of abuse and atrocities they had not previously dared to share. Memories they needed to leave in this world before moving on to the next one.

He took out his cell phone and entered a name into the police's Social Security register with a stiff index finger.

CHAPTER

5

THE CELL PHONE rang somewhere under the piles of
paper. Heloise Kaldan's desk at the *Demokratisk Dagblad* was, as usual, littered with notebooks, clippings, and
court documents of various kinds.

She grabbed the phone before it stopped ringing. "Hello?"

"Y'ello!" Schäfer's voice crackled good-humoredly on the
other end of the line. "Do you have a moment?"

"Yes, if it's very short." Heloise moved the phone into her
other hand and continued writing the notes she was preparing. "I have an editorial meeting in three minutes."

"All right, I just wanted to say that I've researched that
name you gave me last night."

"You have?" Heloise stopped writing. "Thanks, Schäfer,
that's really sweet of . . ."

"Yeah, but I didn't find anything."

Heloise's shoulders slumped.

"But you mentioned that your friend was from Southern
Jutland," Schäfer continued, "so I called a guy named Peter
Zøllner, an old buddy of mine from the police academy. He
is an investigator and lives in Gråsten. Until the mid-nineties,
there was a large police station in the city, but it's shut down
now, and—well, I don't even think they have any police in
town anymore. The nearest duty officers are probably in
Sønderborg now, at least Zøllner is, so . . ."

"I only have a few minutes, Schäfer."

"Well, I asked if he knew someone named Mads Orek. You know, whether that's a name that has ever come across his desk in some way or another. And it had, he said, but the person he was thinking of was called Mázoreck. Not Mads Orek."

Schäfer spelled the name for Heloise, and she wrote it down on a slip of paper.

"It's German or Polish or something along those lines, so do you think you might have misunderstood Fischhof and that's why I haven't been able to find anything in the archives?"

"Maybe." Heloise chewed on her lower lip as she thought about what Schäfer had said. "So it's a surname, you say? Mázoreck—with stress on the first syllable?"

"Mázoreck, yes. Tom Mázoreck. He's from Rinkenæs."

"Okay, at least that's the right place. That's where Jan Fischhof was born and raised. What can you tell me about him?"

"Not a lot. I haven't dug very deep into the matter, but I see that he died in 1998 and that he . . ."

"So there is a case?" Heloise straightened up in her chair.

"No, it was an accident of some sort. It doesn't look like there's anything to go after."

"But who was he? Do you have anything on him?"

"Only an old criminal record. We're talking bar fights, unpaid parking tickets—small stuff. My buddy there says he wasn't someone they ever had in their sights for gross violations."

Heloise's fellow journalist, Mogens Bøttger, passed by her seat and tapped lightly on her desk. He pointed to the meeting room and signaled that she should finish her call.

"Schäfer, I gotta go, but that criminal record of his— could I see it?"

"No, you can't, and you already know that. But you can find the death certificate on the Danish National Archives website if you put on your little journalist's hat and take the trouble. You need to look for August 1, 1998."

Heloise couldn't stop smiling. She finished the call, grabbed her computer, and headed for the meeting room.

6

"**A**LL RIGHT!"
The editor of the investigative group, Mogens Bøttger, slapped his palms against each other and looked out over the assembly. The six journalists were seated around the big conference table. Bøttger was the only one in the room standing up. His dark hair looked freshly cut and styled, the suit clinging to his six-foot-tall yoga-trained body.

"You know the drill. The editor-in-chief would like an update on what we have in the pipeline. What is the status of Ibiza-gate, Bo?"

"I'll have a draft ready this afternoon," said journalist Bo Refslund, pointing to the computer in front of him. "I still need a comment from the bank, but they've had twenty-four hours to respond to my inquiry and I haven't heard anything yet, so I think we should run the story before they have more time to put up a smokescreen."

The story they were talking about involved the branch manager of Danske Bank in Holte, who had bought a vacation home in Ibiza with money whose source nobody seemed to know. In the wake of Denmark's biggest money-laundering scandal, more bad press and more dubious employees were the last thing Danske Bank needed.

"Sounds good! I'm ready to read it as soon as you have something," said Bøttger. He moved on to one of the other reporters, and Heloise zoned out of the conversation.

Opening her computer, she logged onto the National Archives website, and it took her no more than a few minutes to locate Tom Mázoreck's death certificate. She clicked on the link, and a scanned document from Danish archives unfolded on the screen.

Heloise's eyes swept across the page.

The death certificate issued by the coroner appeared at the top of the document. Mázoreck's name and Social Security number showed up in the right corner, and a column of standard questions ran down the left side. All answers were entered with a pen, the oblique writing intricate and blurred in patches.

Heloise squinted her eyes and tried to decipher the words.

Full name: Tom Mázoreck.
Manner of death: Consequence of misadventure.
Cause of death: Lack of oxygen by drowning.
Livor, rigor, putrefaction: No, no, no.
Place of death: Rinkenæs, 6300 Gråsten.
Date of death: August 1, 1998.

Mázoreck's date of birth was May 12, 1951, and at the time of his death he had an address in Rinkenæs, a small suburb of Gråsten that was located all the way down by Flensburg Fjord, about twelve miles from the German border. The death certificate did not say much more.

Heloise opened a new browser and wondered for a moment where she would be able to find more information about the accident. She logged into Infomedia, the database where most media news items are recorded over time: news, interviews, editorials, feature articles and notices from all the country's media—everything she wouldn't find in a regular Google search.

She typed Tom Mázoreck's name in the search box and hit Enter. Three results popped up, and she clicked on the first—a short notice from *Gråsten Weekly News* dated August 3, 1998.

Fatal accident on Flensburg Fjord

"On Wednesday evening, Flensburg Fjord claimed another victim when a Nimbus 3000 motorboat sank off Stranderød in Gråsten. *Gråsten Weekly News* spoke to restaurateur Kurt Linnet, 51, who witnessed the tragic accident.

'One minute I saw the boat coming around the point, and the next it turned into a pillar of flames. I called the police and they arrived quickly, but unfortunately it wasn't fast enough,' he said, pointing out across the fjord from his terrace where he stayed that fateful night.

The skipper, local resident Tom Mázoreck, 47, had to surrender to the waves just a few hundred yards from the shore. According to police investigations, a faulty engine caused the fire. Tom Mázoreck is the third drowning victim in Gråsten in just two years.

The family has been informed."

* * *

Heloise took a screenshot of the article and clicked on the next link from Infomedia. It was a note on passedaway.dk. An obituary that had been published in *Jydske Vestkysten* in the days after Mázoreck's death.

Our dear son and brother

Tom Mázoreck

* May 12, 1951   † August 1, 1998
taken from us far too soon.
In the heart hidden, but never forgotten.
On behalf of the family,
Renata and Kjeld.

Heloise noted the names of the relatives and then clicked on the third and final search result from Infomedia. It was an article from *Jydske Vestkysten* dated the year before the accident, June 4, 1997. At first, she didn't understand why it had appeared in the search, but then spotted Mázoreck's name some distance down in the text and started reading.

Missing Gråsten Girl Sought Internationally

"South Jutland and Southern Jutland Police have sent out a call via Interpol for 19-year-old Mia Sark, who has been missing since Saturday. This is based on testimony leading the investigation in a southern direction.

The young woman was last seen on Friday May 31st at the Tin Soldier pub in Gråsten, where she arrived in the company of friends around eleven PM. Late that night, she left on her own, ostensibly to get some air, and she has not been seen since.

Hundreds of volunteers have been out looking for Mia Sark in and around Gråsten. One of them is local Tom Mázoreck. He is one of several witnesses who have given the police concrete clues to go after. 'We saw the girl leave the Tin Soldier that night, and now that she hasn't been seen since, those of us who were there have talked about what could have happened to her,' he said to *Jydske Vestkysten*. 'A few of us had noticed a man sitting at the bar earlier in the evening—a bald guy in a leather jacket. He didn't speak Danish, and he seemed to be there alone. Us regulars hadn't seen him there before, and now we all wonder if he could have something to do with the case,' said Tom Mázoreck.

Police confirmed that they had received calls from several locals describing the man from the bar.

'Granted, it's odd that a stranger shows up in town at the same time that a young girl disappears,' says Peter Zøllner, head of investigations in the case. 'But we also know that many trucks drive through the area on their way to the border, and drivers regularly stop in town to eat or sleep before traveling on. So we can't conclude anything from the scant information we've received, but it is clear that it is a line of inquiry we take seriously and are following up on.'

Mia Sark is described as having an average build. She has long, dark-brown hair and measures 5 feet 5 inches. She was last seen wearing a black Saint-Tropez sweater, light-blue Levi's jeans, and a pair of black Bianco sandals.

The police are asking anyone with information about the case to contact the authorities at . . ."

"Kaldan?"

Heloise looked up from the screen.

All eyes in the room were turned toward her, and Mogens Bøttger smiled, waiting.

"How's it going with the Vigil piece? You about done?"

"Uh, no. Not yet," Heloise said, finding herself dodging Bøttger's gaze.

A month had passed since the last round of layoffs at the newspaper, the third in two years. The employees had been notified in advance that twenty-eight jobs would go up in smoke, and they had all been prepared for it being their turn to clear out and update their profiles on LinkedIn. When the day came, Karen Aagaard, editor of the investigation group for the past five years, was the first to get kicked out. She had taken the firing without flinching: firm handshakes all around and then "later'gator." She was fifty-seven years old and unemployed in an industry where young people were getting younger and the demands for long working hours were increasing.

Heloise had made the cut, and so had Bøttger. But it was to him that editor-in-chief Mikkelsen had handed the reins, and the promotion had created an imbalance in Heloise's relationship with the colleague with whom she had previously been a foot soldier. Now he had become the one you gave a little bow to at the sight of; the one who issued orders, directives, and gave you hell. Heloise didn't want the job herself—that's not what bothered her. She just couldn't stand the fact that Bøttger was now her superior.

"The article isn't ready yet?" He frowned with his dark brows. "You've had weeks to write it. What's going on?"

"Well, it's not like I haven't produced a hundred other articles in the meantime," Heloise protested.

"Right, and thank you very much for that. But what about this one?"

"Some information has come to light that I would like to examine more closely before writing the story."

"Isn't this guy you're visiting on the verge of dying?"

"Yes, but I think there may be a bigger story there."

"Such as?"

"Such as . . ." Heloise hesitated. "I have found some articles about a fatal accident that I would like to take a closer look at. I think Jan Fischhof may know something about it."

Everyone at the table looked up.

"A fatal accident?" repeated Bøttger.

"Yes. A man who perished in Southern Jutland, who I . . ."

"Wait, did this happen just now?"

"No, back in 1998. I don't know much about the matter yet, but I think there's something bigger behind it. Fischhof has a daughter who might be able to help shed some light on . . ."

"Okay, but you'll have to look into that at another time." Mogens Bøttger looked over at the board where the plan for the coming week's articles was lined up. "Right now, it's the Vigil story that we need to have in place. When do you expect to have something ready?"

"Jan Fischhof is still alive," Heloise said. "Shouldn't we wait with the article until he's . . ."

"No, we're making a series out of it—Vigil: Parts 1, 2, and 3. The first meeting, an introduction to the service. What it is about, how you sign up—that kind of thing. After that, an article about your relationship, the bond one forms with the dying, and so on. And then, finally, the grand finale, the last farewell. Can you have the first part ready by the start of next week?"

Heloise stared without expression at Bøttger, who awaited her answer.

"Kaldan? Monday?"

Heloise cleared her throat.

"As I said, I would like to take a closer look at this death, and there is also another case that I have just found. A young woman who disappeared in . . ."

"Right, but as *I* said, there is no time for that right now. If it's an old case, then it's not going anywhere. Be sure to get an appointment in place with the photo editor regarding the Fischhof guy. By the way, is this something that needs to be cleared at the Vigil? Can we take pictures out there, are they cool with that?"

Heloise did not answer.

"Good!" said Bøttger. "We agree that there will be a first draft of Part 1 ready on Monday, and then I'll reserve a space in the Wednesday newspaper." He nodded toward those assembled. "I think that's it. Work hard and have fun, folks!"

The other reporters stood up and slowly trickled out of the meeting room.

Heloise remained seated.

When they were alone, Bøttger looked at her with raised brows.

"Is there anything we need to talk about?"

Heloise met his gaze. "I don't think I can write the series of articles you're asking for."

The vertical furrows in his forehead became more distinct. "Why not?"

"Because . . ." She took a deep breath as she thought about her answer for a second. "I don't feel like it."

"You don't feel like it?"

"Nope."

Bøttger laughed. "Are you shittin' me?"

"No, I am not shitting you."

Heloise held his gaze as an unfamiliar tension grew between them. Bøttger's facial expression was difficult to decipher, but then his features hardened, and the smile disappeared. He moistened his lips and turned his palms upward.

"What's going on?"

"What's going on is I tell you I've got the scent of a story and then you shoot it down." She shook her head. "You never would have done that before."

"But we had agreed that you would write about the Vigil, so . . ."

"And what amazes me most is that you're not even *curious* about what I have to tell."

"Okay, then!" He leaned against the wall and crossed his arms. "I'm listening!"

Heloise recounted in detail what Jan Fischhof had said to her and told him about Schäfer's call concerning Tom Mázoreck.

Bøttger shrugged. "And?"

"Mads Orek, Mázoreck," Heloise said. "What are the odds that it's not this Tom Mázoreck that Fischhof is referring to? They are from the same small town—it *must* be him. That sounds like something damn well worth investigating."

"Yeah, for the police, maybe. But where is the journalistic angle?"

"Jan Fischhof said that he was afraid of having to answer for Mázoreck, so if he has somehow played a role in his death, then . . ."

"Then our readers couldn't care less. It's a police case and it happened more than twenty years ago."

Heloise pulled her chin back and narrowed her eyes. "Where has investigative journalist Mogens Bøttger gone?"

"What the hell are you talking about?" He threw up his arms in irritation. "This is a matter you have taken a *personal* interest in. It has fuck-all to do with your work as a journalist."

"Christ, you know, you're starting to sound like Mikkelsen!" Heloise nodded in the direction of the editor-in-chief's office at the far end of the building.

"Yes, strangely enough, that's how it works when you're given some responsibility. We can't react to every whim we get, because we actually have a business to run. We're here to sell newspapers, you know that, right?"

"And here I thought we were here for the sake of the story."

"The tree that falls in the forest, Kaldan. If no one reads the newspaper, does your story even exist?"

"Do you know what I think Mogens?" Heloise looked him up and down. "I think that this promotion has gone to your head."

"Gone to my head?"

"Yes."

"Wow!" Mogens Bøttger's smile was devoid of joy. The protruding Adam's apple bobbed up and down in his throat a few times. "Are you jealous? I would never have believed that about you."

Heloise lowered her gaze.

Her comment was way over the line, and she knew it. But she couldn't bring herself to take it back.

"Well, I guess this is where I have to put my foot down," Bøttger said. "You drop that story and focus on the Vigil—done, boom! Your deadline is Monday."

He turned to leave.

"I have vacation days," Heloise said.

Bøttger stopped and looked at her over his shoulder.

"Excuse me?"

"Vacation."

She stood up.

"I haven't taken more than a few days of vacation in the last three years, and I'm taking a week now. If that's a problem, you can fire me."

Mogens Bøttger stared at her for a long moment. Then he turned around and left the room.

7

THE CALL TO the small house in Dragør was answered after the third ring, and Heloise immediately recognized Ruth's small voice.

"Is he awake?" she asked, closing the door to the meeting room so that the noise from the open-plan office on the other side died down. Ruth scrabbled a little with the receiver, and Heloise could hear her talking to Fischhof in distinct croaks, as if the disease had affected his hearing as well as his lungs and mind. There was a little more scrabbling, and then Jan Fischhof's hoarse voice sounded at the other end.

"Heloise?"

"Hi Jan. How are you today?"

"Excellent!" The answer fell promptly and dryly. "Ruth isn't quite as stingy with the beers as she used to be."

Ruth protested in the background, and Heloise smiled down into the receiver as she pulled up the death certificate on her computer.

"Jan, listen, I'm calling because I've been thinking a little about what you said yesterday."

There was silence at the other end. Only Fischhof's breathing came through.

"That man you told me about . . . Was his name Tom Mázoreck?"

"No, Heloise, no, I can't . . ." Jan Fischhof's voice fell to a whisper. "Forget what I said yesterday. I guess I said some awful nonsense."

"But is it him, that you . . ."

"Forget it, I said. Forget that name! It . . . it's a thing of the past." There was an odd tone in his rusty bass.

"What are you afraid of, Jan? If you tell me about it, I can help you."

Jan Fischhof did not answer.

"Is this about your daughter?" tried Heloise. "Does she have anything to do with all this?"

What at first sounded like a soft laugh simmered in the phone. When Fischhof spoke, Heloise realized he was weeping.

"You can't help me," he cried. "No one can help me. It's too late. Far too late."

"No, nothing is too late," Heloise insisted. "But it requires you to tell me a little bit about what happened between you and this Mázoreck guy and why you're so afraid of him. He can't come after you if that's what you think. I see in the news archives that he died in 1998, but when I search for his name, only a few obituaries pop up, and then a single article about a girl who disappeared from a pub sometime a hundred years ago. So if you can tell me a little bit about . . ."

"You mean Mia?" He snuffled softly into the phone. Heloise blinked a few times.

"Yes," she nodded. "Her name was Mia."

"If you rake this up, they'll come after us. Both of us!"

"Do you know anything about that case, Jan?"

"They'll come after us. They are coming . . . they . . . come," he repeated in strange staccato thrusts, as if trying to speak and yawn at the same time. His voice suddenly sounded both childishly puzzled and sleepy. "They'll come . . . in coats of wool with torches and spears and eyes popping out of their heads."

Heloise frowned. "What are you talking about? Torches and spears?"

"The drawers in the house, Heloise. They have messed with them. I can see it. They have stolen my papers and . . . Yes, they took them. They took the papers!"

"No, Jan, wait! Stay with me for a moment!"

Heloise knew he was on his way out. It wasn't the first time she'd seen him go from coherent to confabulation in a few seconds.

She held her pen clear of the notepad.

"Tell me about Tom Mázoreck."

Nothing.

"Hello? Are you there?" Heloise raised her voice to make him react. "JAN?! HELLO?"

There was silence on the phone for a long moment. Then she heard Ruth's voice.

"Heloise? Are you still there?"

"Yes, what's going on? Where's Jan?"

"He's sitting here in his chair. He had put the phone in his lap."

"Has he fallen asleep?"

"No, I don't think so. Are you sleeping? Jan? . . . No, he's not sleeping, but he's not himself right now. I think he needs rest, so if you . . ."

"Has anyone been in the house today, Ruth?"

"In the house? What do you mean?"

"He says someone has stolen some things from the drawers—something about some papers?"

Ruth clicked her tongue. "He's talking nonsense! You know that. Yesterday he claimed there were suspicious noises on the phone and insisted he had been bugged. This morning it was the postman he barked at. There hasn't been anyone here but me."

"Just tell him that no one is coming after him and that he shouldn't be afraid."

"Who would he be afraid of?" snapped Ruth, sounding at once alarmed and annoyed. "There is no one here but me."

"Just tell him I'll figure it all out so he doesn't have to worry, okay? Tell him!"

"Yes, yes." Ruth was silent for a moment. "Are you coming out here today?"

"No, I . . ." Heloise hesitated. "I'm not in Copenhagen for the next few days, so if something happens, you'll call me, okay?"

"Is there something wrong?"

"No, but I . . . I'll try to sort this out. Find out what is bothering Jan."

"You have got to stop with these tall tales, both of you. He has absolutely no idea what he's saying!? Why don't you come out here and . . ."

"No," Heloise said. "I know you think I'm the one keeping him alive, but I'm starting to think it's something else. I think he refuses to check out because he's afraid of the bill."

"The bill?"

"Yes. Paying the check. From the higher powers." "But . . . that's ridiculous!" laughed Ruth.

"Is it? You said yourself that it's our job to do what we can to ease the grief of saying goodbye to life. That it's our job to send them off well."

Heloise interpreted Ruth's silence as agreement.

"That's all I'm trying to do."

8

HELOISE WALKED WITH quick steps through the investigative editorial office and took the stairs down to the second floor two steps at a time. She opened the door to the research department and scanned the room. At the largest desk in the room sat Morten Munk, a mountain of a man. He had two screens in front of him and two keyboards, on which he typed simultaneously with the grace of a concert pianist and fingers as thick as cucumbers.

"Hey, Munk?"

He turned the office chair in the direction of the sound. The sunlight that surged through the open windows fell mercilessly on his face. He was thirty years old, but his stretched skin gave him a younger appearance, and Heloise could easily imagine what he had looked like as a child.

"Miss Denmark!" he said in an airy voice and smiled, his eyes disappearing behind his big cheeks. "What brings you hither?"

"I need your help, and it's a bit urgent, so if you want to throw yourself into it right away, I'll owe you the world's largest gin and tonic."

Munk spun around on the chair and held his hands ready over the keys. "What do you need?"

"I need a phone number and an address for a woman. She is a Danish citizen—at least she has been—and she lives, as far as I know, in Stockholm."

"Name?"

"First name unknown, last name Ulvaeus."

"Do we have a date of birth?"

"Nope."

"Approximate age?"

Heloise thought of the family picture in Fischhof's living room. Of the daughter's acid-washed jeans, the suede jacket, the giant shoulder pads of Alice's neon-colored Marc O'Polo blouse.

"She must have become a teenager in the early nineties, so I'm going to guess she's my age, maybe a few years older. Her last residence in Denmark was probably in Dragør." She gave him Jan Fischhof's address.

Munk's fleshy fingers danced away on the keyboard as he whistled the melody to *Mamma Mia*.

"Anything else?" he asked.

"Yes, give me everything you can find on a Tom Mázoreck." Heloise gave him the Social Security number. "He died in 1998 in an accident in Flensburg Fjord, and I need to know who he was, where he worked, his family relationships—the whole shebang. Anything you can find about him."

Munk nodded and typed.

"Check and check!" he said. "What are we working on?"

"Yeah, that's the next thing we need to talk about." Heloise looked over her shoulder. None of the other researchers seemed to have noticed that she was there.

She turned her gaze back to Morten Munk. "Don't say anything about this to Bøttger."

Munk's left eyebrow formed an arch over his eye. He leaned back into the office chair and brushed his fingertips lightly against each other.

"Well, well. Is there drama?"

"No, there is no drama, but Mogens is the boss now, and that changes the rules of the game. So we're doing it ninja style, okay? It's total hush-hush!"

Munk pursed his lips and locked them with an invisible key.

Heloise gave him a kiss on the forehead and left the newspaper.

9

THE TRIANGLE SANDWICHES were lined up on the cold counter at Pret à Manger at the Copenhagen Airport. Heloise grabbed one with ham and cheese and lined up at the checkout. She paid, put the sandwich in her shoulder bag, and was heading for the gate when her phone beeped. She fished it out of her pocket with the one hand while pulling the rolling suitcase behind her with the other.

It was a text message that had come in from Munk.

Heloise stopped in the middle of the busy terminal and opened the message. It contained three links, and she pressed the first one. It was Tom Mázoreck's death certificate—the one she had found online. The next link was a map of Rinkenæs on which Munk had marked Mázoreck's last address, and the third was an overview of his working life.

Heloise's eyes scanned the page.

From 1985 to 1988 Mázoreck had worked as an orderly at Sønderborg Hospital; for the next few years, he was employed at a brickyard in Egernsund; and after that there had been a long period where his income was not registered. In any case, Munk hadn't been able to find anything, even in the form of a transfer income. There was also a missing address in the years 1991 and 1992, but in January 1993 he reappeared in the system and, until his death, was employed partly at Blans Slaughterhouse and partly in an unspecified position at something called Benniksgaard. The last five years of his life he'd had an address in Rinkenæs.

Heloise raised her eyes and looked out over the duty-free area without focusing on anything.

Benniksgaard?

She remembered that Fischhof had mentioned that place several times. Had he worked there? She knew he had worked with animals, anyway. With agriculture of some sort.

She opened a browser and did a Google search on the site. The results showed that Benniksgaard was a four-star hotel in Rinkenæs with an associated golf club and eighteen holes overlooking Flensburg Fjord. Golfers apparently made pilgrimages there from all corners of the world to enjoy a true piece of Danish country bliss, while people in the local area used the place for weddings, christenings, and student parties.

Heloise wrinkled her brow.

It didn't fit with what she knew about Jan Fischhof. He was a dirt-under-the-nails type who had dug ditches and skinned his own dinner. He hadn't supported himself by schlepping rich tourists' golf clubs around or putting chocolate mints on hotel pillows, she was sure of that!

An incoming FaceTime call interrupted Heloise's thoughts. She answered it and smiled at the sight of Gerda Bendix.

"Am I disturbing you?" Gerda asked. The connection was a little fuzzy, but she lit up the screen anyway, her eyes clear and wide-awake.

Lately, Heloise's best friend of more than thirty years had been meeting life with an appetite and curiosity that had been on standby for years. It looked good on her, Heloise thought. Gerda had always been beautiful in a way that triggered multiple collisions in traffic, but it was as if her divorce from Christian had made her look ten years younger. Her inner light shone brighter than ever, while wicked tongues in his social circle reported that he looked like he had grown ten years older.

"You never disturb me," Heloise said, starting to walk toward the gate. "Are you alright?"

"Yes, all is well. I have a break between two clients, so I just wanted to say hello. What about you, what are you doing? You're not at the paper, I see."

"I'm on the go." Heloise turned the phone around so Gerda could see the shopping area at the Copenhagen Airport.

"Where are you going?"

"It's a long story—or . . . actually, it's so short and imprecise that I don't even know what it's about. Jan, who I am a visiting friend of through the Vigil, has told me some things about an old case in Southern Jutland that I think is worth investigating further."

"A case about what?"

"It's a bit complicated, but I think he's afraid of saying goodbye to life and for that reason he has . . ." Heloise remembered something and interrupted herself: "Hey, isn't there something about soldiers writing farewell letters when they are to be sent out?"

Gerda worked as a trauma psychologist in the Armed Forces and worked at the Svanemøllen Barracks. She had also been deployed to war zones several times.

"Yes, everyone in the Armed Forces does that when they get deployed," Gerda answered. "The times I've been in Afghanistan, I've written letters to you, Lulu, and my mother. And at that time, of course, to Christian."

"What do people write in letters like that?"

"It's very different from person to person. I usually write something about how much I love you and that you shouldn't be too unhappy if I don't return home. In the letters to Christian, I also wrote things that . . . you know, things that at that time I didn't want to take to the grave. All the unspoken things."

Heloise nodded slowly.

"Why do you ask?"

"Because I started thinking about needing to lighten your heart before you die."

"To tell your secrets, you mean?"

"Yeah, or . . ." Heloise hesitated. "To confess your sins. It seems like Jan needs some sort of forgiveness."

Gerda frowned. "What for?"

"I don't know. Maybe it's about what you're saying: all the unspoken things, the secrets. It seems like there's something from his past that he's never processed, and I'd like to try to ease the burden for him. Plus . . ." Heloise shrugged. "You know me. I have to know what it is."

"Hmm," said Gerda, and looked like she had worked up to saying what was on her mind. "Just remember to take care of yourself, right?"

"I always do."

"Yes, but still. In just a few months, you've bonded a bit too closely with a man old enough to be your father, and perhaps you've projected your own past and your own unprocessed feelings into the relationship."

"Yeah, yeah," Heloise said, resisting the urge to roll her eyes. "I can see what it looks like, and of course you're right—you are! But the thing is, I . . ." Heloise took a deep breath and gave a little smile. "I really like him! I just need to make sure I'm not wrong about him."

Gerda opened her mouth and looked for a moment as if she wanted to say more, but pressed her lips together instead.

"Okay," she nodded.

"Okay," Heloise said in a tone that emphasized that the subject was closed. She didn't feel up to being psychoanalyzed today.

"So where did you say you're going?"

"I'll be flying to Sønderborg shortly to . . ."

"Sønderborg?"

"Yes. Jan was born and raised in Southern Jutland," Heloise said.

"Isn't that also where Thomas lives now?"

"Thomas who?"

Gerda smiled indulgently. "Thomas *who*? Don't give me that!"

"You mean O'Malley?"

"Are there any others?"

"Uh, yes, Gerda. There are other men in the world named Thomas."

"Not in *your* world."

"Agh, I don't know . . ." Heloise lowered her gaze and smiled briefly. "I haven't seen Thomas Malling since he moved to the U.S.A., and that was—what?—seven years ago."

"But doesn't he live in Sønderborg now?"

"Yeah, I think so," Heloise said. She had stopped paying attention to what Thomas was doing and where he was in the world, because every time she googled his name or picked at the wound in some other way, she slept badly and woke up with a tight feeling in her chest, as if she had slept with an elastic band around her heart.

She sat down on a bench at the gate and looked out over the landing pads where an Emirates Airbus A380 was taking off. The last time she had seen O'Malley, as he had been called since school, they had been standing a few hundred yards from where she was now, in the Kiss & Fly zone in front of the airport. He had been on his way to New York to start his new job as a news editor at one of the world's biggest media houses, and Heloise had promised that she would follow suit as soon as her temporary job at the *Demokratisk Dagblad* ended.

Five weeks later, Mikkelsen had offered her permanent employment in the investigative group.

"Thomas has a wife and kids now, so it doesn't really matter where he lives."

"Was there something about him being the editor-in-chief of one of the regional newspapers down there?"

"Yes."

Gerda made a compassionate grimace. "Well, that's quite a long fall from the *Huffington Post*, huh?"

"You could say that," Heloise nodded.

"Well, so you're flying to Sønderborg now?"

"Yes."

"And when will you be back home again?"

"That depends on what I find down there. If Jan gets worse, I'll come home right away, but I've rented a house in Rinkenæs for the week—a place called Gerda's Momento, I kid you not."

Gerda smiled. "God, that sounds perfect."

"Doesn't it? I found it on Airbnb for 240 kroner a day, so it's still affordable even if I suddenly have to ditch it all and go home."

"Well, the newspaper is picking up the check either way, right?"

Heloise shook her head.

"Not this time. I'm flying solo on this one."

10

T HE AIR QUIVERED in the heat as Carl Roebel parked the car and got out. He straightened his glasses and scouted the beach, where the waves washed ashore in long, lazy laps. Vemmingbund Beach in Southern Jutland was an anthill of bathing nymphs, playing children, and retirees who sat under the beach's many orange-colored umbrellas enjoying the hottest summer in a hundred years.

Carl's eyes found the ice-cream parlor on the boardwalk and spotted the old man sitting on a folding chair next to the small wooden shed. The man sat on the edge of the seat, resting his hands on a cane that stood on the patch between his pointed knees. His skin was tanned, his muscles long and sinewy, and he was dressed in a white undershirt and a pair of black Speedos. His long, gray hair was damp with sweat, framing a face with sharp cheekbones and narrow lips, while his eyes were hidden away behind a pair of mirrored sunglasses.

As Carl approached, the man looked up.

Carl stopped in front of him and held out his hand. "Hi Jes."

Jes Decker nodded once, but remained seated with both hands on the cane.

Carl pulled his hand back and glanced at the row of people lining up to buy popsicles. He was just about to ask if

there was a place they could talk in peace when Jes Decker
stood up and signaled with a sideways nod for Carl to
follow.

The old man stepped out onto the sand and, on precari-
ous legs, headed for the water's edge.

Carl followed in his footsteps.

A couple of boys with crew cuts and freckled shoulders
came sprinting up to them so that the sand swept around the
ears of the beachgoers who were sunbathing. They had scooped
a jellyfish the size of a manhole cover onto a tennis racket, and
the red-violet tentacles protruded through the mesh. The
eldest boy held out the jellyfish and squealed joyfully.

"Look, Grandpa! Look what we've found!"

"Not now, boys. Not now." The old man waved them
away with a single movement of his hand.

He continued to the water's edge. Then he turned to
Carl.

"Take off your clothes," he said. His voice rasped, the
tone said this was not up for debate.

"But . . ." Carl smiled nervously and looked down at
himself. He was dressed in a short-sleeved shirt and a pair of
gray pants with pleats. "I really can't . . . Well, I haven't . . ."

"Take them off!"

Carl met the old man's gaze. Then he unbuckled his
leather belt and dropped his pants around his ankles. He
stepped out of them so that they fell on top of his shoes in the
sand and unbuttoned his shirt. He took it off and threw it on
the ground. Then he folded his hands in front of the fly of his
boxer shorts and swallowed hard.

"Now what?"

The old man raised his cane and pointed in the direction
of three men who were standing in water up to the navel a
fair distance after the second sandbank. Only now did Carl
notice that it was a 7-iron he held in his hand.

"They're waiting for you out there."

Carl turned his attention to the men. Thunderclouds
hung low on the horizon behind them, threatening to roll in
and ruin the day.

He smiled uncertainly. "This, it's not necessary, Jes. I wouldn't think of . . ."

"Go!" The man gave Carl a nudge in the chest with the golf club.

Carl began to walk into the water while pebbles and seashells scraped against his feet. The three men watched him as he moved in their direction, and Carl recognized one of them: Jes Decker's son, René. He was a man of medium height in his forties with short golden hair and muscles so well developed they looked like they were painted on. Carl hadn't seen the other two before, but their bull necks and crossed arms indicated that they were a pair of Jes Decker's Eastern European handymen.

René Decker greeted Carl with a nod as they faced each other.

"There's no reason to meet out here," Carl said. He looked nervously from one praetorian to another. "I would never dream of recording our conversations or otherwise . . ."

René Decker spread his hands out. "I'm sure you're a stand-up guy, Roebel. But you know what they say about trust and control." He smiled and lay a heavy hand on Carl's naked shoulder. "This way, we're sure we can stay friends, right?"

Carl nodded.

"Good," René said, crossing his arms. "So what's this all about? A delivery? Are there any problems with the product?"

"No, it's, um . . . it's Glenn."

"What about him?"

"He works for you, doesn't he?"

The corners of René Decker's mouth turned downward and he shrugged. "Perhaps. Why?"

"Because he was at Penny Lane last night bragging about a job he'd done for you in Hamburg recently. He didn't say specifically what it was about, but you got the impression that it was drug-related, so if I were you, I might just put him in his place. Once he gets some drinks in him, his mouth runs, and maybe he needs a . . . a reprimand."

René Decker ran his fingers over his chin and nodded.

"Okay. I'll have a chat with him." He patted Carl on shoulder. "It's good you keep your ears open out there, Roebel. Your loyalty will be . . ."

"There's something else too." Decker met Carl's gaze.

"I . . . I've heard something I thought you all should know."

"Okay?" René Decker nodded to get him to continue.

"Someone called in to the station this morning. A homicide investigator from the Copenhagen Police."

"And?"

"And he asked some . . . some questions that I thought might be of interest."

"Questions about what?" Decker frowned. "We have no axe to grind with Copenhagen."

"He asked if anyone knew anything about Pitbull."

René Decker's lips parted. He was quiet for a long moment, as his eyes bore into Carl's.

"Are you sure?"

Carl nodded. "He asked Peter Zøllner if the police knew anything about how he died."

"What else did he say?"

"Nothing else."

René Decker hesitated. "Do you know if . . . if they've found anything?"

Carl shook his head.

"And he called from the homicide department, you say?"

"Yes. It was Zøllner who talked to him, so I only heard fragments of the conversation."

"What was his name?" René Decker lifted his chin and looked toward the beach where his father was waiting. "The one who called—what was his name?"

"Schäfer," Carl said, straightening his glasses. "Erik Schäfer."

CHAPTER

11

THE BLOOD LAY in large, dried-up lakes in the entryway and all the way down the hall of the stately apartment; black-violet and cracked like Japanese raku. It was smudged in those places where feet had stepped, and there were tobacco-brown imprints of hands, elbows, and shoulders that had been thrust up against the white walls and panels.

Erik Schäfer stepped over a brass waiter cart lying in the middle of the hall, squatted down, and watched the blood seeping into the wormholes of the old wooden planks.

He raised his eyes to look for splatters on the ceiling from a weapon in motion, but couldn't see any blood splashes on the prisms of the large crystal chandelier or in the vaulted space above it.

He closed his eyes and breathed in slowly through his nose.

Beyond the clear, metallic smell of blood, the apartment's aroma was fresh with soap flakes, sun, and open windows. The only smelly thing to be found came from a handful of Mikado-esque sticks poking out of an overturned, amber-colored bottle on the dresser in the hallway. Cèdre du Fil de Fer was written on the label. Home fragrance.

The resident could not have been dead for long.

Schäfer stood up and looked down the long hallway, where the police photographer's flashes went off in uninterrupted clicks.

The corpse sat at the end of the hallway, back against the wall, legs slightly spread. The face and torso were hunched over toward the groin, so all you could see of the head was a bald scalp surrounded by semi-long, silver-gray hair. The cream-colored suit the man had donned for what was to be his last day on earth, was drenched in blood and urine.

Schäfer shook his head.

"Lester, you old rascal," he muttered. "Who the hell did this to you?"

The door to the staircase behind Schäfer was open, and he heard the sound of soles striking the steps.

Profiling expert and former police psychologist Michala Friis appeared in the doorway. Her fair hair was gathered in a ponytail, and she was dressed in tight black jeans and a black T-shirt with a bateau neckline that accentuated her tanned shoulders and collarbones.

Bertelsen's words reverberated again like a delayed echo in Schäfer's thoughts. Michala Friis stopped at the threshold and peered into the entryway.

"What do we have here?" she asked.

"A regular bloodbath." Schäfer nodded in the direction of the corpse and held out a pair of latex gloves to her. "Are you coming in?"

She accepted the gloves and smiled.

"I thought we were going to meet at Bistro Bohemia," she said, referring to the restaurant situated diagonally across from the property they were in.

"Lunch is postponed," Schäfer said.

"Yes, I gathered. Apparently, you'll do anything to drag me back into the police."

It was the usual joke, but there was more than a grain of truth in it, and Schäfer gave her a wry smile.

Until about a year ago, Michala Friis had been a permanent part of the investigation unit, but now she worked primarily as an adviser in the private sector. Schäfer had persuaded the police commissioner to earmark a pool of money for profiling so that they could pull her in as a consultant in particularly challenging cases, and he used every opportunity to remind her that she belonged with the police, not among property speculators and other financial assholes. She was the best in the country at what she did, and Schäfer had reproached her—yes, been almost furious at her—for quitting her job with the police.

He had never considered that her motives were anything but financial.

"I was parking in front of the restaurant when I spotted the blue flashes over here," Schäfer said. He had caught sight of the officer standing on the sidewalk in front of the staircase interviewing a middle-aged woman with blood on her clothes and a look of condensed horror in her eyes.

Michala Friis stretched her neck and peered down the hall. "Wow, this went savagely, didn't it?"

Schäfer nodded.

"A stabbing?"

"Can't say yet. I can't see the lesions while he's sitting *there*, and we can't move him around until Oppermann has been here."

The state coroner was on his way, and he had to examine the body before they could begin to narrow down the hunt for a weapon and a perpetrator.

Michala Friis took a step past Schäfer and looked into the first of three large adjoining rooms. The entire apartment had painted white walls and floors, and with the exception of a few works of art that leaned toward the avant-garde, the home was decorated with French vintage furniture, church roofs, mirrors, and thingamabobs in a romantic style. It was a long way from Copenhagen to Versailles, but Louis XVI's spirit was alive and well in the three-hundred-fifty-nine-square-yard stately apartment at the corner of Grønningen and Esplanaden.

Michala Friis whistled softly. "Old money?"

"Self-made."

She looked down at the corpse. "What did the deceased do?"

"It's Lester Wilkins."

She raised her brows in surprise and met Schäfer's eyes. "Jetset-Wilkins?"

Schäfer nodded.

Lester Wilkins, born Poul Næssøe Andersen, had in his early days been a kingpin in the international jazz world, and the millions had rolled in. He had been the darling of the tabloid magazines, intimate with the royals, friend of the ladies, and whatever else there was of jet-set clichés, but in recent years he had become the worst cliché of all: a washed up has-been. A sad end to an otherwise fine life.

"Who on earth would hurt him?" asked Michala, looking at the corpse. "And why?"

"Yes, exactly. Why?"

This was always the starting point when Schäfer began a homicide investigation. The first question was never who, but why. What was the motive? It was always one of seven options: jealousy, profit, revenge, ostracism, fanaticism, lust, or excitement. Sometimes they overlapped each other, but all killings could be attached to at least one of the seven motives, and that's where, among other things, Michala Friis came into the picture. She could go through a location, a murder book, listen to a suspect's voice, observe their posture or facial expressions, and see the slain person's belongings. Based on details that police would not consider of value, she could help narrow down probable motives, and thus the pool of potential perpetrators.

Schäfer looked around. Most of the apartment looked nice, only the entrance area and hallway were ravaged.

"It looks like he was assaulted here at the front door, and he probably let the perpetrator in himself, because there's no sign of burglary," he said. "I think they were arguing, because it looks like Ragnarok out here. Things on the chest of drawers are overturned, the brass waiter, that painting there . . . It seems overly violent, doesn't it? Aggressive!"

Schäfer pointed to a painting hanging on the wall in the entryway. It was cobalt blue and looked as if it had been painted with a roller, and there were four vertical gashes in the middle of the canvas where someone had stabbed into it with a knife or other sharp object.

"What does that tell you about the perpetrator?" asked Schäfer. "Does anger play a special role?"

Michala Friis squinted her eyes and walked over to the painting.

"It looks like a Lucio Fontana."

"A what?"

She grabbed hold of the frame and pulled the painting out from the wall so she could see the signature on the back of the canvas. She frowned slightly and nodded, impressed.

"I'll be damned. It is!"

"What is it?"

"A genuine Fontana. So you can probably rule out profit as a motive—that's what it tells me about the perpetrator," she said, letting the painting slide back into place on the wall. "That, and the fact that Wilkins has what looks like a Rolex Submariner on his wrist."

Schäfer turned his gaze to the corpse and saw the gold strap peeking out from under his sleeve.

He pointed to the painting. "But what about the gashes?"

"They are Fontana's hallmark. He was the founder of what is called spatialism, where the artist tries to break through the two-dimensional image."

"Are you telling me it's supposed to look like this?"

"Yes, and it's worth a lot of money. We're talking millions! To think that it is just hanging here in an apartment in Copenhagen." Michala Friis viewed the painting with wide eyes. "It should be lying in a safe. Or better yet, hanging at the National Museum, or at the Louisiana Museum of Modern Art."

Schäfer noticed that her breathing had accelerated in excitement, and small beads of sweat had trickled into the recess between her upper lip and nose.

"I'm sorry but are we looking at the same thing here?" he asked in a flat tone. "A blue canvas with four holes in it!?"

Michala smiled at him and nodded.

Schäfer gave her a pointedly blank look. Then he shook his head and continued down the hall.

"Did Wilkins live alone?" asked Michala from behind him. "He did, didn't he? He had no wife or children."

She opened a door and stepped into Lester Wilkins's bedroom. The large double bed was made, the sheets chalky white and unwrinkled. She looked around the room and sat down on the foot of the bed.

"Yeah, he lived alone." Schäfer had poked his head through the doorway at her. "And I think he was pretty shabby here in his old age. A heavy drinker and depressed, as far as I know. So who knows what else he'd gotten himself into? Drugs? Hookers?"

Michala Friis leaned back so that the bed frame creaked and propped herself up on her elbows as she looked around the bedroom.

"If these walls could talk," she said. "Wilkins supposedly bedded all the fashion models in the seventies and eighties, but I don't know how much action there's been in here in the last several years. Probably not much," she added, nodding in the direction of a pair of crutches that stood in the corner of the room next to a whitewashed dresser, on which lay a self-service table of arthritis medication, beta blockers, anti-anxiety drugs, and other stuff that didn't immediately point to a wild and spicy sex life.

Schäfer looked at Michala Friis as she half sat, half lay on the bed, and thought: maybe in another life.

She met his gaze and smiled. "What's on your mind?"

Schäfer cleared his throat. "Bertelsen said something to me earlier today that . . . something that I can't help but wonder about." He scratched his forehead with a finger.

Michala looked at him without blinking. "Yes?"

"Yeah, I told him that the two of us were going to meet to talk about the poison killing on Holbergs Street, and then he hinted that, um . . . that I no longer pick up signals as clearly as I once did. He claimed I've lost my touch."

She lowered her gaze and moistened her lips.

"Any thoughts on that?" asked Schäfer. "Is he right?"

She pulled her shoulders up to her ears and half smiled. "What do *you* think?"

"I think it would be a real mess." His tone was warm, but it was not open for negotiation. "And I can't do my job properly if there's too much discrepancy between things as I see them and things as they are. I have to be able to trust my gut." He patted his stomach.

Michala got up from the bed and straightened her clothes. She walked over to Schäfer in the doorway so they stood face to face.

"You're a brilliant investigator, Erik– if that's what we're talking about . . ." Her gaze rested on his mouth for a moment, and she looked like she was about to say more when they were interrupted by knuckles banging hard against the entrance door at the other end of the apartment.

She and Schäfer walked out into the hallway, where a young officer was waiting for them. He was the first to arrive at the address, and Schäfer had asked him to knock on the doors along the stairwell to see if anyone other than the neighbor's wife had seen or heard anything.

"Most of the apartments by the stairs are commercial leases," the officer said. "It's only here on the fifth, and upstairs on the sixth floor, that there are residences, and there's no one home upstairs right now." He pointed upward with a thumb. "The neighbor next door says she greeted the victim briefly last night on the stairs and that he looked like he was on his way into town. Nice clothes and in a good mood."

"Did she know where he was going?" asked Schäfer.

"She says he usually sits down at the bar at Bistro Bohemia several nights a week, but I've just been over there and they don't remember seeing him last night."

"What time did she find him?" It was Michala who asked.

"About an hour ago. She was on her way out to walk her dog when she noticed that the door to the apartment was open, so she went in to make sure everything was as it should be. Emergency services received the call at 11:17 AM."

"Does that mean that the shoe prints here," Michala Friis pointed to a maroon stripe on the floor where it looked as if someone had slipped in one of the blood pools, ". . . might be from her? From the neighbor?"

The officer nodded. "She says she went to check if he was still alive, so she touched him, took his pulse—and so on."

"Where was the dog in the meantime?" asked Schäfer.

"What do you mean?"

"You said she was taking her dog out when she walked past the open door. So what did she do with the dog when she walked in here?"

The officer shrugged and looked around.

"All right, make sure the guys from the NFC get the neighbor's finger and shoe prints," Schäfer said, nodding toward the team from the National Forensic Center who were fully engaged in dusting for fingerprints and securing other clues. "Does she have an alibi for the evening and the night?"

"She says she was home."

"Alone?"

The officer nodded.

Schäfer's mobile phone vibrated. He pulled it out and looked at the display.

KALDAN, it said.

He hesitated and looked from the phone to the corpse. Had the media already gotten wind of Lester Wilkins's death?

Fucking Facebook and Twitter!

You could no longer get a moment of peace to do your work before photos of murder victims, conspiracy theories, and fake news of various kinds circulated on the Internet. It was only a matter of minutes before the news trucks rolled up on the sidewalk in front of the stairway and newspaper websites were plastered with pictures and bombastic words about Wilkins's life and death.

Schäfer tensed his jaw muscles and dismissed the call. He turned his gaze on the officer.

"The neighbor is, as far as we know, the last one to see Wilkins alive, so take her to the station and have her retell what she saw and when she saw it. It may be that something interesting will pop up that she didn't think to communicate to us the first time around. A confession, for example."

The officer nodded and left the apartment the moment forensic scientist Jakob Sandahl walked through the door, medical bag in hand.

"Sandahl?" said Schäfer in surprise. "I thought John Oppermann was on his way?"

"Yeah, that was the plan, but they rolled one in just as he was walking out the door— a minor. So he chose to stay at the Institute to look after that, and I'll take care of Wilkins here in the meantime."

Jakob Sandahl had been employed at the Department of Forensic Medicine for only five months, but he had enjoyed superstar status from day one because he came from a high position as chief of Service de Médecine Légale at the University Hospital of Montpellier. He was young—at least, younger than Schäfer—and arrogant, which he had plenty of reasonto be. He was also infuriatingly good-looking, with his thick, gelled hair and dark brows, and although he didn't take up as much space in the landscape as Schäfer, he exuded a confidence that made him seem ten feet tall. He made no secret of the fact that he expected to take over the reins from Oppermann when the state auditor retired next year, and in truth he was a gift to the Copenhagen police.

They benefited from a forensic scientist with his know-how, and Schäfer had no good reason to despise him. Still, he didn't like what Sandahl represented: new times and the handing off the baton to a snot-nosed kid who thought he knew more than the operators who had been in the profession since Adam and Eve were kids.

Jakob Sandahl turned his attention to Michala Friis.

"We haven't met," he said, holding out his hand.

She acknowledged Schäfer's displeasure with a smile and accepted Sandahl's hand.

Sandahl continued down the hall and squatted down next to the corpse. He lifted Wilkins's head up, showing his twisted, lifeless facial expression. Then he grabbed his chin and tried to close the open mouth, but rigor mortis had already occurred in the small muscles, and Wilkins's jaws were locked in a silent scream. He examined the mouth, tongue, and throat. Then he grabbed the body's left leg and gave it a push up toward his torso. The leg gave in to the pressure and bent its rusty hinges.

"Rigor has occurred in the upper body but has not yet reached the lower body," Sandahl said into his Dictaphone without lifting his gaze. He took the temperature of the corpse and pressed the bruises to see if they faded. "I would estimate the time of death to be . . ." He looked at the watch around his wrist and tilted his head from side to side. "Somewhere between five and seven o'clock this morning."

"Are we talking blunt force? Or a stabbing? It would be nice if we could start looking for a murder weapon."

"It seems to be a natural death."

"A natural death?" Schäfer's eyebrows rose to his forehead, and he gestured dramatically toward the blood that was spread throughout most of the hallway. "This looks like a damn massacre!"

Sandahl shook his head. "It's drinking."

"Drinking?"

"Yes. The man was a notorious drunk, right?"

"Allegedly. So what?"

"Based on what I see here, my preliminary guess is varicose veins in the esophagus, which are caused by increased pressure on the venous circulation. These kinds of varicose veins burst easily, and when they do, blood spurts out of your mouth. It looks violent, as you can see; nevertheless, it is a natural death. The technical term for the disorder is esophageal varices, and the most frequent cause is cirrhosis."

"Cirrhosis?"

"Yes."

Schäfer scratched his neck as he watched Sandahl with narrowed eyes.

"Of course, I need to get him on the table before I make a final assessment," Sandahl said, standing up. "But anything else would surprise me a lot."

"Huh," said Schäfer, looking down the hall at all the blood.

"He probably came home late, locked himself in, and got ill in the entryway. A hole appeared in a varicose vein and blood streamed out of his mouth—and we're talking gushing streams here. Like an open fire hydrant! He panicked no doubt and then groped his way down the hall, where he collapsed and bled to death."

"Huh," Schäfer repeated skeptically.

"I can assure you that I have yet to come across a single case of esophageal varices where the investigator did not initially believe it was a homicide," Sandahl said, pulling off his latex gloves. "It looks like the Niagara Falls of Death. A hell of a mess! But you know how it is." He patted Schäfer on the shoulder with a patronizing air. "Things aren't always what they seem."

Two paramedics brought a stretcher into the apartment. They lifted the body, placed it in the open body bag lying on the stretcher, and pulled the zipper up so that Lester Wilkins's wide-open eyes and open, bloody mouth disappeared under the black plastic material.

"I expect to perform the autopsy tomorrow morning," said Jakob Sandahl. "Shall we say eight thirty?"

Schäfer nodded silently, and the coroner took his leave from the apartment.

Schäfer turned and reluctantly met Michala Friis's gaze.

The ponytail holder around her hair had loosened slightly and a lock of hair had fallen over one of her eyes.

She smiled encouragingly.

"He's right, Erik. You can't hit the mark every time, and a couple of mistakes doesn't mean you've lost your touch. You know that, right?"

Schäfer heard the pity in her voice and winced.

He pursed his lips and nodded. There was no need to belabor the point.

"Well," he said. "Should we go get that lunch?"

12

THE SKIES OVER Sønderborg Airport were cloudless when the wheels hit the landing strip, but the smell of rain on hot asphalt revealed that a shower had just washed over the area. The trip had been surprisingly short, Heloise thought as she made her way down the stairs from the black propeller plane: a piddling thirty-five minutes from takeoff to landing; thirty-five minutes from the deep baritone of the capital to the wondrously clear silence that now enveloped her.

She turned the phone's airplane mode off while she waited to receive the keys to the car she had rented, and a text message popped up from Morten Munk as soon as there was a signal:

> *The woman you are looking for in Sweden is named Elisabeth Ulvaeus. She is the registered owner of that house in Dragør you gave me the address of. I've sent you telephone number etc. via email. / MM.*

Heloise signed the car rental papers at the Enterprise counter and a few minutes later located the white Renault Clio out in the parking lot in front of the terminal. She got into the car, which smelled artificially of new-car spray, and pulled up Munk's e-mail. It was filled with various attachments, and she first settled for pressing the one marked "Ulvaeus."

She skimmed the document.

According to Munk's research, Fischhof's daughter worked as a marine biologist for a German-owned company in Stockholm, and her home address showed that she lived in somewhere called Smedslätten, some distance west of the Swedish capital.

Heloise tapped out the phone number and put the phone to her ear. The call went straight to voicemail, and she waited for the beep.

"Hi Elisabeth, my name is Heloise Kaldan," she said, pulling the shoulder strap across her chest. "I'm calling because I'm friends with your father, and I have some questions about your time in Southern Jutland that I need your help to get answers to. After all, he doesn't remember so well anymore, so . . . If you'd be kind enough to give me a buzz as soon as you get my message? Thank you very much!"

Heloise left her number and hung up, then she tried to catch Schäfer again. She had called him from Copenhagen Airport, but he had declined the call with an automated message saying he was busy and would call back later.

He still didn't pick up his phone so Heloise texted instead.

Just landed in Sønderborg. On the way to talk to the police. Your colleague down here was called Peter Zøllner, right? Just give me a call!

Heloise typed the address in on the GPS and put the car in gear.

13

H ELOISE HAD ONCE been robbed at broad daylight in New York City. A handsome elderly gentleman wearing a soft hat and a Baileys-colored suit had sat down next to her on a bench on the corner of Mulberry and Spring. He had smiled and nodded, politely drawn her attention to the 9mm Luger he had in his inner pocket, and asked her to hand over her wallet and cell phone. Heloise had obeyed, and when she arrived at the 5th Precinct in Little Italy half an hour later to report the robbery, she had been shocked at how dirty and dim it was inside the beautiful old building—and how *unsafe* it felt. There had been a cacophonous spectacle of phones ringing, detainees yelling and screaming, coffee machines hacking and coughing, and indignant citizens reporting everything from theft to noisy neighbors, sexual harassment, wife beating, and murder, while the city that never sleeps raged outside its doors.

By comparison, the police station in Sønderborg, which she now found herself in front of, was reminiscent of a modern crematorium. It was dazzlingly bright and desolate, and the yellow-brick building seemed to have been designed by an architect who had gone out of his way to avoid being considered for the Pritzker Prize.

Heloise stepped in through the automatic sliding doors and went inside. She walked over to the counter, where a brick of a stationary telephone stood flashing silently on the table next to a cup of coffee.

The cream in the coffee had separated, so the fat had accumulated at the edge of the mug, and it seemed to have been several hours since it was poured. There was no one in the waiting area or on the other side of the counter, and it was so quiet you could hear the birds whistling outside through the closed windows.

"Hello?" she called, looking around the empty rooms. "Is anyone here?"

She heard the sound of a toilet flushing at the other end of the building, and a moment later a young officer strolled into the reception area with a copy of *Everything for the Ladies* in one hand and a cell phone in the other.

He picked up speed when he spotted Heloise.

"I'm sorry," he said, putting the magazine down on a shelf under the counter. His cheeks flushed red, and his eyes searched the floor. "I didn't realize there was anyone out here."

"That's alright," smiled Heloise. "I would like to talk to one of your investigators, a Peter Zøllner."

She handed her press card across the counter to the officer, who accepted it and read with furrowed brows.

"Heløjse Kaldan?"

"It is pronounced Élois. It's French." If she had a dime for every time . . .

"Zøllner is not here right now," the officer said, handing the card back to her. "He's on patrol."

"Do you know when he'll be back?"

"Maybe later today, maybe tomorrow. He drives around the municipality, so it depends on whether something urgent arises that he needs to take care of. What is it about?"

"I'm researching an article for the *Demokratisk Dagblad*. One of my sources is an investigator with the Copenhagen Police, and he referred me to Zøllner."

The officer straightened his back in a way that revealed it wasn't every day a reporter from a national media outlet stopped by.

"Oh?" he said, his face forming attentive wrinkles. "And it's nothing I can help with?"

"Well, maybe. It's a bit of a long shot, but I'm wondering if you have any information about an old case from 1998? It's about a boat that went down off of Rinkenæs somewhere. There was a man who perished. I have the death certificate here."

She pulled out the printed certificate from her bag and placed it on the counter.

"I would have liked to talk to Zøllner, because he's a bit older than you and therefore may remember the case from that time."

The officer skimmed the page. "It wasn't a criminal case?"

"No."

He pursed his lips and nodded.

"Yes, then it probably *is* Zøllner you need to get hold of. There have been major changes in the region over the last several years due to police reforms. Several police stations have been closed, and a lot of old case materials have been destroyed."

"What about old criminal cases? Do you still have them here?"

"Yes, but only open criminal cases. You can find the closed-case documents in the Danish National Archives department in Aabenraa, where you can apply for access to documents if there's something you . . ."

"There was a young woman who disappeared in 1997. A Mia Sark. Does that mean anything to you?"

"Sark," the officer repeated with a thoughtful expression. Then he shook his head. "Rings no bell."

"The articles that exist about the case are dated in the years after she disappeared, and I haven't been able to find follow-up coverage, so I'm not clear about whether she ever reappeared. Could you perhaps see if you have anything on hand— that is, whether the case is unsolved?"

"Yes, but . . . it will take me some time to work that out."

"Thank you!"

The officer smiled apologetically. "No, you see, cases that go back so many years do not appear in the electronic database. They're downstairs in our archive room, which . . ."

"That's great," Heloise said, holding his gaze. "I'll just wait here."

The officer nodded reluctantly and then disappeared from the room. Twenty minutes later he was back with flushed cheeks and a brown cardboard box in his arms. He set it down on the desk behind the counter and emptied the contents onto the table.

"Well, let's see then," he said.

He picked up a case file and flipped through it in silence for a few minutes. He pulled out a photograph from the folder and handed it to Heloise.

"This must be her here, right?"

Heloise nodded, even though it was the first picture she had seen of Mia Sark. It was an old passport photo from a time when they weren't supposed to look like expressionless mugshots. The young woman's aquamarine-blue eyes were marked with black eyeliner in the picture, giving her a harsh expression, and her mouth was split into an open smile with teeth that were spotted with white and pointed in various directions. Her skin was light, and her long dark hair hung like curtains around her heart-shaped face.

She was pretty without being beautiful, Heloise thought. Hard without seeming cold.

"There's another one here," the officer said, handing Heloise another picture.

It was a group photo of three young people, two girls and a boy, sitting at a brown-lacquered wooden table filled with beer bottles, dice cups, and tealights. Mia Sark was sitting on the far right, closest to the camera, and it was clear that she hadn't wanted to be in the picture. She had a cigarette in the hand she was holding up to stop the photographer; she looked drunk and uneasy. The open smile she had in the first photo was now a narrow line in the pale face, and the camera's flash revealed a pair of angry, bloodshot eyes. She no longer looked pretty, just hard. And cold! Most of all, she looked young,

Heloise thought. Nineteen years old was evidently a lot younger than she remembered that age being.

She turned the picture over and saw that something was written on the back:

The Tin Soldier, May 31, 1997. Mia, Johan, and Marie Louise.

So it came from the night Mia Sark disappeared.

"The case was actively investigated for . . . for a little over a year, I see, and was then put on hold on August 3, 1998." The officer held up the document so Heloise could see the final note of the investigation. "There hasn't been any development since."

"So she never showed up again?"

"No."

"Was there any theory about what had happened?"

"Yeah . . ." He flipped a little further through the folder. "Early on, the investigation indicated that she might have been abducted and transported south. There's reference to the Palermo Protocol in the log just a few days into the investigation, I see."

"Palermo Protocol?"

"Yes, it's a UN resolution on human trafficking!"

Heloise thought of the article in *JydskeVestkysten*.

"There was something about a truck driver?"

"Yeah, there were clues leading toward Germany, and I can see Interpol got involved at the time." The officer read on and then shook his head slowly. "But no . . . no, nothing was ever found."

"Were there any other suspects in the case? Other than the truck driver?"

"The thing is, I cannot disclose any more to you because it's an unsolved case." The officer smiled regretfully. "I'm only allowed to share the information that was already made public."

"One of the last people to see the girl alive was the one I told you about before," Heloise continued, unmoved. "The guy who died in that boat accident. Can you see if there is anything about him in the file there? His name was Mázoreck. Tom Mázoreck."

"Unfortunately, I'm not allowed . . ." The officer closed the case file and put it down on the table. "As I said, it's an unsolved case."

Heloise cocked her head and studied the lines in his face. The nice eyes. The pulse that was clearly pounding in his neck.

"What is your name?" she asked.

"Oliver."

"Oliver," Heloise repeated, holding his gaze. "This case is more than twenty years old. You know as well as I do that it won't be cleared up as long as it's in a box in your basement gathering dust." She stood on tiptoe and looked across the counter. "What's on that videotape, there? Is it footage of interrogations, or what is it?"

She pointed to a VHS tape lying on the table next to the file. On the label on the back of the tape was written in felt-tip pen and in capital letters: SARK, M. HUSH-HUSH, DECEMBER 8.

"I can't . . ." He shook his head slightly and began to put things back in the cardboard box.

The automatic sliding doors facing the parking lot behind Heloise slid open, and a young female police officer walked into the reception. She had long, reddish-blonde hair in a high ponytail and crossed the terrazzo floor with purposeful steps. Her breasts were clearly fake and stood straight out in the air so that the gaps between the buttons of the light-blue police shirt gaped, and Heloise had a hard time not staring at them.

The woman greeted her colleague with a nod as she passed the counter and proceeded to a door at the back of the room. She opened the door, and Heloise spotted an elderly plainclothes officer sitting at a desk in the adjacent room.

"Hey, might that be Zøllner in there? Is he back?" she asked, nodding in the man's direction.

The officer looked over his shoulder. "No, that's Carl Roebel."

"Is he also an investigator?"

"Yeah."

"Could you please ask him to come out here for a minute? I'd like to ask him a few questions."

The officer walked over to Carl Roebel and bent over him to say something Heloise couldn't hear. She saw the investigator lean back in the office chair and felt his gaze on her. He stood up and regarded Heloise with an appraising look as he walked toward her.

She held out her hand when he reached the counter.

"How do you do," she said. "Heloise Kaldan."

Carl Roebel took her hand and nodded without introducing himself. Then he put his thumbs under his belt and tilted his head back slightly.

He was a tall man with slender arms and weak shoulders under the short-sleeved shirt, and Heloise guessed he was in his mid-fifties. His eyes were small and watchful, and his hair grew thin over his forehead.

"I want to know if you can assist us," she said. "Young Oliver here has already been kind enough to help with some information about the Mia Sark case." She smiled at the officer who had appeared at Roebel's side. "But there are a few questions he doesn't know the answer to because it's an older case. So, I thought maybe you knew a little more about it?"

Carl Roebel looked at her without blinking. "The Mia Sark case?"

"Yes, she was a young woman who disappeared in Gråsten in 1997."

"I know who Mia Sark was."

"Did you help investigate the case?" asked Heloise.

Roebel regarded her with a skeptical eye. "Why do you all suddenly care about something that happened so many years ago?"

"You all?"

"Yeah, one of your colleagues called this morning too."

"One of my colleagues?" Heloise frowned and looked alternately at Roebel and young Oliver.

Could it have been Munk who called in connection with the research on Mázoreck? Surely it wasn't Bøttger, who had taken an interest in the matter after all, was it?

"An Erik Schäfer," said Carl Roebel.

"Oh," Heloise smiled and shook her head. "Schäfer is not my colleague. He's a homicide investigator."

"What section do you work in?"

"I'm not . . ." She shook her head, confused. "I'm not a police officer. I'm a journalist."

Carl Roebel turned his gaze to his young colleague and looked for a moment as if he was considering grabbing his collar.

"You said she was from the Copenhagen Police."

"No, I . . ." Oliver shrugged his shoulders up toward his ears and raised his eyebrows in defense. "I said she had been *referred* by the Copenhagen Police."

Carl Roebel pursed his lips. Then he turned his gaze to Heloise.

"Can I see some credentials?"

Heloise took out her wallet again and placed it on the counter in front of him so he could see the press card behind the plastic pocket.

Roebel looked from the card to Heloise.

"Why are you interested in Mia Sark?"

"Because her name has come up in connection with a story I'm working on, so it would be a big help if you could tell me what you remember about the case."

Carl Roebel regarded her for a moment with his chin raised, as if trying to decode her. Then he shook his head and ushered her away.

"We don't talk to the press about unfinished investigations."

"But I just want to know whether . . ."

"We don't talk to the press!"

After leaving the station Heloise got into the driver's seat and slammed the car door. She pulled out her notebook to

record what she had seen and heard before it all faded from
her mind.

> Trafficking. The Palermo protocol. How was Interpol
>   involved in the investigation?
> Suspects? Interrogation on videotape—who was
>   questioned?
> The case was put on hold after only fourteen months
>   . . . Why so fast?
> The last photo of Mia Sark—what preceded that
>   night? Johan, Marie Louise—where are they
>   now?

She lifted the pen from the paper and stared out into the
air, thinking about Carl Roebel's reaction. The lack of coop-
eration had not surprised her. The police were rarely enthusi-
astic about the press, and few investigators could be persuaded
to bypass chains of command and relax the rules, no matter
how charmingly you smiled at them. What puzzled her was
Roebel's reaction when she had asked about the Mia Sark
case—the immediate connection to Schäfer's call. Heloise
had not told Schäfer about Mia Sark. When he had called the
South and Southern Jutland police this morning it had been
to inquire about Mázoreck.

There was a hard knock on the window, and Heloise
jumped in her seat, causing the notepad to fall out of her
hands and onto the floor.

"Christ!" she exclaimed, placing a hand on her chest.

Heloise looked at Oliver, who was standing at the car
door. She turned the key halfway in the ignition, rolled down
the window, and laughed.

"You scared me!"

"I'm sorry," he said, smiling. "You forgot this in there."

He handed her wallet through the window, and Heloise
took it.

"Thank you. I'm sorry if I got you in trouble with that
Roebel guy," she said. "He seems like the fairly grumpy type."

"Yeah, he wasn't happy with the situation, but don't take that personally. He's always like that."

"Did he chew you out?"

He shook his head and looked around the parking lot. "No, actually, I don't even know where he went."

"Well, in any case, thanks for your help."

"You're welcome," he said. "I'm sorry I couldn't help more, but maybe you could try contacting the regional newspapers. Since it's regarding a local accident, they may have covered it in the past, and they may still have notes and sources and things like that. Otherwise, you'll have to try taking it up with Zøllner when he's back."

"I'll get in touch with one of my news contacts," Heloise said, turning on the engine.

Oliver took a few steps away from the car, then changed his mind and walked back again. He put a hand on the roof and leaned down towardher.

"I was thinking . . . I'm get off in an hour or so. Do you want to grab a cup of coffee?"

Heloise met his gaze and smiled. How old was he—twenty-four? Twenty-five?

"Thank you for the offer," she said, "but I have to get going."

Oliver lowered his gaze and nodded. Then he turned around and disappeared through the door of the police station again.

Heloise pulled out her phone. She typed a name in the search bar on Google and stared at the screen for a long time, doing nothing.

"This is a really bad idea," she said aloud to herself and took a deep breath.

Her body quivered as she pressed Search.

14

THE WOMAN PLUNGED her fingers deep into the cleft between her breasts and fished out a small, cylindrical glass container. She took the lid off and sprinkled the white powder on the bar counter.

"Here, baby," she said. She scooped up the powder with a long, blood-red fingernail and held her finger in front of René Decker's face.

He shook his head without looking at her. His gaze was fixed on the closed door that led to his father's office at the other end of the club. Since meeting Roebel on the beach he had been waiting for a moment alone with his father, but when they'd returned, the Germans were here. Accounts had to be settled, money counted. René knew it could take up to an hour. Maybe more.

The woman snorted the cocaine. She wiped her nose with her fingers, sniffed a few times, and leaned against René, who sat on the bar stool next to her.

She lay her hand in his lap and began massaging him in long, mechanical strokes, kissing him on his neck and breathing in his ear. He let her do it but didn't respond to the touch, and felt nothing. He sat perfectly still on the bar stool, his eyes fixed on the closed door, waiting while she moaned and panted and accelerated the strokes that had no effect on him. He turned the pint glass in his hand clockwise on the counter, around and around. His eyes were on the door, his thoughts on Mázoreck.

"You like that?" she asked, trying to kiss him on the mouth.

He pulled his head away. Her breath smelled of metal, and the breasts she pressed against him were hard as stone.

"You like that, baby?"

"No," he said, taking a sip of the beer. He still didn't look at the woman.

She pulled her chin back slightly and regarded him with furrowed brows. She smiled questioningly and ran a finger under her nose.

"What do you mean?"

René Decker turned his gaze on her for the first time since she had sat down.

She was in her mid-twenties, but the made-up face made her look older. Her lips were distended and shone like water balloons filled to bursting point, and they looked unnaturally large in the small face. The brows were tattooed on, the long extensions in various maroon shades were fastened with bands in the worn-out hair and matched the dress—a chestnut patent-leather number the size of a stamp. Her stage name was Luanna—an alias his father had come up with—and all the guys at the club had hit her several times, including René. Now it struck him that he didn't know what her real name was.

He met her gaze.

"You're not my type," he said.

The woman laughed uncertainly. She moistened her lips, lowered her gaze, put her hand in his lap and began to rub again.

He looked at her with dead eyes.

"You have a child, right?"

Her smile faded. She pulled her hand back and looked at him for a long moment. Then she reached for the glass container again and began sprinkling cocaine on the bar counter.

"You have a child," he continued, glancing pointedly at his Omega watch. "It's a quarter past one on a Thursday afternoon, and you're sitting here snorting coke while your kid is running around alone out there somewhere. Aren't you ashamed?"

She emptied the entire glass container onto the table decisively and found a credit card in her bag.

"Do you think I can get a hard-on for a drug whore like you who can't figure out how to take care of her own child?"

"You used to get hard like a rock back in the day," snorted the woman. She began chopping into the cocaine with the card, dividing the drug into small, thin lines.

"Have you seen yourself lately?" asked René, looking her up and down. "Plastic tits and fake lips. Fucking strangers for money. For coke!"

"Fuck you," she muttered, putting a rolled bill to one nostril and leaning toward the counter.

Ren grabbed the woman's hair and pulled it back with a quick jerk, causing her to let out a howl. He stood up and dragged her halfway across the room by the hair on her neck.

"Get the fuck out of here!" he shouted, giving her a hard push toward the exit.

The woman sobbed softly and staggered out to the cloakroom. The other girls present in the club watched her briefly with languid glances. Then they returned to their customers. To their own problems.

The door to the office at the opposite end of the club opened, and René turned his head toward the sound.

Laszlo— a big, bald Croat who spoke broken English and faithfully followed René's father everywhere—looked out from the office and gave him a nod.

René straightened his shirt and walked over.

Jes Decker sat in his chair behind the mahogany desk in the dark back-room office. He was still wearing the dark-blue velvet robe he had dressed in after the beach trip. The hood was pulled up over his head as if he were a boxer about to enter the ring.

It struck René how old his father had become—how frail and emaciated he looked. His pointed shoulders were clearly noticeable under the dark fabric, and his hands shook as he gathered the bundles of money lying on the table in front of him into tall stacks.

The old man raised his head and met René's gaze. His eyes were still the same, he thought. Dead, just like his own. Uncompromising.

"Did you get ahold of Glenn?" his father asked.

"I sent someone out to get him," René replied. "He'll be here any second now."

The old man nodded and lowered his gaze. "We can't have him going around running his mouth like that."

"What about the other thing?" asked René, clasping his hands at his sides so that his knuckles turned white. "What Roebel said?"

"That's a thing of the past," Jes Decker said without looking up. "Leave it there."

"But there's a policeman from Copenhagen asking questions, and we need to investigate what he . . ."

Jes Decker held up a hand to stop him.

"We don't need to attract the attention of policemen we don't know. It's too risky."

"Then we have to find out what he knows *without* attracting attention."

The old man looked up and tilted his head slightly. He regarded his son with a searching gaze.

"What do you think this cop knows that we don't know?" The corners of René's mouth sagged and he shrugged. "Maybe they've found something over there. A DNA trace—something or another that proves that it was . . ."

His father snorted and brushed off the idea with a wave of his hand.

"Wishful thinking," he said.

"Why the hell would a homicide investigator from Copenhagen care about something that happened twenty years ago at the opposite end of the country?" asked René.

Jes Decker leaned on his golf club and got up from his chair with difficulty. He walked on uncertain legs toward his son. He pressed his lips together and exhaled heavily through his nose.

"I thought you'd put all this behind you, boy."

"Put it behind me?" René Decker stared at his father in disbelief. "Every time I pull the trigger, I picture Mázoreck's face."

"You need to move on."

René looked down and shook his head.

"I can't. Not until I've found out what happened that night when he . . ."

They were interrupted by a knock on the door, and it was opened slightly.

Laszlo poked his head into the room.

"Sorry for disturb, boss, but Glenn is arrive."

Jes Decker sent his son a long look. Then he nodded to Laszlo, who opened the door completely.

A few seconds later, Glenn Nielsen, a stocky man in his early fifties with shoulder-length hair and an obsequious door-to-door salesman smile, stepped into the room and threw out his arms as if they were best friends.

"What's up, boys? Are you keeping warm? Shit, you'd think we were in the Congo, huh?"

He was wearing black sweatpants that were buttoned up on the sides, and a red-checkered shirt with cut-off sleeves. Beads of sweat trickled onto his temples under the dark hair, which was gathered in a low ponytail at the nape of his neck.

René didn't like Glenn and had known all along that one day he would be dead weight that they would have to part with. They had kept him on the payroll until now because, on the plus side, he was small-minded and willing to do any-thing for money; he therefore took on tasks none of the oth-ers would touch with tongs of fire, most recently the job of driver on a high-risk job in Germany.

On the minus side, he was small-minded and willing to do anything for money.

They couldn't trust him.

"What's up, junior," Glenn said, holding out a clenched fist to René. "All good?"

"No, Glenn, all *not* good," René said, ignoring the fist. "I have a small problem that you need to help me solve."

"It happens to even the best," Glenn said, dropping his arm. "But isn't it better if you get one of the girls out there to help you with that kind of thing?"

Glenn looked from René to Jes Decker to Laszlo and chuckled. He fished a cigarette out of his shirt pocket and tucked it between his lips.

"Any of you have a light?" he asked, patting his pockets.

"I hear you're shooting off your mouth in the city," René said.

Glenn raised an eyebrow and took the cigarette out of his mouth.

"Shooting my mouth off? Shit, people are so busy, man. I haven't said a damn thing."

"So how do you explain that the police know you were in Hamburg last month?"

"The police? Hey, man, I sure as hell haven't . . ."

René Decker reached behind his back and pulled out a gun. He aimed it at Glenn's head and fired a single shot.

The bullet went in through the right eye, and Glenn collapsed like a house of cards. The cigarette slipped out of his hand and rolled some distance along the floor, stopping at René's feet.

René squatted down and picked it up.

He remained seated, watching the blood as it slowly spread under Glenn, whose legs convulsed for a moment before lying completely still.

René sensed that his father was approaching from behind.

"Maybe that was a little excessive," said Jes Decker in an inquisitive tone of voice. "A bullet in the knee would have been fine too."

René said nothing.

Laszlo looked questioningly from one to the other. Then he shrugged and started tracking down a saw and a floor mop.

"Well, but let it pass." Jes Decker put a hand on his son's shoulder and gave it a squeeze. "What is it you'd like us to do with that cop, the investigator from Copenhagen?"

René put the cigarette in his mouth and lit it. "Can you do without Laszlo tonight?"

CHAPTER

15

THE BLADES OF Dybbøl Mill were standing still as Heloise drove past, and the wide expanses of sunny-yellow rapeseed fields sloped down in front of her toward Sønderborg Bay. On soil fertilized with blood from the war with Germany in 1864, a handful of mansions lay with white-washed walls and black, glazed roof tiles that glittered like freshly minted coins in the sun. Heloise slowed down completely as she approached one of the houses. She slowly rolled past the driveway and looked at the name on the mailbox.

MALLING, it read.

She drove twenty yards down the road and pulled over, letting the engine run, and rested her arm on the frame of the open window as she peered over at the property.

Her heart was beating so hard that she could feel her pulse in her fingertips.

There were two black 4x4s in the driveway, and several of the bay windows on the second floor of the house were open. The sand-colored curtains moved easily in the wind.

There had to be someone at home.

Heloise spotted a swing hanging from a large oak tree in the yard and suddenly felt her heart grow heavy. She had known it would be difficult to see Thomas like this. As someone's dad. Someone's husband. But seven years is a long time, and feelings fade. At least that's what she'd told herself on the drive here.

Now she was no longer so sure.

She jumped as the front door of the house opened and a woman with shoulder-length blond hair walked down the stairs with quick steps. She was wearing a form-fitting white dress that went all the way down to her ankles. One of her hands lay protectively on her pregnant belly, which was large and distended under the elastic fabric, and in the other she had a gym bag.

She put the bag in the trunk of one of the cars, then turned to the house and clapped her hands.

"Come on, boys, we need to hurry. The game starts in half an hour!"

There were children's voices from the open front door, and two medium-blonde twin boys came out on the stairs wearing soccer outfits. They laughed and shoved each other with their elbows.

Someone appeared in the doorway behind the children, and Heloise stopped breathing.

His face was more marked than she remembered it, jaw-line clearer. The hair was also different. When he was younger, it had always been allowed to grow randomly in dark, unruly locks. Now it was short and well-trimmed and somehow made him look even better. More adult.

Heloise had been wrong. Time hadn't changed anything.

She shouldn't have come.

The children got into the back seat, and Thomas Malling was left standing on the stairs and waving as the car rolled out of the driveway. When it was out of sight, he turned to go back into the house, and at the same moment the ringtone from Heloise's cell phone broke the silence.

She hurriedly rejected the call. Then she turned her head and looked over at the house.

Thomas had stopped. He stood on the stairs leading up to the front door, shielding his eyes from the sun with a hand as he peered in her direction.

Heloise slid herself down into the seat and held her breath.

Did he see me?

Fuck, what am I doing here?

She carefully stretched her neck and looked out the window.

Thomas's gaze was still directed toward the car.

Ten heartbeats ticked by.

Then he started walking toward her.

Heloise watched him disappear in a cloud of dust as she put her foot to the accelerator and stepped on it.

CHAPTER

16

THE FIELD ROAD was dusty and bumpy, and the tall elephant grass along the shoulder hung over the ruts and whipped at the car. Heloise drove over tree roots and potholes, and for a moment wondered if she had entered the wrong address into the GPS. It had all happened so quickly when she planned the trip earlier in the day. Half an hour after she had made the decision to leave, she had been in a taxi on the way to Copenhagen Airport and had managed to buy a plane ticket, be at home in the apartment on Olfert Fischers Street to pack a suitcase, rent a car, and find a place to spend the night. She hadn't grasped the fact that the house she had rented was so isolated. So far out in the middle of nowhere.

She could see from the map that it was a mile, maybe a mile and a half, to the nearest neighbor, and twice as far to anything resembling a grocery store. In Copenhagen she had everything she needed within a hundred-yard radius and could sense life around her on the stairs and in the neighborhood at any time of the day: the constant buzzing of hissing vacuum cleaners and spinning washing machines; chair legs screeching across old wooden floors; children's voices in the early hours of the morning; and howls from emergency vehicles. The Doppler effect from the pulse of the big city in rising and falling tones.

The road she was driving on stopped at a dead end in front of the property. Heloise turned off the engine and raised her brows in amazement.

For 240 kroner a day, on the outskirts of Gråsten, you apparently got what, with a little goodwill, reminded you of the Hermitage Castle—at least in terms of size. Gerda's Momento looked neglected, though. The old pink paint clung to the walls, and the maroon roof tiles lay helter-skelter at the peak of the roof. But the house was beautifully situated in a glade surrounded by large beech trees and weeping willows that looked as if they had stood there for hundreds of years, while the rest of the vegetation on the plot grew youthfully and uncontrolled in a lush chaos of a thousand green nuances.

Heloise found the key under the top log in the woodpile at the back of the property as agreed, locked herself in, and looked around. There was a faint, sweet smell of decay in every room, and although it was fully furnished, everything in the big house looked abandoned. Forgotten. There were white sheets all over the furniture in the living room, and the wicks of the candles on the dining-room table were squashed into the hardened candle wax, as if someone had extinguished the flames hastily with an angry thumb.

Heloise opened the double doors that led out onto the lush garden and let the sun come into the house as she walked around, pulling sheets off the furniture so that the dust swirled in the golden light. She sat in the doorway and ate the sandwich from Pret à Manger while she read the new e-mails that had come in from Munk, and everything she could find in print about the Mia Sark case.

There wasn't much to go on. The media interest had apparently died down in 1998 along with the case. Heloise had not run into any new information in the articles she had been able to find from the time before, and Tom Mázoreck's name did not figure into any mentions of the case other than the one she'd found on Infomedia. It was just the same recurring story. No new clues, nothing new under the sun.

Heloise tried to catch Schäfer again, and he answered the call on the third ring.

"Hey," she said. "Am I disturbing you?"

"Yes, a little. What's up?"

Heloise sensed a bite in his voice that hadn't been there earlier in the day.

"Are you okay?" she asked .

"I'm busy. What can I do for you?"

"If you don't have time now, I can just call later," Heloise said, pausing to give him the opportunity to end the conversation. She could hear the sound of cutlery and clinking glasses, a buzz of voices in the background, and she glanced at her wristwatch. It was approaching one thirty PM.

When Schäfer said nothing, she continued.

"I just wanted to let you know that I'm in Southern Jutland to see if your buddy Zøllner can help me with . . ."

"You drove to Southern Jutland?"

"No, I took the plane over here, but yes, I've come down here to find out more about Mázoreck, and now there's something else I've stumbled on: a case from 1997 that the police believe is a trafficking case. There's some talk about a young woman who may have been kidnapped and driven out of the country on the back of a truck. She never showed up again and the case was forgotten."

"So what?"

"I think the two cases are connected in some way."

"What two cases?"

"Tom Mázoreck's death and Mia Sark's disappearance, and I think Fischhof knows something about it. He started crying when I mentioned the girl. He knew her name, and an investigator I spoke to today also left me with the impression that there is a connection there."

"Mia Sark?"

"Yes, that was her name," Heloise said. "The one who disappeared. I inquired about her today when I was at the police station in Sønderborg, and the investigation was apparently put on hold after only fourteen months."

Schäfer said nothing.

"Fourteen months!" repeated Heloise, as if that ought to trigger a stronger reaction. "Do we agree that this is incredibly quick to call off work on such a case?"

Schäfer grumbled noncommittally. "You can't say that so categorically. It depends on a lot of things."

"But it's a short time, yes?"

"Yes, but again, I need to know more about the specific case to have an opinion about it."

"Tom Mázoreck saw the girl the evening she disappeared. He was in town at the same tavern and spoke to the press about the case, gave testimony to the police and so on. Then he drowns on August 1, 1998, and two days later the Sark investigation is put on hold. Unsolved, period."

Schäfer was quiet.

"Hello, are you there?" asked Heloise.

"Yes, I'm here, but I'm waiting to find out what this has to do with *me*?"

She frowned. "Why are you so pissed?"

"I'm not pissed."

"You sound really annoyed! Are you sure there's nothing wrong?"

Heloise could hear Schäfer breathing heavily on the other end.

"There's nothing wrong," he said. "It's just been a long day so far."

Heloise was quiet for a moment. Then she continued: "Well, don't you think it's a strange coincidence? With those dates?"

"It's a coincidence. I don't know if it's strange."

"Can you put me in touch with Zøllner? I saw that he was the investigating officer on the Sark case, but he wasn't at the police station today." Heloise got up and went into the kitchen to throw the sandwich wrapper in the trash. "And by the way, do you know an investigator down here named Carl Roebel?"

"Roebel? No, that doesn't ring any bells. Why?"

"I met him today and he seemed a little shady."

"What do you mean?"

"He seemed kind of . . . well, I don't really know. I got a weird vibe from him, and he automatically linked your call this morning to my questions about Mia Sark. Isn't that weird?"

"Didn't you just say that Tom Mázoreck had been a witness in the case?"

"Yes, but . . ."

"Then I guess it's makes sense."

"Well, sure, when you put it that way, but . . ." Heloise took a deep breath, searching for the words. She couldn't explain what it was that had caused Carl Roebel to hit her radar.

She heard a woman's voice in the background.

"Are you with Connie?" she asked.

"No, I'm in a meeting, so if there's nothing else?"

"Are you sending me Zøllner's contact info?"

Schäfer mumbled something and hung up.

Heloise stuck the phone in her back pocket and looked in the fridge. There were four bottles of beer in there from a German brewery she didn't know, Krombacher Pils, and a red bag of Gevalia coffee.

Otherwise, it was empty.

She made a mental note to buy a few small things on the way back to the house after she had been at Benniksgaard. Morten Munk had sent her a summary of Jan Fischhof's address and place of work in the nineties, and Heloise had remembered correctly that Jan had both lived and worked on the farm at the same time as Tom Mázoreck.

She went into the living room and put her notebook and iPhone in her bag. Then she walked out into the hallway and shut the front door behind her.

17

I T WAS NO wonder that Jan Fischhof had chosen to settle in
Dragør when this was where he had grown up, Heloise
thought as she drove into Rinkenæs. The cities were similar
and entering both was like stepping into an old *Shu- bi-dua*
song about Summer in Denmark: grain billowed in the fields,
the whitewashed church tower stretched its neck so it could
be seen from up on the main road, and Flensburg Fjord lay
gleaming in the background.

Heloise parked in the courtyard in front of Benniksgaard
Hotel and headed for the main house: a white, two-winged
property in a neoclassical style with a thatched roof and blue,
barred windows.

At the reception desk, she was greeted by a woman with
short, henna-colored hair. She was dressed in a long summer
dress that fluttered behind her and wore eight rings of amber
on her fingers: large, petrified pieces of resin in various shades
of yellow-brown that made it look as if she had donned brass
knuckles of gold.

Her gaze drifted over Heloise, and she smiled
obligingly.

"Welcome! Can I help with anything?"

"I hope so," Heloise said. "I'm looking for anyone who
can tell me something about what this place was like before
it was turned into golf courses and a hotel."

The woman nodded and reached for a stack of brochures
lying on the counter. She put one of them in front of Heloise
and turned to page one, where an old black-and-white photo
filled the entire page.

"For many hundreds of years, Benniksgaard was a traditional farm. The farm was built in the year . . ."

Heloise held up her hands to stop her.

"We don't have to travel back that far in time," she said.
"I'm only interested in the nineties."

The woman closed the brochure. "Is there anything specific you'd like to know?"

"Yes, I . . ." Heloise hesitated as she tried to judge the
woman's age. She appeared to be at least ten years younger
than Fischhof. "I know someone who worked here back then,
but I think he's a lot older than you. His name is Jan Fischhof, does that ring any bells?"

The woman pursed her lips in regret. "No,
unfortunately."

"Maybe one of your colleagues can help?" Heloise peered
out toward the back room. "Could any of them have been
here then?"

"The owner of Benniksgaard is the same as always, but
he is in Scotland and won't be home until next week, so you
might want to try contacting Hans Gallagher. He undoubt-
edly has a lot of stories from that time."

"Who is he?"

"He managed the mink farm out here back in the day.
He has a pig herd now, not far from the old church, and—
yeah, who else is there from that time?" She drummed her
fingers on the counter. "There's Dres Carstensen, who was a
herdsman out here for many years."

Heloise wrote the names down in her notebook. "You
said something about a mink farm?"

"Yes, it was over there where there's a driving range now."
The woman pointed out the large floor-to-ceiling windows.

Heloise turned and looked out over the links where a
gentleman in white sent a golf ball in a high arc into the sky.
He remained standing with the club raised over his left

shoulder and his body in the characteristic hip-twisted stance while he followed the ball's curve with his eyes.

"When was that, did you say?" asked Heloise. "When was there a mink farm here?"

"That was during the period you're interested in." The woman pointed at Heloise and nodded. "But there were so many problems with it at the time that it was closed after just a few years. I can't remember the year, but I wonder if it wasn't before the turn of the millennium?"

Heloise looked up from her notepad. "What problems are we talking about?"

"Well, there was so much talk about the ethics of it, so much hassle and fuss, so . . ." She shrugged.

"And his name is Hans, you say? The one who managed the mink farm?"

"Yes, Hans Gallagher. He rented the land from the Benniksgaard family in his time, but as I said, it wasn't long before he closed it down and left for good."

"Was that something he lost money on, do you think?"

"Oh, I don't have any idea," said the woman.

"He lives right down here, you say?" Heloise pointed in the direction of the church she had passed on her way there.

"No, out by the Old Rinkenæs Church. It's located a few miles outside the city."

Heloise wrote this down on her notepad.

"My friend mentioned something about him living here at Benniksgaard in his time. Can that be true?"

"Yes. There were three worker residences at the time that sat side by side, and I know some of the employees lived here permanently for a number of years, but all three buildings were destroyed in the fire."

"Fire?"

"Yes." The woman looked in the brochure again and pointed to a bit of text somewhere in the middle of the booklet. "There was a fire on the farm where the worker residences and parts of the old granary burned down to the ground. It was in . . ." She looked for the right place in the text. "December, 1998."

"Was it a deliberate fire, or what was it?"

"Deliberate?" The woman pulled her chin back, amazed at the question. "No, no, it was . . . well, I don't actually know if it was a gas stove exploding or what it was, but it was something along those lines at least. It was an accident."

"And all this," Heloise threw her arms out and pointed around at the various buildings. "It was all a farm back then?"

"Yes. The main house where our suites are located was once the farm owner's private residence, while the wing, as you can see over there," she pointed to the other side of the courtyard, "served as a stable with horses and sheep and chickens and whatever else belonged to it. It was in that building where they skinned the minks."

"Is there still anything to see over there? Anything left from that time?"

"No, the entire farm has been completely renovated. It's all a hotel now."

Heloise thanked the woman for her help and searched for Hans Gallagher's name when she was standing out in the courtyard again. She found his phone number and made a call.

The voice answering the call sounded cheerful and good-humored.

"Hello," Heloise said. "Am I speaking to Hans Gallagher?"

"Who's asking?"

Heloise introduced herself and said she worked for the *Demokratisk Dagblad*.

"I understand that it was you who ran the mink farm at Benniksgaard back in the day?"

The question made him squirm a little.

"Uh, well, but that was many years ago, and I don't do fur production anymore, so I'm not interested in . . ."

"That's not why I'm calling either. I'd like to know if you can recall Jan Fischhof, who worked at Benniksgaard back then?"

Hans Gallagher was quiet for a moment. When he spoke again, Heloise could hear the smile in his voice.

"Fischhof? God, yes, I certainly remember him. He worked for me you know!"

Heloise pointed the car key at her Renault, unlocked it, and began to walk toward it with quick steps.

"Can I stop by? I have some questions I would like to ask you. It won't take that long."

Hans Gallagher sounded puzzled by the question.

"Why, yes, but . . . I'm in Kollund, and it'll be a few hours or three before I . . ." He took the phone away from his mouth, and Heloise could hear him talking to someone else. Then he was back. "I can be home by five thirty PM. Is it going to work?"

"On the pig farm? At the old church?"

"Yes."

"See you out there."

Heloise hung up, opened her notebook, and looked at the name she had jotted down when she had read the articles about Mia Sark. She considered calling first for a moment, but then brushed off the idea and got into the car. Although it was a lousy method usually reserved for journalists from the tabloid press, everyone in the profession knew that it was strategically unwise to warn sensitive sources that you were on your way to see them. You usually got a better story out of knocking unannounced on their door. Catch them with their guard down

18

"Yes?"

Dark, painted eyes looked questioningly at Heloise and the porcelain crowns glowed white in the measured smile. The woman in the doorway had to be in her early seventies. Her pageboy hair was blue-black, and her skin stretched tightly over full cheekbones, pale and translucent like the skin of a drum.

"Ingeborg Sark?" asked Heloise.

"Yes?"

"My name is Heloise Kaldan."

Heloise held out her hand, and the woman hesitated for a moment before accepting it. Her hand felt fragile in Heloise's. Large, but powerless, like a child's.

Despite her height, Sark didn't look like it would take much more than a light gust of wind to knock her over. Her long, lanky figure was wrapped in a black suit, and from this dark getup two arms stuck out, thin as toothpicks, and a pair of naked, knotted feet.

"Can I help you with something?" she asked. Her voice sounded tiny, almost childish.

"I'm a journalist," Heloise said. "I want to know if I can ask you a few questions about your daughter."

Ingeborg Sark let go of Heloise's hand and let her own fall limply down along her body.

"Mia?"

"If I could come in for a moment, I can explain."

Ingeborg Sark looked at Heloise with her chin raised, but said nothing.

"I see that it has been many years since anyone last wrote anything about the case," Heloise said when it became clear that she would have to argue her way into Ingeborg Sark's home. "When such cases are forgotten, it rarely benefits the investigation. The police need testimony, and often it is ordinary people who contribute the crucial information: people who have read about an old case in the newspaper and suddenly remember something they saw or heard. It could be a perpetrator who has talked over the years to a friend or a colleague, who then puts two and two together and contacts the police because . . ."

"Perpetrator?" Ingeborg Sark put a hand on her chest. "Is there something new on the case?"

"No, no." Heloise shook her head and took a step closer to the woman. "That was clumsily put. What I'm trying to say is that media coverage can help kickstart a stalled investigation."

She held her hands out to Ingeborg Sark with upturned palms.

"I have just visited the police in Sønderborg, and there was literally dust on the file. No one is working to find out what happened to your daughter anymore—no one but me."

"But . . ." Ingeborg Sark shook her head slightly. "Why are *you* interested in the case?"

Heloise hesitated for a moment.

"I'm investigating another case, and your daughter's name has come up in relation to that."

Something indefinable flickered in Ingeborg Sark's eyes. She swept the pageboy hair behind her ears and pursed her lips slightly.

Then she nodded and took a step back into the hallway. "Who do you work for?"

Ingeborg Sark sat on the edge of a black leather armchair and rocked slightly from side to side as she watched Heloise

with narrowed eyes. She held a water glass in her hands. It
had been sitting on the coffee table when they sat down in
the living room and was two-thirds full of a straw-yellow liquid with a faint, greenish glow that indicated Sauvignon
Blanc rather than tap water.

"The *Demokratisk Dagblad*," Heloise said. "I work in the
investigative department, where we go in-depth with things,
researching and unraveling subjects a little more than a news
journalist normally has the opportunity to do. ."

Ingeborg Sark nodded to herself, as if that was an answer
she could live with.

Heloise looked around the living room, where all the
curtains had been drawn. It was dark in the large, detached
house and so empty and quiet that she wouldn't have been
surprised if a tumbleweed had rolled across the living-room
floor as in a ghost town in the post-goldrush Klondike. The
walls were painted in a burnt-red color, and the large, dark-
brown tiles on the floors cooled the house down.

Outside, the sun beat down, but in here you didn't feel
the heat.

"Do you live alone?" asked Heloise.

Ingeborg Sark nodded.

"You don't have any other children?"

"No."

"Do you have a husband? A boyfriend?"

Ingeborg Sark directed a distant gaze to the wall behind
Heloise. "Not anymore."

Heloise took a recorder out of her bag.

"Do you mind if I record our conversation?"

The woman shook her head, and Heloise pressed the
record button.

"How long have you lived here?" she asked.

"In Gråsten or here in the house?"

"Both."

"I was born and raised in the city, and I've lived in this
house since 1987. Mia was nine when we moved in, and I've
considered moving many times. There are too many memories in these rooms—too many good ones, too many bad

ones, but . . . I've always thought that . . ." Ingeborg Sark lowered her gaze. "Yes, I know people think it's silly, but I've always thought that if I move, she won't be able to find her way home." She looked up and met Heloise's gaze with an uncompromising face.

"That's what keeps me going," she said. "That's how I survive. There are no other options. She might come back home."

Heloise nodded, because it was the kind thing to do, and a heavy silence descended over the room.

"I've read some about the case, so I know she left the bar alone that night," Heloise said. "But I don't know anything about who she was or what state of mind she was in at the time."

Ingeborg Sark turned her face away. "We . . . we had argued that day."

"The day she disappeared?"

She nodded.

"Do you remember what you argued about?"

"Yes, but . . ." She shook her head slowly. "It wasn't any- thing serious. At least not compared to what happened next, and she was normally such a good girl."

"Any information could have an impact on the case. Even if it seems unimportant," Heloise said, and nodded encouragingly to get her to continue. "You had been arguing?"

Ingeborg Sark was breathing heavily and shaking her head slightly. "It actually started several months earlier. Long before Mia disappeared."

"What was it about, the quarrel?"

"Well it . . . it was about something as stupid as ciga- rettes. And money!" She took a sip of the wine. "It was just a foolish, inconsequential thing. I'd discovered that she had started smoking. We had an agreement that I would pay for her driver's license if she stayed away from such things, but now I had found cigarettes in her bag. So I informed her that she had to take care of the expenses herself—said that a deal was a deal. A driver's license cost in the region of ten thousand kroner, and she didn't have that kind of money at all, so I figured it would be a long time before she could afford it—a year, maybe two. But a few months later she came in waving a bundle of cash. I couldn't understand how she had scraped together so much in such a short time, and of course I became suspicious."

"Where did she get the money?"

"Yes, I wanted to know that too," said Ingeborg Sark, nodding. "That's why we got into an argument, because she lied to me. Said that she had saved one half and that the other half was a gift from her father. But—smoking or not—he would never have given her money for that driver's license."

"What's his name?" Heloise looked up from her notepad. "Your ex, I presume?"

Ingeborg Sark narrowed her eyes slightly and nodded.

"His name was Henning Sark, and he died many years ago. We divorced when Mia was little, and we weren't very good friends after that, to say the least. When she disappeared, he told the police that he wouldn't be surprised if she had run off to get away from me. He didn't help look for her, and I don't think he ever thought about her again."

"I'm sorry to ask, but could he have been right?" asked Heloise cautiously. "Could it be that Mia ran away from home?"

Ingeborg Sark shook her head slowly.

"We had argued that day, but it wasn't symptomatic of our relationship. She was always such a good girl. Such a *good* girl," she repeated, lost in thought for a moment. "Besides, she was of legal age. If she had wanted to move, she was free to do so. No one forced her to stay here."

"If we can just go back to the argument," Heloise said. "You say that Mia claimed that she had received half the money from her father and had saved the other half herself."

"Yes."

"Then what happened?"

"I said I didn't believe her and demanded to know where the money had come from. Because I have to admit that I honestly . . . I thought the worst."

"What was that?"

"That she might have stolen it. Maybe from that place, from the . . . the café she worked at, but I still have no idea. I just don't see where else it could have come from."

"What kind of café was it?"

"A place that's out in Broager. She managed to work there for half a year, two evenings a week. Until she disappeared."

"Do you know if it still exists?"

She hesitated. "Yes, but . . . it has changed a lot since that time. It's no longer what it was—it's become so shabby. Seedy!"

"What's the name of the café?"

"Celeste. Something-Celeste."

Heloise switched tracks. "What type of person was Mia? Was she a happy girl? Did she have many friends?"

"Yes, she had friends, and yes, she was . . ." Ingeborg Sark went silent and sat for a long moment, staring into space. "But she seemed different . . . the last time."

"In what way?"

"I don't know, she was just . . ." Ingeborg Sark lay a hand against one of her cheeks, and her eyes went blank. "I could see that she cried a lot. The last few weeks she was . . . her eyes were completely ruined with crying, discouraged, but she wouldn't tell me what was wrong. I asked several times, but she didn't want to talk about it, she said. She seemed strange . . . despondent."

"Could it have been a romantic heartbreak, do you think?"

She shook her head uncertainly. "I think she was seeing someone, but she never told me about him. The only boy she ever brought home was Johan, and they were just friends."

"Johan—he was the one she was in town with that evening, wasn't he?"

Ingeborg Sark nodded. "He's never really recovered from what happened."

"Do you know where he lives now?"

"He still lives in town. He has an auto repair shop not far from here. A sweet boy. Every year on the anniversary he stops by to see how I'm doing. I think it's comforting for both of us to talk to someone who knew Mia. Someone who remembers her as she was before she became the girl who disappeared." With a gesture, she encapsulated the last three words in air quotes. "There aren't that many of us left."

"What about the other girl who was in town with them that night? There were three of them out together, right? A girl named Marie Louise?"

"Malou Yang," she nodded. "No one called her Marie Louise back then."

"Were she and Mia friends?"

"More than that. They were inseparable for a number of years." Ingeborg Sark stared into the fireplace on the other side of the coffee table. The hearth looked like an open mouth, empty and black with soot.

"It sounds silly when I say it out loud, but I could get quite jealous of how close they were—they almost acted like they were in love. But that changed as they got older. They started to grow apart in the last few years. At least that's what Malou said to the police at the time. She was also the one who told them that Mia had been seeing some guy during that spring."

"A boyfriend?"

Ingeborg Sark shrugged.

"Was he questioned in connection with the case, this guy?"

"No, because no one knew who he was. Malou had just seen them together a few weeks before and said that Mia had been secretive about it. She thought they might have gone away together, but . . . no." She shook her head. "Without saying anything to me? And without coming home again? No. She never would have done that."

"Does Malou come and visit you once in a while?" asked Heloise.

Ingeborg Sark snorted slightly and shook her head.

"She started medical school in August the year Mia disappeared, and I haven't seen her since. I heard she works at Hvidovre Hospital now. That she's a *pediatrician*." She sneered at the word and laughed a quiet, joyless laugh. "I often find myself thinking: I wish it had been her. I wish it had been Malou who disappeared back then instead of my daughter. And then I imagine Mia in a white coat with a stethoscope around her neck in the children's ward of a hospital somewhere." She met Heloise's gaze. "Does that make me a bad person, do you think?"

Heloise shook her head. "It makes you human."

"I sometimes meet some of the mothers of Mia's old classmates when I'm at the store, and I can see them thinking: Thank God it was Ingeborg's daughter this happened to, and not mine. "

"They're also just human," Heloise said. "I'm sure they don't mean any harm by it."

"Well, I don't know . . ." Ingeborg Sark looked down and took a sip of her wine.

Heloise leafed through her notes.

"In one of the first articles written about the case, a witness from the pub speaks out—a Tom Mázoreck. Does that name mean anything to you?"

Ingeborg Sark looked up and blinked a few times. "Tom?"

"Yes. Did you know him?"

"Yes, I . . ." She narrowed her eyes. "Why are you asking about him?"

"How did you know each other?"

Ingeborg Sark shrugged slightly, and red blotches appeared on her cheeks.

"He helped look for Mia when she disappeared, and he . . . he was there for me in the aftermath."

"Were you dating?"

"No, we weren't what you'd normally associate with being in a romantic relationship. It was more . . . unconventional."

"But did you have a . . ." Heloise raised her brows and nodded, ". . . a physical relationship?"

Ingeborg Sark pulled deeper into the black suit and shook her head halfheartedly.

"It was, above all, a *spiritual* relationship. Tom was very affected by what had happened, and it bound us together for a while. I honestly have no idea how I would have gotten through the first few months without him. He took care of me, made sure I got something to eat, comforted me, bathed me. He helped me with all the paperwork, with the conversations with the police—he was by my side through it all. But as time went on, the visits came less and less frequently." She stared down at her glass. "I couldn't blame him. It wasn't his grief, of course."

"Were you in love with him?"

Ingeborg Sark lifted her chin, and her eyes hardened. "That certainly isn't any of your business."

Heloise met her gaze with a conciliatory smile and let a few seconds pass in silence to reset the mood.

"Did you know him already?" she asked. "From before Mia disappeared?"

"I knew *of* him. Gråsten is a small town."

"Do you remember if he worked at Benniksgaard during the period when you were seeing each other?"

"Yes. He did."

"Do you remember Jan Fischhof, who also worked there?"

Ingeborg Sark started. She stared at Heloise for a long moment, then swallowed so hard it was audible.

"Do you know if Mia knew him?" asked Heloise. "Or have you ever heard her mention him?"

"What are you doing?" whispered Ingeborg Sark. "You knock on my door. Pretending to want to help."

Heloise raised both brows. "I don't understand what you . . ."

Sark stood up.

"Please go," she said.

"If you'd just sit down again, Ingeborg, then you can explain . . ."

The water glass exploded in the fireplace. "GET OUT!"

Heloise stood up, picked the recorder up from the table, and walked out into the hall.

At the door, she turned around.

"If you change your mind," she said, holding out her card. "I'll stay in the area for a few days, in case you want to talk after all . . ."

Ingeborg Sark looked down at the card without taking it. She fixed misty eyes on Heloise, and her chin quivered.

"Mia is out there somewhere," she said. "Do you understand? She's out there somewhere."

Heloise didn't have time to say anything before Ingeborg Sark closed the door.

CHAPTER

19

"WELL THEN, YOU'LL have to go in and wake him up. It's important!" said Heloise into the phone.

She got out of her car and slammed the door behind her.

"No, I won't," Ruth said on the other end of the line. "He has been extremely anxious since you spoke this morning, so whatever it is you're doing over there in Jutland, I don't think it's something that will help him."

"I just need to talk to him for a moment," Heloise said. "I have to ask him a few questions."

"I think it's a bad idea."

"Duly noted. Now, please wake him up!"

"I can't! The doctor was here to give him a shot of something to calm him down, and now he's finally asleep, so it'll have to wait until tomorrow."

Heloise turned her head toward the sound of a car approaching at high speed on the main road.

An off-white Range Rover with dried mud up the sides crashed into the courtyard and braked hard into the gravel. An elderly man with a suitcase of an upper body jumped out of the car and headed toward her with short, targeted steps.

Heloise asked Ruth to make contact if Fischhof woke up during the evening and hung up.

The approaching man was wearing a camouflage sweater, dark-blue jeans, and a pair of knee-high rubber boots. His face was wide and tanned. His narrowly set eyes crackled cheerfully, and his silver-gray locks waved over a hairline that didn't look like it had ever moved an inch.

There was something instantly disarming about Hans Gallagher, Heloise thought. A warmth that flowed out of every pore of his body.

"Mornin'!" he said, smiling happily at the sight of her. He held out his hand, and Heloise took it. His skin felt rough and warm against hers, and the handshake was so firm that it nearly buckled her knees.

"Hans Gallagher," he said. "Sorry about the delay. You're coming from a ways away, I believe?"

He let go his iron grip.

"Yes," Heloise nodded, discreetly stretching the fingers of her right hand to feel whether all the bones were intact. "I'm from Copenhagen."

"Oh, yeah? A big city girl! Can you stand it?" He wrinkled his nose at the manure smell and smiled with his whole body.

Heloise looked around and took a careful breath.

"It smells a bit like Inner Copenhagen on an early Sunday morning, so I would venture to say that I am in training," she answered, and smiled.

Hans Gallagher laughed loudly and thumped Heloise on the back, nearly causing her to lose her balance.

"That's good," he said, motioning with a sideways nod for her to follow. "I'm a little busy, so if the stench doesn't go to your gut, maybe you can join me in the barn while we talk?"

"Yes, of course."

"Multitasking, right? Isn't that what you women claim you're so good at?"

He started walking toward the large stable on the other side of the courtyard, and Heloise had to trot to keep up.

"So you know Jan Fischhof?" he asked over his shoulder, pushing open the doors to a pigsty the size of a football field. The noise inside was inhuman, like ten thousand knives screeching against porcelain, and the stench of ammonia made Heloise have to struggle to keep her stomach at rest.

His Gallagher looked at her out of the corner of his eye, and the corners of his mouth curled upward into a smile.

"Everything okay?"

Heloise manned up and nodded. She looked down at the barn floor for a place to step with her white Converse sneakers so they wouldn't get smeared with pig crap.

"Jan Fischhof and I are friends," she said.

"How is he?" asked Hans Gallagher, and started walking down the middle aisle of the barn. "You know, it's been many years since I last saw him."

"He's not doing so well."

Gallagher stopped and turned his head toward her, looking at her with furrowed brows.

"He has terminal-stage lung cancer, so he doesn't have long now," Heloise said.

Gallagher turned his gaze to his rubber boots, put his hands to his sides, and shook his head.

"Satanic shit, that cancer. It took my daughter—oh, and Jan's wife too, by the way! Breast cancer, both of them." He bit his lower lip lightly and set his gaze infinitely far away as he thought back. "That was a terrible time for both of us back then. Now that we've reached a certain age, the death toll is beginning to climb in earnest, and it's that damn cancer behind most of it, you know. Damned satanic filth!"

"Yes, it's bad," Heloise said, nodding. "In addition to lung cancer, Jan has also started to suffer from dementia, so I'm here to try to help him remember life as it was at Benniksgaard back in the day. There was something about you two working together back then?"

"I wasn't employed on the farm like Jan, if that's what you mean, but I had a stake in the mink farm that was there for a number of years, so I went over there from time to time, and Jan worked for me for a few years, but that was a long time ago, of course. What would you like to know?"

"Do you remember a guy named Tom Mázoreck?"

"Tom Pitbull? Oh, yes! What about him?"

Heloise frowned. "Why do you call him that?"

"What? Pitbull?"

"Yes."

He shrugged. "It was just a name, you know. Just something you said. Mázoreck, Tom, Pitbull—it was all the same."

"What can you tell me about him?"

"Yeah, well . . . what can I tell you?" Hans scratched his neck with a bear paw of a hand. "He was a fun character, I'll give him that. And unfortunately, he died very young."

"Wasn't he in his forties?"

"Well, he probably was," Gallagher said. "That's no advanced age, though."

"How well did you know him?"

"We didn't see each other privately, if that's what you mean, but he worked both at Benniksgaard and in Blans, so I ran into him regularly."

"You mean at the slaughterhouse in Blans?" Heloise remembered the job summary Munk had sent her.

Hans Gallagher nodded.

"He wasn't afraid of rolling up his sleeves. Nowadays, it is completely different with the workforce. Young boys cry like bitches when they are asked to work harder, and it all comes down to trade unions and representatives and claims for damages for broken nails and whiplash and a lot of pissing and moaning. Tom Pitbull had several jobs at once, and he never whined. He was old school. A real man."

"What else do you remember about him?"

Hans Gallagher frowned and shrugged.

"He was funny. Had a sense of humor, and a rather dark one at that. He was also nice enough, at least he always said hello nicely and stuff, but he was also a bit of a scoundrel, so we didn't move in the same circles."

"A scoundrel? In what way?"

"He was always involved in fights and that kind of stuff. Gråsten is a small town, and naturally people talk, so you knew he was a troublemaker."

"What was his relationship with Jan Fischhof, do you know?"

Hans Gallagher narrowed his eyes and lifted his chin. "What do you mean by 'relationship'?"

"Were they friends?"

"Oh, I see." He laughed in relief. "Well, I don't know . . . They were both on the farm for many years, so they worked really closely with each other, but if they saw each apart from that . . .?" He tilted his head from side to side. "They may well have had a beer together every now and then after work, I couldn't say for sure. But more than that? No, I don't think so. Jan was always such a nice guy. Our daughters went to school together, and the wives drank some coffee every now and then. I've often considered contacting him, but you know what it's like. One day flows into the next, so . . ." He pursed his lips in regret.

"What do people say down here about Tom Mázoreck's death?"

"What do folks *say*?"

"Yes, you said it's a small town and people talk. So what do they say?"

"Nowadays, folks don't say much anymore. It was a lot of years ago, but . . ." Gallagher shrugged, hesitant. "Well . . . it was an accident. Tragic!"

"And what else?" Heloise held the pen ready over her notebook and looked at him, waiting.

Hans Gallagher took a deep breath and scratched under his nose a little.

"Yeah, well . . . He had a sailboat of some sort. It may well have been a motorboat, I can't quite remember. Be that as it may, some problem arose out on the water some distance from Providence, and . . ."

"Providence?"

"A restaurant located down by Stranderød, out toward the fjord."

Heloise noted down the name in her notebook.

"As I said, there was some problem. The engine came off, something like that. And this was before people had cell phones with them all the time, keep in mind." He held up a finger. Then he dropped his hand again and shook his head. "No one knows what happened next. Maybe he tried to fix the engine—who knows? In any case, the piece of shit caught fire, and—yeah!" He threw out his arms. "Then it went the way it went. It's tragic, but that kind of thing happens on a regular basis in a community like ours that's out on the water."

"That people drown, you mean?"

"Yes."

"Does it happen often?"

"Define 'often.' It certainly happens more often here than it does in the Sahara. It's simple math."

A young guy wearing what looked like waders came over to Gallagher and handed him a marker and a clipboard with a document on it. They exchanged a few words that Heloise didn't understand any of while pointing around the various stalls in the barn. Gallagher nodded and wrote something on the document. He handed the board back to the guy, then turned his gaze to Heloise.

"Was there anything else?"

"Yes, in the obituary the family placed some days after Mázoreck's death, there are two names." She flipped through her notebook to find them. "Renata and Kjeld. Does that mean anything to you?"

Gallagher nodded. "Tom's mother and older brother."

"Are they still around? I haven't been able to find anything on the family name."

He shook his head. "The mother died a few years ago. She was an old lady at the end and not quite playing with a full deck, but I guess she never really was."

"And his brother? Kjeld?"

"Yes."

"He passed away a few years after Tom."

"How did he die?"

"It was a traffic accident. An unknown driver hit him at a hundred and ten miles per hour out on the E45 somewhere."

"So there are no other family members left?"

"Not as far as I know."

"And he didn't leave behind a wife or partner or anything?"

"Tom?"

"Yes."

"No, not in Denmark."

Heloise looked up from the notebook. "What do you mean?"

"He had a regular girl for a number of years. I don't know if they were married. They went to Thailand together and were away for a few years, but Tom couldn't live with the heat over there, so he came back home."

Heloise thought of the list Munk had sent her of Mázoreck's residential addresses over time, and about the years when he hadn't been able to find anything on him.

"What about the girlfriend?" she asked.

"She stayed over there."

"Do you remember her name?"

"Mmm, Vicki, I think. Or Becky. Something like that. I only met her once or twice, and many a lady came after her. Tom was also a slick character in *that* area," said Gallagher, winking.

"But he was living alone when he died?"

"Yes, he slept around a little here and there, depending on which broad he was seeing, but he mostly lived with his mother. She had an old country estate where there was a small guesthouse, and he lived there for many years."

"Do you know where it's located, that country estate?"

"Yes, it's not that far from here." Gallagher gave Heloise the address. "The house has been up for sale since Renata passed away, and I can't imagine a buyer showing up any time soon. It's just decaying.'Course, it belongs to the state now."

Heloise leafed through her notebook.

"Was there anything else?" asked Gallagher, looking at his wristwatch. "It's almost dinner time, so . . ." He patted his stomach.

"Yes, in my research I've come across some articles about a young woman who disappeared back then. Does that ring any bells?"

"Sure. Nina. What about her?"

"No, Mia," Heloise said, looking up from the notebook. "Her name was Mia Sark."

"Oh, you're talking about the Sark girl. Yes, I do remember that story."

Heloise frowned. "Who did you think I meant?"

"I thought you meant Nina Dalsfort." Hans Gallagher made a subtle movement with his hand in the direction of Benniksgaard. "Because we were just talking about the mink farm."

Heloise stared at him without blinking as a shiver spread up her neck.

"Nina Dalsfort?"

"Yeah, it was another case that caused a lot of media hubbub."

"What happened?"

"With Nina?"

"Yes."

"She ran away." Hans Gallagher sprinkled a shovelful of feed into one of the troughs.

"Ran away?"

"Yes, she was part of a group of young idealists who had worked each other up and were looking for trouble. Some PETA fanatics who had been mad at us mink breeders. Back then, all the outrage was directed at fur production, you see. I never thought I'd say that I actually long for those times, but nowadays you can't eat meat or fly to Prague or buy a bouquet of roses for your wife without being lynched for the carbon footprint your lifestyle leaves. You are also not allowed to whistle at pretty ladies, sing old Danish songs, or scold your children, because then you will be reported for sexual harassment, racism, and psychological violence. Today, the condemnation is spread over everyone and everything, but back then it was only us mink breeders who were targeted."

Heloise cocked her head and gave him an indulgent smile.

Gallagher met her gaze and chuckled slightly.

"I'm not whining, I'm just explaining to you what it was like," he said. "This group of activists had planned actions against two mink farms here in the area: Benniksgaard and Padborg Mink. The plan was that they would let the animals out and set fire to the farms, but they didn't get that far. Not with us, at least. We'd gotten wind of their plans and were ready when they snuck onto the farm in the middle of the night."

"What happened?"

Hans Gallagher cleared his throat. "They got busted. All four. Charged with vandalism and aiding and abetting the release of mink in three other places in Jutland. They were also charged with arson and death threats."

"Death threats?"

"Yes, the Dalsfort girl had letters on her when she was arrested that the group had planned to leave for us at the farm. Addressed personally to those of us who worked there."

"What did they say?"

"They said that if we resumed work, they would do to us what we did to the animals: kill us and skin us."

"And you're saying it was four young people who participated in this action?"

"Yes. The girl and three guys. She was the only one of them who was under the age of eighteen at the time of the crime, so she was released while they awaited trial, and a few days later she was gone. It was a big circus down here because of her family."

"What kind of family is it?"

"Dalsfort?"

Heloise nodded.

He smiled wryly. "You really do come from far away, don't ya?"

"Yeah, I can't deny that. Who are they?"

"The parents' names are Ole and Lisette Dalsfort. They own Dalsfort Industri."

"Dalsfort Industri, which . . ." Heloise dug deep into her mental filing cabinet. ". . . produce valves and the like?"

"Yes, exactly. It's now a huge company with offices in thirty countries or so."

"And no one ever found out where the girl had gone?"

He shook his head.

"The police's theory was that she had gone to Germany, and where she went from there is anybody's guess."

"And Jan and Tom Mázoreck were both involved in this case with the activists?"

"Yes, certainly, because the death threats were directed at them personally—and then of course at me and another guy named Dres Carstensen. When the case went to trial, all four of us testified against three of the louts and against Nina Dalsfort in absentia, because by that time she had long since run away. In order to shut down all the crazy stories that had been circulating because of the marks on the girl's arms and the neighbors who had heard gunshots and screams and everything, we explained what had happened."

"What kind of marks on her arms?" asked Heloise.

Hans Gallagher hesitated for a moment. He lowered his gaze and scraped his heel a few times across the barn floor.

"We were lying in wait that night, ready for them to show up. At that time we had not yet informed the police that we had heard rumors of an impending attack. We thought we'd first deal with it ourselves, so when the scoundrels showed up with their hedge clippers and their petrol cans and whatnot, we surprised them. Dres Carstensen had one of his hunting rifles with him, so he fired a warning shot into the air, and the three of them surrendered immediately— one of them pissed in his pants with fright. But the girl went on unaffected. She headed for the cages, so Jan and Tom ran after her and tackled her down aways on the dirt road—over there, where hole two is now. We had brought plastic strips in case we had to make a citizen's arrest, so they tied her hands behind her back and dragged her back to the courtyard where the rest of us were waiting."

"And then what happened?"

"Well, that girl—Nina—she was lying on the ground yelling and screaming like a stuck pig. She was completely hysterical, so one of the neighbors—a guy named Lorentz— called the police. He thought she was about to be killed or something because she sounded so crazy. The other three had kind of grasped that the jig was up, but not her! She lay there thrashing around on the ground, pulling the strips to get free, which then bit more deeply into her skin."

"What did the police say when they came?"

"They said thank you!" Hans Gallagher cackled contentedly. "The thing was that the group had struck at Padborg Mink before they showed up at Benniksgaard. They had let the minks loose out there, and the animals lay dead by the hundreds out on Fjord road, hit by trucks heading for the border, drivers who couldn't see them in the dark. That's what these activist freaks don't understand. They think they're giving the animals freedom."

He shook his head.

"Anyway, my point is that the police were already looking for the vandals when they showed up at our place, so they just came and scooped them up, and thanked us for the help. The girl, of course, screamed about abuse and violence, claiming that the strips had been tightened so hard that she could not feel her hands. But I had recorded it all on video just to make sure we were in the clear in case the slightest thing should occur, so I wasn't worried about what it would look like in other people's eyes. Not at that point anyway. Back then, I didn't know her name or who her parents were. But the mother sure came after us later, I kid you not. Thought we were the ones who had driven her daughter away."

Heloise felt the adrenaline tingle in her blood, and she tightened her grip on the pen.

"Hans, you wouldn't happen to still have that video recording?"

20

A BLACK LABRADOR LIFTED its head from the dog basket as they entered the utility room, sleepily registering that there were people in the house before it lay down again. Hans Gallagher stepped out of his rubber boots on the light-yellow tiled floor and opened a small refrigerator that stood on the floor next to the dog basket. He took out a pair of Ceres lagers, opened one bottle with the top of the other, and held it out to Heloise.

"No thanks," she said, taking off her shoes.

He put one beer back into the refrigerator.

"It's in here," he said, leading the way through the house in his stockings.

It smelled of browned butter, meatballs, and freshly chopped parsley, and Heloise suddenly became aware of her watering mouth. It was almost six o'clock, and she had eaten nothing all day but a soft-boiled egg and a dry airport sandwich.

In the large, south-facing living room, Gallagher walked over to a bookcase that filled the entire end wall. It was tightly packed with books, binders, folders, and old VHS tapes. There were four or five yards of vinyl records on the bottom shelf, and on the floor in front of the bookcase lay old, yellowed newspapers and magazines in knee-high stacks.

He ran his fingers slowly over the videotapes, as if he were doing a count. He grumbled with frustration and started over several times.

"Well, I don't know where the hell I put it," he said, irritated, and gave up the search. "You might be lucky enough to find fragments of the footage on *TV 2*. They did a broadcast about the challenges we had, which was shown on *TV South* on a debate program called *45 minutes*. I remember they used some clips from the incident."

He took a bottle-green photo album off the shelf and made himself comfortable in an armchair.

"But I know I have some old photos from the mink farm in this one," he said, flipping through the album. "Ah! Here's one of Jan!"

He took the photograph out of its plastic pocket and handed it to Heloise.

She looked down at it, and it made her smile.

In the picture, a young Jan Fischhof stood with his arms folded over his chest and his head leaning back in laughter. It had been taken at a time when he was Heloise's age, perhaps a few years older, and he had a clear, open countenance that revealed he was living a good life at that time, when he had not yet experienced either illness or grief.

He looked strong. And infectiously happy!

Heloise found herself wishing she had known him then.

The wire cages ran in a long line behind him on the left, and hundreds of minks of different colors latched onto the sides with sharp claws. At his right shoulder stood a man in an army-green thermal jacket and blue fireman's pants. He was leaning against a feeder that looked like a cross between a tractor and a wheelbarrow, and it appeared that he was the one who had said whatever it was that had made Fischhof burst out laughing. The man sucked his cheeks into a confidently delivered smile, clearly enjoying the applause.

"Who's the other one?" asked Heloise, looking up.

"That's Tom Pitbull!" Gallagher pointed the beer bottle at her and nodded eagerly. "Mázoreck! I think it was taken immediately after the mink farm opened, so it was about nineteen ninety . . ." he rocked his hand in a seesaw motion, guesstimating, "ninety-three."

Heloise turned her eyes back to the image and zoomed curiously in on Tom Mázoreck's face.

He didn't have the same warmth in his eyes as Jan, or the same robust charisma. He was slimmer, and his skin was more worn-out, sun-damaged, and raw. His eyes were set close to his wide cheekbones, and even though he wasn't what you'd call a handsome man, there was still something that drew you in. The dark pupils that sucked in the light. The way the corners of his mouth curled upward. The self-satisfied look.

"And you don't know why they called him Pitbull?" asked Heloise, taking a photo of the picture with her cell phone. She had imagined that the name was a reference to Mázoreck's appearance, but he exuded reptile rather than muscle dog. More rattlesnake than pitbull.

"Well, yeah . . . how did the story go?" Hans Gallagher took a deep breath and held the air in his lungs as he thought for a moment. Then he turned his head toward the door behind him and shouted.

"GRETHE?"

The answer resounded from one of the adjoining rooms: "YES?"

"Why was it that Tom Mázoreck was called Pitbull?"

Hans Gallagher had switched into a full-on dialect which, to Heloise's ears, sounded like a mixture of German and Danish, and she had to make an effort to understand what was being said.

A woman who Heloise guessed was Gallagher's wife appeared in the doorway. She was a small, fair-haired lady in the shape of a snowman—soft and curvy, with dimples so deep that they must have remained there even in her sleep. She greeted Heloise with an unpretentious face that revealed she was used to people waltzing in and out of her home.

"Pitbull?" she asked, wiping her hands on her apron.

"Yes, what was it? Something about a fight at a town festival or something?"

"It was at the ring riding. But that was many years ago."

"Yes, but what was it that happened? They got into a fight, didn't they?"

"Yeah. Tom Mázoreck and Jes Decker."

"Oh, yes, that's the way it was," Gallagher nodded. "Now I remember!"

"Who is Jes Decker?" asked Heloise.

The leather in the armchair creaked under Gallagher and he exchanged a glance with his wife.

"They got into a fight," said the wife, as if she hadn't heard the question. "And it got out of control. They were rolling around on the ground kicking and punching each other like complete lunatics."

"What were they fighting over?"

"I think it was something about a girl. I believe one of them had been a little too fresh with the other's girlfriend. Something along those lines."

"Who won?"

"Decker did," said the wife. "But it wasn't entirely fair play. He had his dog with him, a pit-bull terrier. The type that is illegal today because they are completely unpredictable and very aggressive. The dog attacked Mázoreck while he and Decker were rolling around, and it held on tenaciously." She put a hand on her husband's shoulder and dug her nails in to illustrate how it had happened. "It caught one of the major arteries and Mázoreck got hurt really badly. It almost killed him."

"Yes, he was hospitalized for weeks, right?" asked Gallagher.

The wife nodded. "He survived, but the dog didn't. It was found in Jes Decker's fridge immediately after Mázoreck had been discharged from the hospital—cut into pieces and wrapped in grease paper like butcher steaks. It was René who discovered it. Jes's son."

"Was Mázoreck the one who had killed it?" asked Heloise.

"I guess no one ever found out, but he seemed like the most obvious candidate. Who else would have an interest in killing that dog?"

Hans Gallagher added, "I definitely think it gnawed at Mázoreck to be humiliated like that in public."

"So they called him Pitbull because of that story?"

"Well, a lot of people did. As I said before, Mázoreck, Tom, or Pitbull—it was all the same thing."

"And what about this guy Jes Decker? Is he still around?"

"Mm-hmm. Yes."

"What kind of guy is he?"

"Yeah, well . . . Decker is . . ." Gallagher pinched the tip of his nose with a couple of fingers as he chose his words. "Let's just say, he's not the type you would want get on the wrong side of."

"Why not?"

He frowned slightly, waving the question away as if it wasn't worth bothering with.

"Are you scared of him?" asked Heloise.

"Scared?" Hans laughed a little too loudly, and the color in his cheeks flared up. "People down here have . . . we have respect for him."

"Because you fear him?"

"Because he does what he wants. He doesn't care about laws and rules, and they say the police are in his pocket, supposedly including several local politicians—no one can touch him. He cooperates, as far as folks know, with some creepy types down across the border."

"Cooperating on what?"

"I don't know, but there are rumors about it."

"What do the rumors say?" Heloise made a rolling motion with her hand to speed up the narrative.

His Gallagher cleared his throat. "Yeah, well . . . some say smuggled goods. Others say drugs. Pornography. Prostitution."

"Hans . . ."

Gallagher looked at his wife, who gave him a warning look.

Heloise looked from one to the other.

"But if this Jes Decker is as hard as nails as you claim, why did he let Tom Mázoreck get away with killing the dog?" she asked. "Why didn't he take revenge?"

"Maybe he did," Gallagher said, shrugging his shoulders. "No one knows what happened on the boat that night. A mast breaks, a sail splits, or whatever it was . . . The engine cuts out and suddenly the shit explodes, causing Tom to fall overboard and drown."

He looked up from his beer and met Heloise's gaze. Something like a challenge sparkled in his eyes.

"That's mighty unfortunate, isn't it?"

21

"WHAT ARE YOU doing? Turn it back. I was watching a show!" Connie placed the box of *After Eight* mints on the coffee table next to the coffee pot and smacked Schäfer affectionately.

"But it's *Butch Cassidy and the Sundance Kid*," he protested. "Bank robberies and six-shooter gunfights, honey. It's a classic!"

"Which you've seen a hundred times." She sat down on the couch next to him and pointed at the screen. "They were just about to test their skills with the secret challenge."

"Didn't you say it was an old episode?"

"Didn't you say you had to work?"

Schäfer chuckled in surrender. He flipped back to *The Great Danish Bake-Off*, bowed his head, and handed her the remote control with both hands as if it were a samurai sword.

"Cake Duel. Voilà!"

He tilted the lid of the cardboard box that sat on the floor in front of him, picked up a file, and began to go through the various documents.

"Have you been busy today?" asked Connie, reaching for the chocolate.

"Mmm, ish," Schäfer muttered. He put his feet up on the coffee table and leafed through the documents. "Lester

Wilkins is dead, and with him went a good portion of my afternoon."

"Yes, I saw the headlines. What happened?"

"The coroner believes the death is lifestyle-related."

"What does that mean?"

"Booze."

"But if it was due to booze, why were you summoned?"

"I wasn't. I had a lunch appointment with Michala Friis nearby, so I just stopped by the site to see if . . ."

"Michala Friis?" asked Connie, looking over at him. "You were with Michala today?"

"Yes. We're both working on this one." He patted the documents lying in his lap. "It's a bit of a complicated case, so we met to go through the details and get everything in place before the trial starts next week."

"Huh . . ." Connie raised her brows and nodded slowly. "How is she? It's been a while since you last saw her, hasn't it?" Her tone was strikingly bright and affected.

Schäfer met her gaze and smiled. "Are you jealous?"

"No . . . Not as long as Michala knows her place."

Schäfer's smile grew. "You *are* jealous!"

"Yeah, well." Connie squeezed her eyes shut in confession and said no more. She turned her attention to the television, where a young guy was about to roll out a lump of homemade fondant.

Schäfer flipped further through the file and closely studied the police photographer's photos of the victim in the case: a forty-one-year-old woman who had died of intracranial hemorrhaging after inadvertently ingesting rat poison. In the photo, she was lying on her back on a basement floor. Her skin was milky white, and the blood that had seeped out of her mouth and nose had formed a dark red halo around her head.

"Do you think she's beautiful?" Schäfer looked up.

"Who?"

"Michala."

Connie's gaze was still fixed on the television screen.

"No," he said.

"Sure you do!" Connie looked over at him. "You have eyes in your damn head, don't you?"

"She's not as beautiful as you."

"And she's exciting. She knows all sorts of clever things because of her FBI-psychologist-profiling-hullaballoo."

"She's got nothing on you, babe," Schäfer said with a smile. He cupped a hand around the nape of Connie's neck and pulled her into a kiss. The scent of the evening bath's shampoo still lingered on her, deep notes of grape and patchouli, and he slid a hand into the bathrobe and down onto one of her breasts.

Connie returned the kiss and then pulled away. Not in a quick jerk, but in a slow, polite rejection—the kind that Schäfer had been getting a lot of lately. She used to be the first to shed her clothes, and poison ran in her veins at the thought of Schäfer with another woman. But when he touched her lately, it was as if she stiffened in his hands. As if she no longer took an interest.

Schäfer didn't get it.

You've lost your touch, old man.

He took her hand and gave it a kiss.

"I'm going to bed," he said.

"There are twenty minutes left of this," Connie said, pointing to the TV screen. "I'll come up when it's done."

Schäfer gathered the documents and put them back in the box. He got up, carried it out into the entryway, walked barefoot onto the driveway, and opened the trunk of his battered, black Honda. It was already filled with files and documents and other work items that needed to be brought to the office.

He moved things around to make room for the cardboard box and was standing with his upper body half inside the open yawn of the car when the sound of an approaching vehicle made him look over his shoulder.

It was almost eleven o'clock, but visibility in the summer twilight was still good.

A dark-blue BMW sedan drove along the residential street and slowed down as it passed the driveway. The windows in the car were tinted, and Schäfer could sense nothing but the contours of the driver inside.

As the car crawled past his house, he straightened up and turned around fully to face the street.

The BMW picked up speed a bit and continued down the road.

Schäfer walked out to the sidewalk and watched the red taillights until they disappeared around a corner.

* * *

Schäfer took the toothbrush out of his mouth as the phone vibrated on the table next to Connie's makeup and perfume bottles. He glanced down at the screen and smiled. He accepted the call and put the phone to his ear.

"You're hitting up my phone like crazy today. What do you think Connie is gonna think with all these calls?"

He spit into the sink and put the toothbrush back in the mug.

"Oh, she knows you're not my type," Heloise said dryly.

"No, that's right, you're more into those metrosexual momma's boys who shave their chest hair." Schäfer chuckled softly. He sucked in his stomach and looked at his overgrown torso in the bathroom mirror. When Heloise didn't return the ball, he let his stomach drop into place and said, "That was a joke, Kaldan!"

"Yes, I know."

"Well then, what's up? Is everything okay?"

"Yeah, everything is fine," Heloise said, but Schäfer sensed that she was somewhere else in her thoughts.

"You don't sound like everything is fine," he said, wiping his mouth with a towel.

"Well, it's just . . . I've whipped myself up into a mood, and I just need to be talked down again."

"Down from what?"

"From the thought that I find myself completely alone in an old, abandoned house in Shitsville. There isn't a soul for miles around—or at least, I don't *think* there's anyone for miles around—and that freaks me out. It's altogether too quiet!"

"The only thing you really need to fear where you are is bedbugs. Those fuckers are created by the devil, if there is such a thing."

"I was thinking more along the lines of axe murderers and such," Heloise said, and Schäfer could hear the smile in her voice. "You know, faceless men clad in sou'westers. Dead twin sisters haunting old houses—that sort of thing. I'm not scared of bedbugs."

"You damn well should be! I always burn our odds and ends when we've been to Saint Lucia to visit the in-laws. Swimming trunks, towels, the whole kit and caboodle! Turpentine, light a match—*woosh*! No one should joke about that kind of thing."

"Okay, Grandma. But I think I'll take my chances!"

"That's up to you," Schäfer said. "As for that other stuff, there's not much risk of you being visited by a skipper-clad psychopath while you're there, so if I were you, I'd take it easy."

"If you say so," said Heloise without sounding completely convinced.

Schäfer walked into the bedroom. He opened the window next to the bed and drew the curtains.

"Did you find out more about that guy Mázoreck?" he asked.

"A little, but I'm honestly more confused than I was when I left this morning. For every question I ask, three new ones pop up."

"Such as?"

"I set out to investigate Tom Mázoreck's death and find out what his relation to Jan was, and suddenly I'm digging into old disappearance cases. It seems like it's all connected in some way."

"What do you mean by *cases*? I thought you said there was only one?

"I've found another one. The first one, Mia Sark, disappeared on May 31, 1997, at the age of nineteen. The second one, Nina Dalsfort, has not been seen since September 15, 1996. She was only seventeen when she disappeared, and Mázoreck's name is smeared over both cases."

"Smeared how?"

"In the case of Mia Sark, he was one of the last people to see the girl alive. He was in the same tavern as her—the place I told you about earlier today, the Tin Soldier. He was a witness in the case, and to top it all off, he then began a relationship with the girl's mother in the following month. I can't quite tell if they were screwing or if they were just friends; in any case, he came to the house for a while."

"And in the other case?"

"In the other case, he had clashed with the girl just before she disappeared."

Heloise told him about the goings-on at the mink farm. About how Jan Fischhof and Mázoreck, together with Hans Gallagher and Dres Carstensen, had captured the activists, tied up Nina Dalsfort, and handed her and the other three over to the police.

"There are some coincidences in the cases that just can't be overlooked," she said. "So, do you think this could be what Jan is talking about? Does he know anything about what became of those girls?"

Schäfer sat on the edge of the bed and stretched his neck from side to side so that it cracked loudly.

"What are you thinking?" Heloise asked.

"I'm thinking there's a big difference between investigating a case in Copenhagen and in a small provincial town like the one you're in.

What seems like a suspicious coincidence here, usually has a logical explanation over there."

"What do you mean?"

"Well take Gråsten, for example. There's—what, four thousand inhabitants? Five? Max!"

"No idea."

"So everyone has crossed paths in one way or another. The baker's sister is the aunt of the dentist's daughter, who was in the same class as the pastor's wife, who is married to the bike mechanic's cousin. They're connected in a way you're not used to at home, so the likelihood of your seeing ghosts is pretty high because you're using a calculation method that doesn't fit the demographics."

"How can the pastor's wife be married to the bike mechanic's cousin when you have just said that she is married to the pastor?" asked Heloise dryly.

"The pastor *is* the bike mechanic's cousin. Get with the program, Kaldan, you are in the suburbs now. It's uncharted waters for a snooty little Copenhagener like you."

"I'm not a snooty Copenhagener," Heloise protested, "and tell me, aren't you from Copenhagen too?"

"Yeah, but I went to the military school in Sønderborg when I was young and nailed more than one milkmaid before little Miss Connie Diocesse came along and made an honest man out of me. I know the environment down there. Moreover, I traveled the whole country with the Travel Team in my time, until some idiot of a politician pulled the plug on the department, and I can only repeat what I said before: patterns are different in small towns. I will bet you can go down to the town square in Gråsten and tap any old Mrs. Hansen on the shoulder, and she will have some connection to Mázoreck—or she knows someone who knows someone who played tennis with him."

"So investigation in provincial towns is a bit like Bacon's Law?"

"What's that?"

"It's the thesis that you can connect any actor to Kevin Bacon with six or fewer connections. They call it Six Degrees of Kevin Bacon. Or Bacon's Law."

"Right," Schäfer nodded. "And you're now playing Six Degrees of Tom Mázoreck, although I'd guess there are no more than two or three degrees between him and pretty much everyone else in Gråsten."

Heloise was quiet on the other end of the line.

"What about Fischhof's daughter?" Schäfer asked. "Did you get ahold of her?"

"Not yet, her phone is still off. Don't you think it's weird that it's not on?"

"I guess the battery's just run down."

"For ten hours? Nowadays? And with a father who is dying and could kick the bucket at any time?"

"Mmm," muttered Schäfer.

"What bothers me the most is that Jan is surrounded by people who are strangers to him. I understand that she lives abroad and without a doubt has a busy life. Maybe she has young children, maybe the job of marine biologist is a demanding one—what do I know? But in the months I've been with Jan, I haven't seen her out there even once. It's about to be her last chance, so where the hell has she gone?"

"What's your point?"

"Why isn't she the one holding his hand?"

Schäfer shrugged. "She probably has a good reason."

"Yeah, that's what worries me. I know better than anyone that there are good reasons to stay away from this kind of thing. What's hers?"

"There's the possibility that she isn't a particularly empathic person."

Heloise was quiet on the other end of the line.

"Or maybe *he* isn't," Schäfer continued.

"No, he's cool," Heloise said, but Schäfer could hear a doubt in her voice that hadn't been there before.

If she had been sure of her case, she probably wouldn't have gone all the way to Southern Jutland, he thought.

*   *   *

Heloise opened the bedroom door and looked around in the darkening twilight. The room smelled damp and strangely sweet of old-lady perfume, dust, and mold. She opened the window facing the garden, sat on the edge of the bed, and let herself fall backward with a sigh. Feeling raw from the impressions of the day, she lay staring up at the cracks in the ceiling, thinking about why she had traveled here; why she just couldn't leave the story alone, take Fischhof by the hand, and wish him a happy journey.

The thought exhausted her.

Since returning from Hans Gallagher's, she had sat in the living room until darkness had fallen, writing down notes and keywords about Mia Sark's and Nina Dalsfort's cases, and she had also contacted a former colleague who worked at *TV 2* and asked her to search the archives for the report about the mink farm that had been broadcast on one of the station's regional channels. All her notes were now scattered across the living room floor like loose puzzle pieces. Heloise had tried to piece them together and pinpoint similarities.

Two girls had disappeared without a trace. They had been almost the same age, they had grown up in the same small town, and they had both crossed Tom Mázoreck's path just before disappearing. Was it trafficking, as the police believed? And what about Jan? How did *he* fit into the puzzle, and why had Ingeborg Sark thrown her out when she had mentioned his name?

They will come after us. Both of us!

Heloise took a deep breath and became aware of her body odor, the stench of pigs that her skin and hair had absorbed after a short time in Hans Gallagher's stable.

She got up from the bed, walked over to the large mahogany cabinet at the far end of the bedroom and opened it. There was a moth-eaten bathrobe hanging in there, a raincoat, a couple of knitted sweaters on hangers, and on one of the shelves on the right side a stack of towels in various pastel colors, pre-washed and stiff as planks. Heloise grabbed one of them and was about to close the closet door again when her gaze caught something glinting in the darkness inside. She took her phone out of her back pocket and turned on the flashlight function, pulled the hangers aside with a metallic swish, and lit up the darkness.

At the back of the closet, up against the back wall, was a gun.

Heloise took it out carefully and looked at it.

It was a shotgun—an old, double-barreled Aya Sherwood 12 caliber—and Heloise knew it because her father had had a similar one. She did not have a hunting license herself, but had regularly gone with him on hunting trips to South

Zealand when she was a child. He had taught her about the different rifles and guns, how to load weapons and shoot at tin cans.

She raised the gun and took aim at herself in the mirror above the bedside table. Then she lowered it again and broke the barrel open.

There were no cartridges in the chamber.

She shone the light into the closet, hoping to find a package of ammunition. She would prefer to sleep with a loaded gun under the bed as long as she was alone out here in the middle of nowhere, but there were no cartridge boxes in there.

Heloise put the weapon back in the closet and went out into the bathroom. She took a long shower in the rusty water that sputtered out of the shower head in uneven jets while the old water pipes groaned.

She heard the phone ring as she got out of the shower and crossed her fingers that it was Fischhof's daughter finally returning her call.

She ran naked into the bedroom to answer the call but didn't get to see the number on the screen before her phone ran out of power. She pulled the charger out of her suitcase and set the mobile phone on the bedside table to charge up. Then she pulled the covers aside and tumbled over into the old, creaky, wrought-iron bed.

She reached up and switched off the bedside lamp, turning the room black.

Her heart immediately began to beat faster as she lay trying to identify the sounds in a house that, with the exception of a few sighs from the woodwork, was eerily quiet.

Her eyes took a long time to adjust to the darkness but, little by little, silhouettes appeared like ships through the mist. Her pulse slowly but surely began to stabilize, and she turned onto her side to look out the window. There was no moon visible, but the stars shone brighter than she had ever experienced in Denmark in July.

Her gaze fell on a cluster of stars at the edge of the window frame, a misty, white spot. It looked like a dandelion with bright, fluffy seeds and formed a perfect circle in the night sky.

Heloise thought of her father. And of Thomas. Of all that she had lost.

She closed her eyes, puckered her lips, and blew.

22

S CHÄFER SAT UP with a start.
      The house was dark, and Connie was sleeping next to
him in the double bed. He held his breath for a moment, sat
perfectly still, and listened.

A dog barked somewhere in the neighborhood . . . a car
accelerated on Vigerslev Alley . . . Connie's breathing.

Otherwise, nothing.

Something is wrong.

He swung his legs over the edge of the bed and walked to
the window facing the path that ran along one side of the
house. The window was open, but the curtains were drawn.

Schäfer stood still and listened.

The seconds ticked by. Five, ten.

He was about to turn around and go back to bed when
he heard it again. The voice that had awakened him. A whisper out there in the dark.

He walked to the armchair at the other end of the bedroom and pulled his gun out of the shoulder holster that
hung across the backrest.

"Baby?" whispered Connie sleepily from the bed and
lifted herself up on her elbows. "What is it?"

Schäfer looked at her and put a finger to his lips.

She sat up, suddenly wide awake.

Schäfer walked over to the open window and pulled back the curtain a few inches so he could see out.

There was no clear view of the entire driveway, but he could see long shadows cast on the tiles in the glow of the streetlight. There were soft murmurs out there, and Schäfer stood perfectly still and listened.

Connie got up from the bed. "Erik, what's the matter?"

"There's someone outside," he whispered, handing her the phone from the nightstand. "Call 112!"

He walked out of the bedroom and over to the stairs.

"Don't go out there!" whispered Connie in the doorway behind him. Her look was paralyzed with fear.

He held up a hand to hush her and silently continued down the stairs and out the backdoor of the kitchen.

The night air was crisp and dry, and he wasn't cold even though he was wearing nothing but a pair of boxer shorts and an undershirt. The adrenaline was already pumping hard in his bloodstream, and he couldn't feel anything but the gun— cool to the touch, familiar in his hands. He held it raised in front of him as he walked slowly around the house.

He stopped at the corner facing the road and remained hidden, trying to get an overview of where the voices were coming from.

He leaned forward slightly so he could see the driveway with one eye.

The dark-blue BMW from earlier was parked in front of his house, and the hatch of his own car was open. He could see two men bent over the trunk, rummaging through things. They wore balaclavas and were both at least a head taller than Schäfer. Their shoulders were wide, their biceps enormous, which made their arms looked strangely short.

The cardboard box that Schäfer had placed in the car a few hours earlier lay overturned on the tiles next to the right rear tire. The contents had been emptied out across the driveway, and the papers fluttered lightly in the night wind.

Schäfer heard the men whispering to each other in a language he didn't know, and he stepped out of hiding with his gun raised in front of him.

"THIS IS THE POLICE!" he shouted.

The men looked up.

"POLICE! GET DOWN!"

They slowly raised their muscular arms.

"GET DOWN!" Schäfer nodded toward the tiles without taking his eyes off the men. "DOWN ON THE GROUND!"

The men remained standing as they were. They seemed neither anxious nor dispirited to have been caught red-handed. Rather, they looked as if they were mildly bored. Indifferent, cold.

Schäfer pointed the gun at the largest one, a hulk of seven feet, and narrowed his eyes.

"I said get down! Kiss the fucking ground! NOW!"

The giant's gaze flickered for a split second, and his icy-blue eyes shot to a point above Schäfer's left shoulder. At that moment Schäfer sensed someone behind him, and he spun around in one swift motion.

Something blunt hit him hard across the cheekbone and he fell to the ground. He instinctively touched his face and felt the blood streaming down his cheek.

He turned his head and caught sight of the face hovering over him. It was wrapped in nylon, the facial features distorted and hideous.

"Where are documents?" hissed the face. The foreign accent was thick, the voice dark and masculine.

Schäfer put his hands against the gravel and tried to get up. "I have no idea what you're talking. . ."

The man kicked him in the stomach.

Schäfer rolled around on the ground, breathing hard. It felt like his lungs were collapsing and burning in his chest.

He heard the sound of a gun being cocked and Connie screaming from inside the house. Then he saw the mouth of the barrel approaching his forehead.

"Where?"

The men gathered around him.

"Ne pucaj! On je policajac," said one of them.

"Što on zna o Mázoreck?" said another.

Mázoreck?

The kicks hit Schäfer again, this time from several sides, and his vision went black. He was seriously in for it now.

He rolled up, keeping his face tucked behind his arms.

He heard the sound of running feet.

Car doors slamming.

And then they were gone.

23

"Follow the light with your eyes."

The ambulance doctor stood in the driveway in front of Schäfer and moved the small flashlight from side to side in front of his face.

"Are you nauseous?"

"Nope."

"Does it hurt here?" The doctor pressed a few different places on Schäfer's torso.

"Only when I laugh," Schäfer said, directing a dry look at the doctor. He put the ice pack against his cheek and closed his eyes for a moment. The pain zigzagged up the left side of his face; the cranial bones felt like tectonic plates rasping against each other.

"I'd like to take you to the hospital for a little while so we can get some X-rays to see if there are fractures in the cheekbone or the ribs. There is also a risk of internal bleeding, damage to soft tissues, so I also think we should do a CT scan."

"I'm fine."

"Nevertheless," the doctor nodded, "it's a good idea just to check whether . . ."

"I'm fine!" repeated Schäfer, standing up, and walked to the driveway where the police photographer was taking photos of the documents lying scattered about on the tiles.

Detectives were examining the car's hatch and trunk for clues, and on the other side of the police cordon several of the neighbors along the road had gathered in a cluster. They stood in bathrobes with crossed arms and long faces glowing blue in the patrol car's lights that flashed silently in the darkness of the night. They all looked over at Schäfer curiously.

"They were wearing gloves," he told the fingerprint technician from the National Forensic Center. He put a cigarette in his mouth and lit it. "The only fingerprints you'll find there are mine."

His former partner, Lisa Augustin, crouched down in the driveway and flipped through the documents the thieves had left behind. She was wearing black jeans and a tight white T-shirt. Crossfit workouts had sculpted her body. The muscles of her arms and shoulders stood out clearly. The long hair was history, the nails were short and the face makeup-free. The older she got, the more came into her own, he thought.

Augustine stood up and regarded him with a worried look.

"Are you okay?" she asked.

He nodded.

"What did the doctor say?"

"Doctor things. I'll survive."

"What were they after, do you think?"

Schäfer looked around and shook his head slowly. "I have no idea, but I see they've taken some of my papers."

"And you don't know who they were?"

He shook his head again. "They spoke to each other in a language I didn't understand."

"Do you think it could it have been Farsi? Or Arabic? Did it sound like something from that region?"

"No, it was an Eastern European language of some sort. Russian, Polish, I don't know. I could see through the holes in the balaclava that the biggest of them had blue eyes, and he was fair skinned . . ."

"And the other two?"

Schäfer shook his head.

"One was in shadow and the other had a nylon stocking over his head, so it was hard to see anything, but I heard his voice. He spoke English, but with a Slavic accent, and it seemed organized in some way. They didn't just walk into some random house, going after something specific."

"What?"

"They said they were looking for some documents, but . . ." Schäfer frowned and shook his head slowly without saying more.

Mázoreck . . .

"We know that the Lithuanian mafia has been operating in Denmark for the past few years. There are two different criminal networks, Tamuoliniai and Aquarkiniai—known as Aquas," said Lisa Augustin. "They're involved in a lot of different shit."

"What kind of shit are we talking about?"

"Organized burglary, drug smuggling, trafficking." Augustine held out a finger for each point she reeled off. "Profit, profit, profit."

She took out her phone and found a video recording in her photo-library.

"We're looking for more Lithuanians at the moment who we know are in the area, including this guy here." She handed Schäfer the phone. "Vik Jankauskas. Does that ring any bells?"

Schäfer looked at the video recording.

It was a film sequence from a surveillance camera in a parking garage. It was pixelated and grainy, but still gave a good sense of the person in the picture, his posture and facial expressions. It was a bald, slender man talking on his cell phone and gesturing frantically as he walked over to a black Mercedes-Benz parked in a dark corner stall.

Schäfer pursed his lips uncertainly.

"I don't know . . . Two of them were as big as oxen, but I . . . I don't know. I didn't get a proper impression of the last one—the guy who knocked me down. It all happened so fast."

"And they just showed up in the middle of the night?"

"Well, I saw the dark-blue BMW driving down the street late last night, so maybe they scouted the house and saw me put something in the trunk of the car."

"You didn't take note of the license plate?"

Schäfer shook his head and took a drag from his cigarette.

"The Lithuanians I'm talking about have only one thing in mind," Augustin said, "and that's money— alternatively, stealing something or someone that they can make money from, and, with all due respect, this is an old piece of crap you're milling around in."

She kicked one of the Honda's worn tires.

"In other words, they can't have been interested in that, and even though Connie is beautiful and lovely, she is—no offense—middle-aged and not exactly at risk of ending up in the clutches of a trafficking ring."

Augustine glanced at the small brick villa behind Schäfer.

"Have you started collecting Ming vases and Fabergé eggs since I was here last?"

Schäfer gave her a withering look.

"Okay, so what were they after?" asked Augustine. "Why is someone rummaging around in your trunk browsing old case folders in the middle of the night?"

Schäfer ran a hand through his hair and turned his eyes to the car without focusing on it.

"What are you thinking?" she asked. "What does your gut say?"

Schäfer met her gaze and shook his head.

"Nothing," he lied.

* * *

Connie was sitting at the kitchen table when Schäfer entered the house after sending Augustine and the forensic technicians from NFC home. She had pulled her legs up on the seat and was hugging them with both arms. Her dark eyes shone damply in the light of the dining-table lamp as she looked up and met Schäfer's gaze.

"Shouldn't you go to the hospital?" she asked worriedly. "They told me you should go in for an X-ray."

"I'll do it tomorrow."

"But it can be dangerous, Erik, if you don't . . ."

"I'll do it tomorrow, sweetheart. Don't worry. I'm okay."

Schäfer positioned himself behind one of the chairs. He put his hands on the back of the chair and looked at Connie with serious eyes.

"What's wrong?" she asked.

"The man Heloise is visiting. The old guy . . ."

Connie frowned and pushed her chin back, confused by the change of topic. She wiped a tear from her cheek with a flat hand.

"Jan Fischhof?" she asked.

Schäfer nodded.

"What do you know about him?"

FRIDAY, JULY 12

24

H ELOISE OPENED HER eyes and lay there blinking for a moment before realizing where she was. The room was light and the ghosts of the night had disappeared. She had no idea how long she had slept. In Copenhagen, she never set her alarm clock because she woke up automatically when the Marble Church bells rang at eight o'clock. Here there were no sounds other than the bees buzzing in the flower bed under the open window, birds chirping in the trees.

She reached for her phone and saw the screen was black; the battery was still dead. She plugged the charger into another outlet to see if it made a difference, but it didn't.

She pulled the bedspread off the bed and wrapped it around her, went downstairs and out into the square in front of the house, unlocked the car, and put the phone in the USB port to charge.

Back in the kitchen, she took the Gevalia bag out of the refrigerator and filled the coffeemaker with water. She opened the filter box that was next to the machine and saw that it was empty. The kitchen doors slammed loudly as she searched through cupboards and drawers, and her inner caffeine junkie began to sweat at the prospect of not being able to get a morning fix. She stood on tiptoe and pushed cans and bags of flour and breadcrumbs aside in one of the cupboards, sweeping her hand across the shelf to feel if there were an extra filter box up there. She felt something and nudged it, causing it to fall down and hit the floor with a bang.

A handful of cartridges rolled out across the checkerboard linoleum floor, like mice darting off in all directions. They were red shotgun cartridges with brass coatings that went with the Aya in the closet upstairs. Heloise picked them up, put them back in the box, and placed it on the kitchen counter next to the sink.

She picked up a roll of toilet paper from the bathroom, tore off a long strip of it, put it down in the filter compartment of the coffeemaker, filled it with coffee, and turned it on. Fifteen minutes later, she was sitting on the living-room floor with a cup of coffee that tasted like cotton wool, looking at her notes from the night before.

She stopped at one of the names she had written down: Kurt Linnet, the eyewitness who had seen Mázoreck's boat go up in flames that night. She was about to reach for her phone to search for his address, then remembered that it was out in the car. Her eyes ran over the other names she had noted: Ole and Lisette Dalsfort . . . Jes Decker . . . Johan and Malou Yang.

Heloise drank a sip of her coffee and thought about what Jan had said to her.

Blood. So much blood, Heloise. On my hands, on my clothes. There was blood everywhere!

What had he done?

The double door to the garden was open, and Heloise looked up when she heard the sound of a car pulling up in front of the house. She set the coffee cup down on the floor and stood up. When she opened the front door she saw that a black Range Rover Sport was parked next to her white Renault.

The driver got out of the car, and Heloise's heart stopped.

* * *

There were eleven yards between them, and Thomas Malling stared at her without blinking, while his eyebrows pulled together into a question mark over the bridge of his nose.

Heloise slowly raised her hand in greeting. Then one corner of her mouth curled upward into a careful smile.

Thomas started walking toward her, stopping only when they were face to face. His gaze glided over her face as if he was having a hard time taking it all in.

"Hi," Heloise said nervously. Her heart was beating so hard she was afraid he could hear it.

Thomas said nothing, and Heloise had a hard time decoding his facial expression.

"I'm sorry for showing up at your house yesterday, but . . ."

He put his arms around her and pulled her to him before she could say anything more. Heloise returned his embrace as the memories exploded inside her. His breath felt warm through her hair, and he smelled familiar. Secure.

"I thought I was hallucinating yesterday," he said, holding her in front of him with outstretched arms to examine her more closely. His eyes roved over her face.

Then he cracked a smile.

"Is it really you?"

Heloise smiled and nodded.

He squeezed his eyes shut and shook his head wordlessly.

"But what . . . what on earth are you doing here?"

Heloise met his gaze and at that moment couldn't remember what it was that *had* brought her here.

She couldn't remember anything but Thomas.

25

"HOW DID YOU find me?" asked Heloise. She squinted her eyes in the morning sun and regarded Thomas sitting on the picnic bench across from her.

"Yesterday, when you stepped on the gas and disappeared without a word, I called the newspaper and asked to be connected to you, but your boss wouldn't give me your phone number, so . . . at midnight—and after half a bottle of red wine—I called Gerda."

"You called Gerda?" said Heloise, and couldn't help but smile.

"Yeah, I think I woke her up." He laughed lightly. "She was pretty surprised to hear from me. And yet not."

Heloise lowered her eyes and nodded. "She knows me well."

"She gave me your number and told me you'd rented this place." He glanced at the house. "I tried to call, but your phone was off . . ."

They sat for a long moment without saying anything, just looking at each other, smiling.

"Why did you take off yesterday?" he asked. "Why didn't you come in and say hello?"

Heloise looked down and fiddled a little with the white paint peeling on the picnic table between them.

"The woman who was there," she said without looking up. "Is that your wife?"

"Ex."

Heloise met his gaze without raising her head. "You're divorced?"

"Mm-hmm." Thomas nodded.

"Since when?"

"Since two years ago."

Heloise felt a sting in her heart. Two years, and he hadn't made a sound in all that time?

"Does that mean you live alone in that big house?" she asked.

"No, my kids are with me half the time."

"But . . ." Heloise frowned. "I thought you were employed at a local newspaper?"

"I am."

"Then how can you afford to live there?"

He smiled at her. "How can I afford it? What do you think a house like that costs down here?"

"I don't know, but it would cost eighteen million in Frederiksberg. Twelve in Valby and twenty-four in Vedbæk, so down here I would guess that it costs , , ,"

"Two point four."

"Two point four million kroner!" Heloise's eyebrows rose high on her forehead.

"Yep."

"For a mansion like that with a view of the fjord?"

He nodded. "At least, that's what it cost when I bought it four years ago."

"I have a microscopic apartment in Copenhagen that I paid two point six for, and when I bought it, there wasn't even a bathroom!"

Thomas smiled. "That's the way it is for people who insist on living next to the Marble Church."

"But . . ." Heloise shook her head uncomprehendingly. "How on earth did you end up down here?"

He laughed. "You make it sound like I live on the moon."

"No, no, I just mean . . . I thought it was your dream job that you'd gotten in the USA? Wasn't that why you went there?"

"Oh yes."

"So how did you end up in Sønderborg?"

"Camilla is from here." He took a sip of the coffee Heloise had poured him.

"Camilla?"

"My ex. I met her at a party in New York. She was over there studying, and I was . . . It was right after you'd decided to take the job at *Demokratisk Dagblad*, and . . ." He shook his head and looked at Heloise with a hesitant expression. "I was so angry with you."

Heloise looked down.

"I wanted to punish you for dropping me."

"I didn't drop you," she said, looking up. "I just wanted to have both."

"It didn't feel that way back then."

There was silence between them for a long moment.

"Anyway." He shrugged as if to shake the feeling off. "She got pregnant right away, and as you can imagine that was a setback."

He met Heloise's gaze.

"But then, when the boys were born . . ." He fell silent for a moment, his gaze resting on Heloise's hands. Then he looked up. "You don't have kids, do you?"

Heloise shook her head.

Thomas nodded in a way that revealed he wasn't surprised.

"Well, but . . . It changes you."

"Yes, I can imagine."

"No, it changes you in ways you can't imagine," he said.

Heloise said nothing.

"After a few years, Camilla didn't want to be in New York anymore. She didn't want the boys to grow up over there with school shootings and that kind of thing. She wanted them to have a Danish upbringing, a safe childhood where they could run out to play without us having to worry about them, and . . . yeah, I thought it made sense." He nodded to himself. "So, I quit the job at *Huff Post*, and now I'm here."

"From Copenhagen to Manhattan to Country Bliss?"

He smiled and nodded. "That's what it looks like."

"Why did you get divorced? If you don't mind me asking . . ."

Thomas looked at Heloise for a long moment.

"For the same reason as everyone else who gets divorced I guess. We weren't happy together. But we're good friends now, and it's going fine with the kids—we have them fifty-fifty. It's not ideal, but the boys seem happy. Camilla has a new boyfriend they love, and now they are going to have a little brother soon, so . . . all is well."

"And what about you?" asked Heloise. "Do you have a new girlfriend, too?"

Thomas smiled briefly, and his eyes glided over her face.

"It's strange seeing you again," he said.

Heloise nodded.

"Mostly because . . . it *doesn't* feel strange. Do you know what I mean? It's been so long—an eternity, really—but now that you're sitting here, it feels like it was . . ."

"Yesterday. Yes," Heloise nodded. "I know what you mean."

"How are you . . .? I mean . . ." Thomas shook his head and smiled in wonder. "Are you all right?"

Heloise took a deep breath and nodded slowly. "I'm okay."

"But what are you doing here? Why did you show up at my home yesterday?"

"Because . . ." She drummed her fingers lightly on the table. "Because I need your help."

"My help?" He frowned. "With what?"

"I'm researching a story that involves some old police cases down here, but the cops in Sønderborg aren't super-communicative, so I thought that with your contacts you might . . . I don't know." She shrugged. "You no doubt know whom to reach out to if you want to bend the rules a little."

Thomas's smile lost some of its intensity, and he leaned back in his chair.

"What is it?" Heloise asked. He shook his head.

"Nothing. I . . . I just thought for a moment that you had come because of . . ." He slowed himself down and said no more.

Heloise's gaze fell on his lips.

"I thought you were married," she said.

"I was."

"But you're not anymore."

"No." He brought the coffee cup up to his mouth without taking his eyes off her. "I'm not anymore."

*   *   *

"Dalsfort Industry," Thomas said, clasping his hands behind his head. "It's a big company down here. I interviewed the owner at one point—name's Ole. Nice guy, a bit of a nerdy type, but I think you have to be in that line of business."

"What about the wife, Lisette? Have you met her too?" asked Heloise.

"No, but it's not my impression that she ever had anything to do with the company. Well, I mean, she's a co-owner, but . . ." He shook his head. "I don't think she has an active role in the business—or in the marriage for that matter. At least, Ole Dalsfort flits around the world with his personal assistant and, as far as I know, his wife lives a rather isolated life. She is certainly reserved, very private. I believe she is an anesthesiologist, but I don't think she has worked for many years."

"Do you know where I can get hold of her?"

"They have a house down by the water in Egernsund, and I think she stays there alone most of the time."

"Egernsund, is that far away?"

"No, three or four miles from here. Just on the other side of the bridge." He pointed to the east. "But I don't think you can just ring the doorbell over there and expect to be let in. She's very reluctant to talk to reporters."

"How do you know that?"

"The husband told me it when I interviewed him. I had suggested that we meet at his house, but he refused on the grounds that his wife did not like the press. At the time, I thought it was a bit weird, but now that you're telling me they had a daughter who disappeared, I get it."

"Didn't the story of the girl show up in your research on the family back then?"

"No, but I didn't research the family per se. The article I wrote was about Dalsfort Industry buying a Polish competitor—a company called Vicon—for a few billion so that they could become a more significant player in the valve market. It was a feature for the business section, so we didn't go into Ole Dalsfort as a human being, or his family relationships and things like that. We didn't talk about that at all."

Thomas looked down at his wristwatch and pursed his lips in annoyance.

"What's up?" asked Heloise.

"I have an interview with the CFO of Danfoss here at eleven thirty, and I can't move it. It's been a real battle to set up that deal, so I have to . . ."

"Sure! If you need to leave . . ." Heloise said, even though that was the last thing she wanted.

They both got up and walked through the house together.

Thomas stopped in the doorway facing the driveway and looked at her. "You wanna come over tonight?"

Heloise smiled. "To your house?"

"Yes. You can bring all that stuff and we can look at it together." He made a sweeping motion with his hand toward the living room, where all the notes were lying on the floor. "We can eat some food, catch up . . ."

"Okay."

"Seven o'clock?"

Heloise nodded.

"I guess you have the address," he said, smiling.

He gave her a kiss on the cheek and walked toward his car. He turned around when he was halfway there, took a few steps backward, raised his hands palms up, and shouted:

"HOW CRAZY IS THIS?"

Heloise laughed and felt happy for the first time in years. Really happy.

Right down to the bones happy.

"Seven o'clock!" said Thomas, getting in his car. Heloise watched him as he pulled out of the driveway.

Heloise walked over to her car and took her phone out of the charger. She turned on the phone, entered her code, and immediately the messages started rolling in.

Ding, ding, ding!

Messages from Gerda, Ruth, and Schäfer.

The wording was the same in all of them: CALL!

CHAPTER

26

S CHÄFER GRIMACED AND suppressed a groan as he pulled
his shirt on. Over the past seven hours the bruises had
changed from reddish discolorations to large, blueberry-
colored blotches on his stomach and back, and the newly
sewn stitches above his left eye pulled on his skin. He felt as
if he had been driven through a meat grinder, and the half-
hour of beauty sleep inside the CT scanner hadn't helped.

"You've been lucky," the doctor said, handing him a zip-
lock bag with twenty-four pills in it. Take two of them every
six hours. If it gets really bad, you can supplement with a
single ibuprofen per dose."

Schäfer accepted the bag and stuck it in his back pocket.
"Anything else?"

"Yes, take it easy for the rest of the week, okay?" The
doctor regarded him over the rims of his glasses.

"I thought you said there was nothing to see on the
scan?" said Schäfer.

"There wasn't, but at your age there's no point in thinking you can just fly on after a beating like this as if nothing
had happened. You have to listen to your body."

At your age . . .

These were the same words the police commissioner had
used when he had called this morning.

Put your feet up, Schäfer. Take it easy. That's an order! At
your age, it takes a little while to recover from an event like that.
I don't want to see you before the end of next week!"

Schäfer met the doctor's gaze, raised his chin, and sucked
his cheeks in with a rebellious expression.

The doctor nodded once and left the room just as
Schäfer's phone vibrated.

"Y'ello?"

"Hey, what's up? Are you done at the hospital?" It was
Nils Petter Bertelsen.

"Just now."

"What's the verdict?"

Schäfer looked at himself in the examination room mirror as if looking for the answer there.

"Minced meat on the outside, tiptop on the inside," he
said.

"Well that's good to hear. Go home and let Connie pam-
per you. Take a long weekend and I'll hold the fort for a
while."

Schäfer fished a cigarette packet out of his inner pocket
and shook an unfiltered Kings out of it. He put the cigarette
in his mouth without lighting it.

"Have you been to forensics?" he asked. He had asked
Bertelsen to attend this morning's autopsy of Lester Wilkins
in his place.

"Yes. I just left there."

"And?"

"You were right."

Schäfer straightened up. "Is it a homicide?"

"Yes."

"But Sandahl was convinced that it was something about
some ruptured varicose veins? That the death was due to
drinking?"

"Yeah, but when he opened him up Wilkins had a frac-
ture in his skull that ran from the top of his head down across
his frontal bone. You couldn't see it from the outside because
the skin wasn't split, but he must have been hit with a blunt
object of some sort. Hard!"

One corner of Schäfer's mouth curled upward, and he clenched his fist in victory.

At your age . . . lost your touch. My ass!

"The neighbor," he said, starting to walk toward the exit. "Talk to the neighbor!"

"Yes, that's what I was about to say. They've been interrogating her all morning and they're still in there. It turns out that she and Wilkins had fallen out over something. Something about her dog that they had gotten into an argument over last week."

Schäfer nodded eagerly. His step felt suddenly springy, his mood light and bright.

"Let's get the boys from Forensics out to the site to check the blood one more time."

"I've already agreed with Rud that he will head in there later today and go through the apartment with a magnifying glass," Bertelsen said, referring to Rud Johannsen, who was a specialist in trace analysis and divided his time between the Department of Forensic Genetics at the University of Copenhagen's Department of Health and the National Forensic Center. "Then we'll see if he can conjure something up."

"All right, keep me updated, okay?"

"Don't you think you should relax a bit?"

"I'll relax when I'm old!" said Schäfer, smiling.

His phone beeped and he looked at the screen. He put the telephone to his ear again. "Hey, I've got another call, but keep me up to date, okay? I mean it!"

He ended the conversation with Bertelsen and accepted the incoming call.

"Where the hell have you been?" he asked. "I've called you a hundred times!?"

"My phone was dead," Heloise replied in a defensive tone. "Why? What's wrong?"

"What's *wrong*? I'm at the hospital to make sure that none of my ribs are about to puncture a lung. That's what's wrong!"

"What are you talking about? What's happened?"

"We had a break-in last night, Connie and me. I got a sock in the jaw plus extras."

"Christ, Schäfer!? Are you okay? What about Connie?"

"Connie is fine. I could use an Advil, to put it lightly."

Schäfer stepped through the sliding doors and went outside and sat down on a bench to the right of the entrance. He glanced at the No Smoking sign staked in the ground and fished his lighter out of a pocket.

"I'm really sorry to hear that," Heloise said. "What happened? Did you say someone broke into the house?"

"Into my car." Schäfer lit the cigarette and inhaled deeply. "This Tom Mázoreck stuff you're running around picking at over there. Who have you talked to about it?"

"A handful of people. Why?"

"Who specifically?"

Heloise listed them off. "Why do you ask?"

"Because the gorillas who broke into my car last night spoke some Eastern European language with each other that I didn't understand a whit of—except for one word. Mázoreck!"

There was silence on the line for a moment.

"Are you kidding?" Heloise said.

"Nope."

"But that . . . I . . ." She sounded flabbergasted. "I don't understand . . . There's something *totally* fucked up with this Mázoreck case, Schäfer."

"No shit!"

"What were they looking for?"

"I don't know, but they rooted around in my work files."

"Jan warned me about this," she said. Her voice suddenly sounded far away. "He said they would come after us if I asked too many questions. Something about . . . torches and spears and . . . but I didn't think that . . ."

"Don't talk to that Fischhof guy anymore until we know what we're dealing with."

"What? No, you don't understand, Schäfer! He's not . . ."

"You have no idea what you're running around and sticking your nose into over there. You've set out to tie a bow on the past for a man you don't know shit about. He could be a serial killer for all we know."

"I know him. You don't."

"But you've known him for—what? Two months? Three? You always think the best of people and then you're shocked when they turn out to be assholes. You're not exactly what I'd call a great judge of character."

Heloise was quiet at the other end of the line.

Schäfer closed his eyes tight and ran a flat hand across his face.

"Dammit, I'm sorry! That was . . ." He exhaled heavily through his nose. "Sorry! It's been a long night, okay?"

Heloise said nothing.

"I just don't want you to get hurt. Okay?"

"Mm-hmm."

"Can't you, um . . ." Schäfer threw his cigarette on the ground and stepped on it. "I guess I've been a little preoccupied for the last day or so, so could you tell me what you know one more time?"

"About what?"

"About all this stuff with Fischhof and Mázoreck. The girls who disappeared. Start from the beginning."

For the next half-hour, Heloise spoke and Schäfer listened without interrupting. When she'd finished, she said, "Are you still at Hvidovre Hospital?"

"Yes. Why?"

"There's a woman who works there. She was with Mia Sark the evening she disappeared. Malou, they called her, and her real name is . . . just a sec." Schäfer could hear Heloise flipping through some papers. "Marie Louise Yang. She's a pediatrician."

"What about her?"

"She told the police she had seen Mia Sark with a guy a few weeks before she disappeared. That it seemed secret, and that Mia wouldn't tell her who he was. Yang thought it might be someone she was seeing clandestinely."

"And what do you want me to do?"

"Ask her what she saw, what he looked like, and what happened on the last evening. The mother said that just before she disappeared Mia came home with a lot of money, and she was convinced that she had stolen it. Maybe Malou has an idea about where it came from."

"How much money are we talking about? A duffel bag full, or what?"

"Ten thousand kroner. The mother thought she might have stolen it from the café she worked at."

"Ten thousand kroner is peanuts. It's not an amount you want to break into cars or beat people up for twenty years later. Whatever it is these people are looking for, it's not ten thousand kroner."

"Well then, ask her about the guy she saw Mia Sark with back then. Ask if it was Mázoreck."

"Do we have a description to go by?"

"I have a photo. I'll send it to you," Heloise said.

"All right," Schäfer said. "What about you? What are you doing?"

"I'm on my way to talk to Peter Zøllner."

*   *   *

Schäfer put the phone in his pocket, walked through the sliding doors again, and looked down the long corridor. He studied the signage on the wall and tried to match the wards with the rainbow-colored stripes painted on the floor as guides. Hvidovre Hospital was the country's largest and served more than forty thousand patients a year. Finding your way here was like trying to find your way in a large village where all the houses looked alike, the villagers were clad in the same white uniforms, and all roads led straight to Hell.

Department of Amputation and Wound Care, you say? Follow the green stripe! Clinic for Neurorehabilitation/Traumatic Brain Injury? Blue stripe! The dialysis department? Red! The Gastrointestinal Cancer Unit? Follow the yellow brick road!

He spotted a young guy clad in overalls driving down the hall on a scooter and called to him.

The guy put his heel against the brake and stopped in front of Schäfer.

"Yes?"

Schäfer held up his police badge.

"I'm looking for a doctor named Marie Louise Yang. Can you point me in the right direction?"

"Marie Louise Yang," the guy repeated, fishing a phone out of his lab coat. "You don't know which department she belongs to?"

"She's a pediatrician. I don't know any more than that."

The guy typed on the cell phone.

"Yang . . . Yang . . . Here! You have to go down to Children and Youth Admissions. It's all the way down to the end. In section 411. Just follow the black stripe!"

Schäfer thanked him for his help and walked away.

C H A P T E R

27

THERE WAS A wet plop followed by a fizz. Investigator
Peter Zøllner watched the tablets dissolve in the water.
He swirled the mixture around the glass and gulped it down
in two large mouthfuls, then reached for the whiskey bottle
that stood next to the sink, filled the glass to the rim, and
bottomed it again.

He turned on the tap, and forming a bowl with his hands
under the jet, threw cold water over his face. He put a finger
to one nostril and snorted into the sink, wiped his face with
a towel, then put his hands against the edge of the table,
looking in the mirror with a tired expression. The furrows
under the empty eyes were deep and dark, the stubble long
and patchy silver-gray.

He opened the medicine cabinet and glanced at the razor
sticking out of the mug next to his toothbrush. He took it out
and closed the cabinet. He looked alternately at himself in
the mirror and down at the razor in his hand.

Today was Nicky's birthday. He would have turned
twenty-one. Naomi would have been eighteen.

And Lis . . .

He looked down at the faucet that was still on.

He put the plug in the sink, turned the water on full
force, and watched expressionlessly as the basin filled up
faster than the drain could keep up. The water began to

overflow and pour down the sides of the sink down onto the tile floor in a long ribbon, where it found its way into the grout joints and spread out between the tiles in square channels before finally flooding the floor of the small bathroom.

A few drops of blood hit the water and branched out like downward mushroom clouds when Peter Zøllner put the razor blade against the pad of his thumb and pressed.

He stared ahead without seeing anything, and his breathing quickened.

His inner ear heard the rumbling, thunderous sound of houses succumbing to floodwaters and cracking like dry twigs. Cars and boats and furniture and people that were being crushed against each other. Against lampposts, bridges, and buildings.

The sounds under water, above the water. Screams. Panic.

And then . . .

Silence.

It gave him a start when the doorbell rang, and he turned his head in the direction of the sound.

He turned off the tap and walked out into the hallway, seeing the blurred outline of a figure on the other side of the frosted glass door.

He hesitated for a moment, glancing over his shoulder into the house. Then he grabbed the doorknob and released the lock.

*   *   *

A pungent smell of sweat and frying fat leaked out from inside the house. The man in the doorway squinted his eyes in the morning sun and looked at Heloise with a questioning face. He was bald and slender, tanned, with gray hair on his chest. He was dressed in an open robe, white underpants, and a pair of sweat socks that left dark, wet traces on the maroon entrance tiles.

"Peter Zøllner?" asked Heloise.

"Who's asking?"

"My name is Heloise Kaldan," she said, holding out her right hand as she presented her press card with her left. "I am friends with Erik Schäfer from the Copenhagen Police. I understand you know each other from the police academy?"

He accepted her hand and nodded hesitantly. "Erik Schäfer? Yes. Yeah."

"I'm sorry if I'm disturbing you, but I'd like to know if you have time to talk to me for a moment?"

"Talk to you?" he asked. "About what?"

"If I may come in for a moment I can explain."

"Yeah, okay." He nodded, disoriented, and invited Heloise inside with a wave of his hand.

Zøllner closed the door behind her and led her from the hallway into the open kitchen, pointing to the dining table.

"Have a seat." he said.

Heloise looked around the house discreetly. It was an ordinary single-story house with yellow bricks and traditional white Danish windows, and from the outside looked like all the other houses in the neighborhood. Inside, there was a heavy doomsday atmosphere: everything was in disarray, things were lying helter-skelter, as if someone had ransacked the house.

Heloise cast a glance at Zøllner. There was blood on his bathrobe pocket and on his right hand, and he didn't make any move either to close his robe or to remove the stacks of plates piled with food scraps on the table in front of her.

He seemed strangely confused. And he reeked of liquor.

Peter Zøllner took a seat at the table across from her.

"You, um . . . you know Erik Schäfer, then?" he asked. His eyes wandered.

"Yes. I was involved in a murder case he investigated a few years ago, and he has since become a good friend."

Peter Zøllner closed his eyes for a brief second. "I remember him as a good man," he said.

"Yes, he is," Heloise nodded. "You talked to him yesterday morning I understand?"

His lips parted hesitantly. Then he nodded.

"Yes. He called the station. I must say, I was surprised to hear from him. After all, it's been years since I last saw him. Is he the one who sent you down here?"

"No, I'm actually here on behalf of another good friend. Jan Fischhof, do you remember him?"

Zøllner frowned and looked thoughtful. "Fischhof? Huh . . . vaguely!"

"And Schäfer called yesterday to ask you if you knew a guy named Mázoreck? The one who died in a boat accident, right?"

"Yes. That's correct."

"I've read up on the accident a bit, and I saw you were the one out on patrol that night, weren't you?" Heloise took her notebook out of her bag and clicked her pen.

Zøllner nodded and looked at the notebook with a hesitant expression.

"Do you remember anything from that night?"

"Why?"

"I would like to know how it went. You received a call from emergency services, or how did it happen?"

"Yes, I . . ." He sighed heavily. "Emergency services got a call early in the evening from an eyewitness who told me that Tom Mázoreck's motorboat had caught fire out on the fjord, then I immediately drove off toward—"

"Come again?" Heloise said. "Did the eyewitness tell you during that call that it was Mázoreck's boat?"

"Yeah."

"How could he know that?"

"Kurt lives down by the water and sails himself. He knows the local ships on the fjord and recognized Mázoreck's boat."

"He's the one named Linnet?" She flipped through her notes. "Kurt Linnet?"

Zøllner nodded.

"When I got there, I could see the boat lying a good distance away on the water. There was black smoke coming up from the stern, the engine was burning, and the fire had already eaten half the boat."

"And Mázoreck?"

"He lay in the water a few hundred yards out."

"How did you get him to shore?"

"Kurt had a dinghy moored to the jetty in front of his house, so I rowed out and dragged him in." He shrugged. "But unfortunately, there was nothing we could do."

"He was already dead?"

Peter Zøllner nodded.

"How did you know he had drowned?"

"He wasn't breathing anymore, had no pulse, so there was no doubt."

"But how did you know he had *drowned*?"

"As opposed to what?"

"As opposed to, say, being murdered."

Peter Zøllner pulled a questioning smile. When Heloise's facial expression didn't change, his smile faded, and he straightened up in his chair.

"You're serious?"

"Yes, I'm serious. There was nothing to see on him?" she asked. "Defensive wounds? Signs of violence?"

"Violence? No. No . . ." He shook his head and stared at her without blinking.

"Was he autopsied?"

"Uh, no. I don't think he was."

"Why not?"

"I don't remember, it was so long ago, you know. Either the family opposed it, or the doctor who conducted the coroner's inquest deemed it unnecessary."

Heloise clicked her pen. "I know that Tom Mázoreck testified in the Mia Sark case, whose investigation you led in 1997. Do you remember it?"

"The Mia Sark case?"

"Yes, it says in the existing articles about the case that Mázoreck was present in the tavern the night the girl disappeared."

Zøllner ran a hand through his hair and stood up. "Do you want some coffee or something?"

"No thanks," Heloise said. "Was he ever a suspect in the case?"

"Who?"

"Tom Mázoreck."

Zøllner laughed in surprise and looked as if he had forgotten why he had stood up. "What makes you ask that?"

Heloise held his gaze, awaiting his response.

"No, Tom Mázoreck was never a suspect in the case," he said emphatically. "Why do you ask?"

Heloise flipped through her notebook, ignoring the question. "One of your colleagues out in Sønderborg was nice enough to find the case file and help with some information about the investigation. Do you have a theory about what became of the girl?"

He shrugged. "If you've seen the file, you know what it says."

"Yes, but it's one thing to know what it says. It's another to know what you think *now*. So many years later."

Zøllner looked down and became aware of the blood on him. He reached across the table and took a crumpled napkin that lay on top of a plate.

"What you're talking about is twenty years in the past, and I've investigated a sea of cases since." He wrapped the napkin around his thumb and sat down again. "I wouldn't go so far as to say that the Sark case has been forgotten, because that would be disrespectful to the girl and her family, but . . . the road ended in a blind alley." He looked up. "We found nothing."

"So you're still holding to the trafficking theory?"

"Yes, because that's probably what happened. To the best of my knowledge."

"So the motive was—what? Money?"

He nodded. "Human trafficking is one of the most lucrative illegal businesses in the world, second only to arms and drug smuggling. Worldwide, it generates more than two hundred billion kroner a year. A *year!*" He raised both brows and nodded. "It's organized on a level you can't even imagine.

Then, on the other side, there are people like me . . ." He shook his head. "I was no match for it."

"I visited the mother yesterday, and she seems to think that the daughter will come home again."

Peter Zøllner looked down. He stared at his thumb for a moment and pressed it so that blood seeped through the napkin.

"People grieve in different ways," he said. "Ingeborg Sark needs hope."

"What about Nina Dalsfort?" asked Heloise. "What can you tell me about her?"

Peter Zøllner leaned back in his chair and looked at her with watchful eyes.

"How about you first tell me why you are interested in all this," he said, pointing at her .

"I'm interested because it all seems to be connected in some way, and I honestly think it's a *little* bit weird that no one sees it but me. Two innocent young girls disappear, and—"

"Nina Dalsfort was a criminal," he said.

"She was seventeen years old."

"And the age of criminal responsibility is fifteen. She was old enough to know what she was doing."

"She was also old enough to know that any sentence would be manageable. What was she risking? A fine? A suspended sentence? At worst."

Peter Zøllner eyed Heloise in silence.

"Is the police's theory really that she took off? Because of the events at Benniksgaard?" Heloise narrowed her eyes and shook her head. "That makes no sense."

"No one knows what happened to Nina Dalsfort. The parents blamed the mink-farm workers, and the mother harassed them for years. Hans Gallagher got the police to issue a restraining order against her because she kept on showing up at his home threatening him with death and destruction."

"Why did she do that?"

He shrugged. "I guess she needed someone to blame. I guess it's always easier to blame others than to look inward."

"Are you saying the parents themselves are to blame for Nina's disappearance?"

"I'm saying that, to me, it looked like a classic teenage rebellion. A rebellion against capitalist parents who, for many years, were customers of Birger Christensen Fur. It wasn't so much about animal welfare as it was about giving her parents the finger."

"And how were you assigned to the case?"

"What do you mean?"

"I'm investigating a death, which then leads to a disappearance, which then leads to *another* disappearance. There are several common denominators in the cases, and you are one of them."

"I've been in on all the cases in the Gråsten area for the last twenty-eight years."

"Oh, so you have a lot of experience with investigating?"

"I would say so," he nodded.

"Would you also say you are good at what you do?"

He shrugged slightly.

"And still you found not one single clue in connection with Mia Sark's disappearance," said Heloise. "Not one clue, that can tell us what became of Nina Dalsfort?"

Peter Zøllner said nothing.

"Why was the investigation of Mia Sark suspended after fourteen months?"

"Pardon me?"

"I have researched what is normal for these kinds of cases, and the majority of investigations continue indefinitely, so . . ." Heloise turned her palms up. "What was it that made you decide to label this one unsolved?"

Peter Zøllner looked at her for a long moment without saying anything.

"What about the Dalsfort case?" asked Heloise. "Why was that suspended?"

"I don't know what you are up to," said Zøllner, standing up slowly. "But I think visiting hours are over."

28

Schäfer watched the woman from the doorway into the waiting room. Her hair was short and shoe-polish black, her body shape a bit mannish. She stood bent over a little boy who was sitting quietly on a rocking horse, running her fingers up and down his neck in calm, measured strokes.

"How long has he had a fever?" She turned her gaze to the child's mother, who stood by his side clutching his hand.

"For twelve days."

"Has he complained of a sore throat? Stomachache?"

The mother nodded. Her face was drained of color, her eyes wide and anxious.

"This could indicate that it's mononucleosis. What you call kissing sickness." The doctor smiled at the boy. "Have you kissed the girls too much?"

The boy shook his head shyly.

"I'll send a nurse in here who will give you some magic cream on your arm so you can't feel anything when you have to have a blood test shortly." She smiled reassuringly at the boy. Then she turned her eyes to his mother. "Just take a seat and someone will come get you shortly."

She turned around and walked to the door, where Schäfer blocked the exit.

"I'm sorry," she said, signaling to pass.

"Marie Louise Yang?" he asked.

She raised her eyebrows in a welcoming expression but already held up a hand in front of her, ready to reject any request.

"I'm very busy, so if you . . ."

Schäfer held out his police badge. "It'll only take a moment."

Marie Louise Yang's eyes turned into two slits.

"Is there a place we can talk?" asked Schäfer.

She raised her chin. "What's it about?"

"Mia Sark."

Her forehead became smooth. The face was stiff and expressionless. She looked down at her wristwatch and sighed.

"You get five minutes."

*　*　*

"Could we have the room?" Marie Louise Yang's question was directed at a small, scarf-clad lady who was washing the floor. The woman put the mop in the roller bucket and left the room without a word. Yang closed the door behind her and leaned against it. She put her hands in the pockets of her lab coat and looked at Schäfer with a measured expression.

"Yes, you'll have to excuse me if I seem a little astonished here, but what you're talking about is many years in the past."

"Can you confirm that you knew Mia Sark, who disappeared on May 31, 1997?" he asked.

"Are there any new developments?"

"Unfortunately, I can't tell you that."

Yang smiled and snorted, shaking her head.

"What was your relationship with her?" asked Schäfer.

"What do you mean?"

"What I said. What was your relationship?"

Marie Louise Yang looked at Schäfer for a long moment, and a deep, vertical furrow appeared between her eyebrows. Then she blinked a few times and shrugged.

"Yeah, well . . . I guess we were what you call bosom buddies in those years when being the same age and living in the same city is enough to bind people together."

"You sound like it was a phase that passed?"

"You change as the years go by. The differences become more marked, you develop different ambitions, different values . . ."

"Was that what happened to you?" asked Schäfer. "You developed different values?"

Yang nodded. "During high school."

"How did it come about? The difference."

"I had a plan, a goal I was going for. This!" She threw out her arms. "Mia didn't."

"What did she have, then?"

"I don't know, she dropped out of high school six months into sophomore year, and we never talked about her plans for the future. Overall, she wasn't the type to put many words to what she thought and felt. At that point, we didn't have very good chemistry, but I . . . We knew each other's families. We had followed each other through childhood, and that kind of thing matters. But there was a . . . a darkness in her I couldn't relate to."

"A darkness?"

"Yes, she had a dark side—a hardness inside her that I couldn't understand. As the years went by, that side filled her more and more, and we started to see less of each other."

"But you were together the night she disappeared?"

Marie Louise Yang nodded.

"What do you remember from that evening?" asked Schäfer.

"Is this really necessary?" She looked down at her watch. "I already testified about this twenty years ago."

"And now we're going to do another round," Schäfer said, drawing a circle in the air with his finger. "What do you remember from that evening?"

She looked down. "I remember that . . . that Mia was in a bad mood."

"Why?"

She shrugged.

"Didn't you ask her what was wrong?"

"No, you . . . you don't understand." Marie Louise Yang shook her head. "She was often in a bad mood. There didn't have to be a reason, she was just like that. You didn't really read anything into it, and you didn't ask about it."

"Why not?"

"I don't know, you just didn't. My point is that there was nothing unusual about her mood that night. Was she bad company when she was angry? Yes! Did we attach any special importance to it? No."

"We?"

"Johan and I. A mutual friend who was in town with us that night."

"What happened? Try going through the evening for me. You arrived at the bar at . . .?"

"We arrived at eleven o'clock, drank some beers, smoked some cigarettes, drank some shots, played cards." She rattled off the memories as if it were the multiplication table, and Schäfer had the feeling that it was to avoid seeing the pictures all too clearly.

"At one o'clock, Mia said she wanted to go out and get some air. Johan and I stayed put, and that was it. We never saw her again."

"Did you see if any of the other bar guests accosted her during the evening? Someone she talked to?"

"The Tin Soldier is not a bar, it's a dive," Yang said, as if that were an answer in and of itself. "It's a dirty old pub. That night Mia, Johan, and I were the only ones under forty. I didn't care who else was there."

"When did you discover that she had disappeared?"

"When she didn't come back, Johan and I assumed she had gone home. Again, we didn't read anything into it. We just thought it was because she didn't want to be there any-more. But the next day her mother called me. She couldn't understand why Mia hadn't come home and asked if I knew where she was, and so on. She was worried, of course, and then the police got involved." She nodded once. Like a period. "And now, if you will excuse me? I have patients that I . . ."

"It's going to be another few minutes," said Schäfer. "I understand that you told the police in Gråsten that you saw Mia with a guy, just before she disappeared?"

"Is it really necessary to go through this one more time?" Yang repeated, and Schäfer saw her chin trembling slightly. "It has taken me many years to try to forget what happened. Many years of trying to forget Mia, so I . . ."

"I'm sorry to dig up the past if you'd rather put it behind you, but I wouldn't ask if it weren't important." Schäfer put a hand on her shoulder and gave her a warm look. "Did you see her with someone?"

Marie Louise Yang moistened her lips and nodded.

"When was that?"

"A few weeks earlier. Two, maybe three."

"Tell me what you saw," Schäfer nodded encouragingly.

Marie Louise Yang stared ahead of her without blinking. After a moment, she said: "It was early in the morning and I . . . I can't remember if it was a Saturday or a Sunday, but it was certainly a day off. I was out running in the woods, and then I saw them down by the castle lake."

"Castle lake?"

"Gråsten Castle," she said, meeting Schäfer's gaze. "It's out by a lake bordering the forest, and there was Mia with some guy I didn't know. The first thing that puzzled me was really just that she was up so early, because it wasn't more than seven or eight in the morning, and she always used to sleep in on the weekends . . ."

"What were they doing?"

"At first, they just stood and talked, but . . . there was something about the situation that made me stop and watch them from a distance for a moment instead of going over there and saying hello."

When she said nothing more, Schäfer asked, "What was it? What slowed you down."

"First, he was much older, the guy. I remember thinking that maybe he was a friend of Mia's father, because he must have been at least twice her age, so it seemed . . . off."

"And they just stood talking to each other?"

"Yes, to begin with. But it looked like they were arguing over something because Mia was standing like this." Marie Louise Yang crossed her arms and raised her chin. "But then the man suddenly leaned in and kissed her. Mia pulled away and started to go, but he caught up to her, grabbed her, and kissed her again. Kind of . . . hard! And then she hit him. Slapped him across the face."

"She *hit* him?"

"Yes." Marie Louise Yang stared ahead. "I was on my way over there to ask what on earth was going on when Mia suddenly leaned in toward him and laughed—such strange, happy laughter—and then she kissed him. For real. Without holding back. It seemed like the whole prelude had just been some kind of foreplay." Marie Louise Yang made a sweeping gesture and shook her head. "I had never seen her like this before, and I didn't understand what the hell was going on, so I was startled. Not only because the guy was so much older than she—there was also . . . there was a strange energy between them. I can't explain what it was, but . . . it scared me."

"Did you talk to her about it afterward? Did you ask who he was?"

"Yes, a few days later I asked if she had a new boyfriend, but she denied it. I told her what I had seen down by the lake, but she laughed at me and said I must have been hallucinating." Marie Louise Yang shook her head and looked at Schäfer without blinking. "I wasn't hallucinating."

"What did you think when she disappeared? What was your theory?"

"At first, I thought she might have run away—maybe with him. But as time went on?" She shook her head. "Who would do that?"

"What do you think now?" asked Schäfer.

"I think she's dead. I think he killed her." She nodded hesitantly. "In any case, someone did."

"Would you be able to identify him if you saw him again?"

She pursed her lips and shook her head uncertainly. "It was twenty years ago, I don't know . . ."

Schäfer took his phone out of his pocket. He opened the message Heloise had sent him with the picture from the mink farm and handed the phone to Marie Louise Yang.

"Was it him?" He pointed to Mázoreck.

She picked up the phone and zoomed in on the photo. The frown between her eyebrows disappeared.

She slowly shook her head and put an index finger on the screen.

"No," she said. "It was him."

CHAPTER

29

"CRAP!"

Heloise sighed as the mechanical voice asked her to leave a message. She ended the call, opened a browser on her mobile, and googled her way to the phone number of EnviroMax, the company in Stockholm that Elisabeth Ulvaeus worked for.

The call was answered by a receptionist who, after putting Heloise on hold for several minutes, informed her that Fischhof's daughter was on a work expedition in the Gulf of Bothnia with a team of scientists from Nova Scotia. The woman on the phone didn't know when she would be back or if there was a phone number she could be reached at in the meantime.

Heloise left her name and cell number along with a request to be contacted as soon as possible. Then she hung up.

She turned onto the main road and passed Broager Church, whose two towers had grown together like Siamese twins, and continued to follow the directions of the navigation system. She had expected to be led into Broager Center, but when the GPS announced that the final destination was a hundred yards farther along the route, she found herself in an industrial area where the signs on the buildings she passed advertised courses in archery, cheap car inspections, and custom blinds.

Heloise parked the car and got out.

She looked at the building in front of her— a long, flat, single-story property with large windows the entire way around it, all covered with black foil. On the facade, the name was bent into blue-white neon lights, and either Ingeborg Sark had been right when she said that Club Celeste had changed a lot since Mia Sark had worked here, or it had been a serious slip of the tongue when she had called it a café.

Heloise walked over to the entrance and grabbed the door handle. There was an open sign hanging in the black window, but the door was locked. She knocked and waited.

Nothing.

Gravel crunched under worn tires when a matte Toyota Corolla with flip-lights rolled into the parking lot behind Heloise and stopped some distance from her car. She turned her head at the sound and looked over toward the car. No one got out; the engine kept running.

She was about to turn on her heels when she heard someone rattle the lock on the other side of the door.

The man who opened the door appeared to be in his mid-forties. His hair was light and his skin tanned; his muscles were noticeable under the white undershirt, and he kept an arm behind his back, as if hiding something.

"Yes?" he asked.

Heloise looked him over and momentarily forgot why she was there. There was something about him that set off all the alarm bells at once, yet at the same time he was so handsome that she had a hard time not staring.

The symmetrical facial features, the well-proportioned body . . .

The man looked Heloise up and down. "Are you the one who is supposed to start today?"

"No, I'm looking for the owner," she said. "Is that you?"

"What's it about?"

Heloise met his gaze. "That's between me and the owner."

He pulled his cheeks into a smile and nodded in a way that said, Okay, I'll play along!

He opened the door all the way and motioned for her to come inside.

Heloise stepped into the darkness, where it smelled of smoke and year-old beer that had been spilled on the dark-red plush sofas and the stereo played an old Prince song. She could have been blindfolded and still have known she was in a place like this.

She looked around.

The blackout foil kept daylight out, and in the center of the room was an empty stage with a stripper pole in the middle. There were a couple of young girls lying on one of the sofas, staring at their respective cell phones. They were dressed in knee-length patent-leather boots, lace panties, and not much else.

Heloise turned her attention to the man with the blonde hair and made a slight hand gesture. "Where is he?"

"My father?" He turned to look at the far end of the room, where Heloise could see four doors next to each other. A light bulb was lit next to each room. Three of them were green; one glowed red. "He's a little tied up right now," he said, smiling a smile that gave Heloise the feeling that he meant it literally.

Her gaze fell on the cage in the corner. On the chains that lay inside. The leather whip.

"I didn't get your name," she said.

He held out his hand, and Heloise took it.

"My name is René," he said. "And you are?"

"Hey, Decker?"

The voice that called out belonged to a man sitting at the bar behind Heloise—a monstrosity of a human being. He was sweaty and bald and wore glasses. One of the circular lenses was dark and frosted, the other transparent, and he blinked at them with his one visible eye.

"Laszlo called," he said. "He asked me to tell you he's on his way."

Heloise looked at the blond man in front of her and let go of his hand.

"Decker?" she asked, remembering what Hans Gallagher and his wife had told her. "Are you René Decker?"

"Yes."

"Jes Decker's son?"

He narrowed his eyes slightly. "Do we know each other?"

"No," Heloise said, putting her hand in her bag to get her notebook. "But I want to . . ."

"Woah!" René Decker grabbed her arm. His facial expression was suddenly watchful, his eyes cold. "Keep your hands where I can see them!"

He lifted the bag off her shoulder so that it fell to the floor and swept it away with his foot.

Heloise looked at him, startled, and tried to pull her arm away.

"I just wanted to ask you if you . . ."

The one-eyed one from the bar materialized behind her, grabbed her arms, and fixed them behind her back.

"Hey, what the hell are you doing?" she yelled, writhing. "LET GO OF ME!"

René Decker reached a hand behind the small of his back and pulled out a gun. He pointed it at Heloise and hushed her, as if she were an infant to be comforted. "Shh-shh-shhhh . . ."

Heloise looked down the barrel and swallowed hard.

The man behind her grabbed her harder, and her arms felt like they were about to detach from her shoulder sockets.

René Decker picked up her bag and emptied the contents onto the bar counter. He pushed the notebook and cell phone aside and opened her wallet. He glanced at the press card in the plastic pocket. Then he looked over at Heloise.

There was a crisp, metallic sound as he cocked the gun. He took a few steps toward her.

The one-eyed man pulled on Heloise's arms so that her torso shot forward, and Decker pressed the mouth of the gun against her sternum.

"It's pretty rude not to introduce yourself before entering people's homes," he said, making a tsk-tsk sound as he shook his head. "Journalist?"

Heloise lifted her chin and held her breath. It felt like her heart was about to break out through her chest.

René Decker smiled briefly.

"What do you want to talk to my dad about?" he asked, sliding the gun down her neck. It hit the neckline of her T-shirt, which he slowly pulled down. He looked at her breasts for a long moment, frowning slowly, and nodded approvingly. Then he met Heloise's gaze and raised both brows into a question. "Well?"

"I want to talk to him about Pitbull," she said, writhing in the giant's grip.

"That's what you called Tom Mázoreck, right? Pitbull?"

René Decker narrowed his eyes and slid his arm down his side so that the gun was aimed at the floor.

Heloise had a hard time assessing his expression.

"They say it was you who found the dog in the refrigerator," she said. "Is that true?"

Decker's nostrils flared, and his eyes turned black.

"Do you know anything about the girls who disappeared back then? Mia Sark—she worked here. Do you remember her?"

He stared at her for a long time with dead eyes.

"Lock her up until my dad is done," he said without breaking eye contact.

"No, wait!" said Heloise. "You can't just . . ."

The giant dragged her away. She lost her footing, fell, and was pulled back up. She looked for René Decker, who had taken a seat at the bar, and anxiety pulsed through her entire body.

Her cell phone started ringing on the bar counter, and René Decker looked at it.

"Stop," he said.

He stood up and walked toward Heloise. He held the phone up in front of her so she could see the name on the display.

Erik Schäfer, it said.

"Answer it," he said.

Heloise frowned and stared at him uncomprehendingly.

He swiped to the right, put the speaker on, and held the phone up in front of her face. He pointed the gun at her and nodded.

"Hello?" said Heloise.

"Kaldan?"

"Yes." She met Decker's gaze.

"I just talked to Malou Yang, and guess who she identified? Your new best friend!"

Heloise said nothing.

"The man she saw with Mia Sark back then. It was Jan Fischhof!"

René Decker lowered his chin and looked at Heloise in surprise. He slowly lowered the gun.

"Are you hearing what I'm saying? It was Fischhof," Schäfer repeated. "Hello, are you there?"

René Decker ended the call and regarded Heloise searchingly.

"You know Jan Fischhof?" he asked.

Heloise's lips parted, but there was no sound. Her gaze was still on the gun.

The man behind Heloise shook her. "He asked you a question!"

"Yes," she said, trying to wrench herself from his grip. "Yes, we are friends."

René Decker narrowed his eyes.

"But he must be an older man by now . . ." He made a sweeping motion toward Heloise with his hand, like a silent question.

"He's dying, and I . . . I'm trying to help him."

"Is that why you're here? To help Jan?"

Heloise nodded.

René Decker looked at her for a long moment, saying nothing. Then he turned his eyes to the man holding her and nodded. "Let her go."

The man looked at Decker questioningly.

"Let *go* of her."

The man did as he was told, and Heloise took a few steps away from them both. She straightened her clothes and looked tensely from one to the other.

René Decker looked down and nodded. "Get out."

Heloise took a deep breath and watched him hesitantly. "I still want to talk to your dad," she said.

René Decker looked at her with raised brows. One corner of his mouth curled upward in an impressed smile.

"You have balls, beautiful, I'll give you that," he said. Then the smile disappeared again, and he pointed to the exit behind him with a thumb. "Fuck off!"

The one-eyed guy took Heloise's bag and threw her things back into it. He pushed it hard against her chest.

"You heard what he said. Take your shit and go!"

Heloise walked to the door and stepped outside.

"Hey . . ." René Decker appeared in the doorway behind her. Heloise turned around and met his gaze.

"I'll let you go as a favor to Jan," he said. "Once."

He underlined it with an index finger in the air and zoomed in on her with dead eyes.

An icy sensation spread through Heloise's body.

"Don't come back here."

* * *

Heloise pulled over and slammed on the brakes. White-knuckled, she wrapped her hands around the steering wheel, breathing in restrained jerks as she stared ahead.

It had been too close. *All* too close.

If Schäfer hadn't called at that second, if René Decker hadn't let her go . . .

Heloise closed her eyes hard at the thought of what might have happened. Her whole body quivered, and for a moment she considered driving out to the police station in Sønderborg and telling them about the assault. Then she remembered what Gallagher had said about Jes Decker.

They say the police are in his pocket, allegedly several local politicians too—no one can touch him.

There were also rumors of drug trafficking, he'd said. Porn, prostitution.

Could the Decker family also be involved in trafficking? Were they the ones who had abducted and trafficked Mia Sark and Nina Dalsfort back in the day?

And what about Jan? What did he mean to them? Heloise had seen respect for him in René Decker's eyes.

Why had he let her go?

She remained seated until the adrenaline stopped pricking her nerve endings. Then she straightened up and looked at herself in the rearview mirror, rubbed her hands across her cheeks, and nodded.

She pulled out onto the roadway and pushed her foot down on the accelerator.

CHAPTER

30

THE PEA GRAVEL crunched when Peter Zøllner drove into the driveway. He looked at the house in front of him: a one-story bungalow-style villa in dark-brown brick with shutters on the windows. He had been in the house since celebrating the raising of the last beam in 1986, when he and Steffen had both had hair on their heads and what could be described as visible abs.

Now it felt like a very long time ago, he thought, turning off the engine.

He knocked on the door and walked in without waiting for an answer.

"Hello?" he called. "Is anyone home?"

Miriam appeared in the doorway that led into the living room. She had a cell phone to her ear and smiled at Zøllner, hugging him with her free arm.

"He's outside," she whispered, pointing to the glass wall that separated the living room from the garden. She continued her phone conversation and disappeared into the kitchen.

Zøllner walked through the open sliding doors and saw that Steffen was standing with his back to the house trimming the beech hedge that surrounded the garden. The forest started on the other side of the hedge and continued several miles south.

Zøllner stood for a moment, watching him work, thinking about how to handle this.

He cleared his throat, and Steffen turned around.

"Peter, hi!" He smiled in surprise and put the hedge clippers down on the grass.

"Hi," Zøllner said. "Yeah, I was just in the area, so I . . ." He shrugged.

Steffen came over and shook his hand. He met Zøllner's gaze, and the lines of concern between his eyebrows deepened.

"Are you okay?" he asked. "You look like shit."

"Do I?" Zøllner looked down at himself.

"Yes, you have that feverish look in your eyes. Have you been drinking? Or is your head causing trouble again?"

"No, no . . . That's not why I am . . ."

"You remember to take your pills, right?"

Peter Zøllner nodded.

"Good, because it's important that you don't just quit overnight. It can have devastating consequences if you don't do things by the book."

"I'm taking my pills as I should, and it's been a long time since I last had an episode," Zøllner lied. The thought alone caused his heart rate to increase and anxiety to quiver in his chest. "As far as alcohol is concerned, I haven't touched a drop in six months."

Another lie.

"So what is it?" asked Steffen, crossing his arms.

"I got a call yesterday from a colleague in Copenhagen. An investigator from the Homicide Department."

"Yes?"

"I think he's investigating Tom Mázoreck's death."

The color disappeared from Steffen's face and his eyes widened.

"This morning a journalist showed up at my door and asked questions," Zøllner continued.

"Questions about what?"

"About Mázoreck. About how I could be sure of the cause of death, about what I knew about the girls, about why the investigations were put on hold."

Steffen's eyes bore into Zøllner's.

"You promised me this couldn't happen, Peter."

"I know, but I . . ."

"You promised!"

Zøllner nodded.

Steffen shook his head. "But . . . how? I don't understand?"

"The journalist knows Fischhof. I've looked into it, and apparently he's been living outside of Copenhagen all these years, and he . . . he's started talking."

Steffen grabbed Zøllner's collar hard.

"This can't come out, do you understand? I could lose everything: Miriam, the house, my practice . . . Everything!"

Peter Zøllner nodded.

"You've got to shut Fischhof up, Peter. I don't care how you do it. Just shut him up!"

31

THERE WAS NO For Sale sign in front of the property, but the local realtor had told Heloise that had the house had been on the market for a year and a half, and stressed that they were open to all bids. The public property valuation was around a few hundred thousand kroner, but Heloise would be surprised if anyone were to bid even *half* of that for the old country estate, which, since Renata Mázoreck's death, had apparently been allowed to decay.

The realtor had said that Heloise would not need a key to get in, and he had been right. The front door hung crookedly on the hinges and stood ajar, leading into the old house. It creaked as she pulled on it, and a sweetish stench hit her nostrils.

Heloise looked down at the entryway floor, where flies swarmed around dead flesh. Maggots crawled between uncovered ribs, the pointed teeth were exposed, and Heloise couldn't tell whether it was a fox or a dog.

She pulled her T-shirt up over her nose and stepped over the carcass, walked into the first room by the entrance, and looked around. Water damage had eaten through ceilings and walls and stained the whole house brown, and it seemed that everything sat where it had been left. There were books on the shelves and pots of dead plants on the windowsills, knick-knacks on all surfaces, and everything was covered in dust. A faded edition of *The Home* lay on the living room table next to a full ashtray, and a pair of slippers sat on the floor.

Heloise's gaze fell on the couch. The large, dark-brown blotches of corpse fluid on the cushions reminded her of what the real-estate broker had told her when she had called him earlier: that Renata Mázoreck had been lying there for months before she was found. Yet another person had taken their last breath in total solitude, Heloise thought, and contemplated calling Jan Fischhof.

She hadn't yet spoken to him today and wondered if he was still alive, but there was something that kept her from calling. A nagging doubt that had begun to grow in her.

Why had Ingeborg Sark reacted so harshly to his name? Why had René Decker let her go?

That gate you're talking about . . . Up there . . . I'm not sure they'll let me in.

What had Jan's relationship with Mia Sark been?

What had he done?

Heloise directed her gaze toward a framed embroidery hanging on the wall above the couch and snorted a little. FAMILY IS LIFE'S BLESSING it read in meticulous, red-yarn script. She walked over to the patio door and opened it to let fresh air in and spotted the guesthouse at the opposite end of the large yard.

She left the main house, crossed through the knee-high grass, and grabbed the door to the guesthouse. It was locked, so she put a hand against the frame and pulled. The woodwork was brittle and bone dry as dust, and the door gave way after a couple of tries.

Heloise went inside and looked around. According to Hans Gallagher, this was where Tom Mázoreck had lived. A grown man who had never really left home. What did it say about Mázoreck that he had lived with his mother until he was well into his forties? Who on earth would want that?

Except for a sunbed that stood folded in one corner, the guesthouse was completely deserted and consisted of two rooms: a bedroom and a washroom. The room with the sunbed had windows facing the garden, while the washroom was at the back of the house. There were no windows in there, only a naked light bulb hanging from the ceiling.

Heloise took out her cell phone. She turned on the flashlight app and shined the light around the dark room.

The floor was covered with cracked linoleum, the walls with white tiles, one of which was detaching itself at eye level; it was a fluted tile with a stripe of dark-blue floral patterning, as if it were Royal Copenhagen porcelain. It was not a bathroom, because there was no shower or toilet, only a drain in the floor and a sink hanging on the wall. The mirror above the sink was shattered and showed signs of someone having hit it with a fist or something else hard. The shards of glass around the impact point were rust-red and pointed like needles, and hundreds of silver filiments zigzagged across the mirror's surface.

Heloise stared at her twisted reflection and carefully ran her fingers over the sharp edges, imagining Tom Mázoreck standing in the same place, staring into the same mirror.

What had he seen in there?

She jumped when the phone rang and looked at the screen in her hand. She answered the call and put the phone to her ear.

"Hey!"

"Yo, what's up?" asked Schäfer. "You hung up when I called earlier."

"No, the connection is just so bad out here," Heloise lied, leaving the room. She pushed the door of the guesthouse open and walked out into the garden. "I'm far out in the countryside and the phone network is tricky."

"What are you doing?"

"When you called earlier, I had popped by a place called Club Celeste. That's where Mia Sark used to work. You know, the place the mother thought she might have stolen the money from?"

"Okay. And?"

"Ingeborg Sark made it sound as if Mia had been employed at a café—as if she had served lattes out there. But

I found out that it's a sex club of some kind. Striptease, bondage. That kind of thing."

"And she was employed there, you say? The girl?"

"Yes. I don't know if she worked as a stripper or what she did, but it would at least explain how she could scrape together ten thousand kroner in just a few months."

"Did they remember her out there?"

"Yes, I think so, and they also seem to know both Jan and Mázoreck, but they didn't want to talk to me."

Heloise couldn't bring herself to tell Schäfer what had happened. She was embarrassed to have been so helpless with René Decker—to have felt afraid. Moreover, she knew that Schäfer would just scold and blame her for putting herself in danger.

"What about you?" asked Heloise. "Where are you at?"

"I'm on my way back into town. I went out to talk to Fischhof when I finished at Hvidovre, but it was a bit more difficult than I had imagined."

"What do you mean?"

"Well, first of all, I had to get by a real Bud Spencer of a woman even to be allowed through the door out there—damn, what an acrid lady they've put in charge of him. Gestapo, go home!"

Ruth, Heloise thought, nodding.

"Secondly, I was trying to have a conversation with a person who mostly seemed to be talking in his sleep. Fischhof answered in the east when I asked in the west, and when I mentioned Mia Sark, his eyes went completely blank and he didn't say a word. I have to admit that I have a hard time imagining what the devil you two talk about when you're out there. The man is completely on planet Pluto!"

"He's not always like that. He's super cool when you catch him on a good day," Heloise said. "What did you want him to tell you about Mia Sark?"

"I wanted to ask him to explain what his relationship with her was. You know, the doctor friend said that she had seen them together in her time, but wasn't there also something about a wife once?"

"Yes, Alice. She apparently died of breast cancer when they were still living in Rinkenæs. I spoke to a former employer who said it was a tough time for Jan back then."

"Okay, so you might imagine that he sought solace after his wife's death. Maybe he's visited the club you're talking about and met Mia Sark there."

"At Club Celeste?" Heloise shook her head. "No, I can't imagine that. Jan is not the type at all."

"People in mourning sometimes do things they wouldn't normally do—behave in ways that go against what they normally stand for. If Fischhof was lonely, he may have been looking for company. Perhaps he relaxed his principles or explored a side of himself he had not dared to tinker with before. Did you say something about bondage?"

"Yes, that was my impression of the place out there. There were cages and whips. Chains, leather—that sort of thing. Why?"

"Marie Louise Yang said she saw Mia Sark hit Fischhof."

Heloise narrowed her eyes. "*Hit* him?"

"Yes. She allegedly slapped him good and then they kissed each other."

"Sorry, *what*?"

"Yep."

"I just thought they had been *seen* together? I certainly did not realize they'd *been* together!"

"Allegedly, they were."

"But . . ." Heloise was flabbergasted. "Mia Sark was so young."

"Yes. Nineteen."

"And Jan was so . . . so . . ."

"Yes. Old."

"Seriously, he must have been twenty-five years older than she!"

"Yes, and I know what you're thinking, but she *was* nineteen years old after all," Schäfer said. "So he hadn't done anything illegal. And if she worked as a stripper or worse, she probably wasn't quite the shrinking violet that her mother has tried to make you believe."

"Yes, but . . . still." Heloise bit her lower lip lightly and looked out over the fields that lay at the back of the plot. The earth was black and barren as far as the eye could see.

"Did you get ahold of Zøllner?" asked Schäfer.

"Yes, but he wasn't particularly communicative."

"Well, he doesn't know you. You're a journalist and he's a policeman. Oil and water."

"No, it didn't seem like that was the problem. I got the distinct feeling that he was hiding something."

"Zøllner?"

"Yes, just like that investigator Carl Roebel I told you about. There's something fishy about the police down here, Schäfer. I can feel it!"

"Oh, you can *feel* it? Why didn't you say that right away? That's exactly the kind of tangible evidence Internal Affairs loves."

"You know what I mean. He seemed . . . foggy! And drunk!"

"Did he?" Schäfer sighed in annoyance. "I thought he had regained control of his life."

"What do you mean?"

"Zøllner was in Thailand when the tsunami hit. He lost his wife and kids out there, and it knocked him out."

"Oh god, don't say that." Heloise put her head back and closed her eyes.

"Yes, it was so damned tragic. He was on sick leave afterward for quite some time, suffered from depression, and cracked up completely. He was apparently determined to drink himself to death, but then he turned himself around. At least, that's what I thought, because he came back to work the following year."

"Now I feel bad."

"About what?"

"About the way I behaved. I more or less insinuated that he was either incompetent or corrupt."

"Great," Schäfer said.

"Well, how would I know that he . . ." Heloise sighed. "Maybe you could have told me that story *before* I went out there."

She heard a car approaching the front of the property and turned her head in the direction of the sound. The car slowed down, but then slowly continued past the house, and Heloise returned to Schäfer.

"By the way, I'm at Tom Mázoreck's house right now. Or rather, I'm in his mother's house, where he lived most of the time."

"What can the mother tell you?"

"Not much. She died last year, and the house has been up for sale ever since—a smashed-up, old homestead. All her stuff is still here, it's all rotting. It's insanely disgusting."

Heloise walked around the guesthouse and looked at it from the outside. "What are you doing out there?" asked Schäfer.

Heloise hesitated. Her eyes moved from the guesthouse to the house where Renata Mázoreck had lived, and back again.

"They say he was a ladies' man," she said. "He had a lot of women."

"Who was a ladies' man?"

"Mázoreck. The word on the street is that the women loved him."

"Lucky guy," Schäfer said. "What else is said?"

Heloise was quiet for a moment as she thought.

"The man lived with his mother," she muttered, as if talking to herself.

"Sorry, what?"

"It makes no sense, Schäfer. What woman is attracted to a man who still lives at home at forty? Not a damn one."

"I guess we don't really know if he took the aforementioned ladies home with him, either."

Heloise stared at the guesthouse.

"There's something about this place . . ." She turned her gaze to the main house and suddenly felt ill at ease. The mental image of René Decker pulling out his gun and aiming it at her flashed before her mind's eye, and a wave of unease washed through her.

She rotated around, peering out over the deserted fields and the forest bordering the other side of the house, and suddenly became aware of how exposed she was out here. Completely alone, far from everything and everyone.

Again she heard the sound of a car out in front of the house. This time it seemed to be coming from the opposite direction. The car slowed down, coughed slowly past, and Heloise felt the uneasiness throbbing in her temples.

"Schäfer, I'll call you later," she said.

She ended the call and started walking toward her car with quick steps.

* * *

Heloise drove back to her rental house and took a bath, collected her notes, and put them in her bag. In the car on the way to Sønderborg, she called Jan. Ruth answered the call, and she immediately began harping on Schäfer's visit.

"What a tyrant! I can tell you that it will take a court order if I ever let that man back in."

The visit had apparently left Jan mute and exhausted, and when Ruth held out the phone to him and asked if he wanted to talk to Heloise, he emphatically declined. He sounded hurt and aggrieved, but Heloise also heard something else in his voice, a distrust that until now had been directed at everyone but her, and she felt her heart grow heavy at the realization that she'd lost her special status as the Chosen One. But could she honestly say that her trust in Jan hadn't also changed over the past twenty-four hours?

Heloise hung up the phone and put her foot to the accelerator with the oppressive feeling that she had spoken to Jan Fischhof for the last time. There was still so much she didn't know about him, but she did know him well enough to recognize that there was a real risk that he would never let her in again.

The clock on the dashboard showed 6:40 PM, and Heloise had reached halfway to Sønderborg when she noticed the red Toyota Corolla in her rearview mirror. It was the flip-lights that caught her attention, and she could see the outline of someone behind the wheel. Heloise looked alternately at the road in front of her and the car in the mirror.

Was it the same car as the one that had driven into the parking lot when she was at Club Celeste?

The Toyota kept its distance, but it stayed behind her, and when she reached Dybbøl Mill, she continued straight ahead instead of turning off down toward Thomas's house. She picked up speed and the tires drummed hard across the cobblestones, while the Sønderborg Skyline revealed itself at the end of Dybbøl Banke.

Heloise watched the lights in the rearview mirror and turned at random spots to see if the Toyota was following. She drove around Sønderborg for twenty minutes without shaking it off. Eventually, she headed for the police station.

Heloise drove in front of the building, left the engine running, and jumped out of the car. When she reached the automatic sliding doors, she turned around and saw the Toyota drive by. The driver turned his face to her, but it was going so fast that she couldn't tell if it was a man or a woman behind the wheel.

It lasted a split second, and then the car was gone.

Heloise turned around and went inside.

"You again?" said Carl Roebel with annoyance as she reached the counter.

"Yes, hello," she said, pointing toward the road. "I know it sounds strange, but there's a car that's been following me all the way from Broager, and I . . ."

"Why don't you do us all a favor and go home to Copenhagen?"

Heloise lowered her chin and peered at him in surprise.

"I'm sorry, didn't you hear what I said?" she asked, and pointed demonstratively toward the road. "Someone is following me!"

"*Following* you?" Carl Roebel's face wrinkled into a caricature for a moment. Then the unimpressed expression was back. "It's probably someone who's grown tired of all your questions."

Heloise stared at him.

"Tell me, what is it you're afraid I'll find out, Roebel? What are you hiding?"

"I'm not hiding anything," he said with a snort. "I just don't have time for la-de-da types who come down here and brag about their press credentials and their Copenhagen ways and expect us to fall all over ourselves about it."

Heloise watched him silently for several seconds. Then she shook her head, turned around, and left.

She got in the car and was aware of her surroundings as she drove back into town, across the bridge, and up to the mill.

Little by little, she began to relax. Maybe it was all something she had imagined.

She didn't see any red Toyotas in the rearview mirror anymore. No one was following her.

32

THE BARRIER TAPE stretched across the open door, and Schäfer could see that Rud Johannsen and a younger technician from Forensics were busy mapping spots, drops, splashes, and patches of blood in the entrance hall and all the way down the hall to the place where Lester Wilkins's body had been found.

Schäfer knocked on the door frame and they both looked up.

"Am I disturbing you?" he asked.

"No, no, come on in!" Rud waved him inside and pulled the mask down over his chin. "We were just about to pack up."

Schäfer bowed and went under the tape.

"What happened to you?" asked Rud, nodding in the direction of his black eye.

"Connie," Schäfer said. "She thought I was being a smart-ass."

Rud smiled.

"What's up?" asked Schäfer. "Are you finding anything useful?"

"Yes and no," Rud said. He pushed his glasses up on his forehead. His medium-long white hair was hidden under a net, and his gaze, as always, was focused, devoted to the task. "Since the skin was not broken by the impact, and according to Sandahl there was one blunt blow above the hairline as opposed to several strokes one after another, there is no spattering up here." He pointed to the ceiling above them. "On the other hand, there are many elongated drops of blood angled obliquely, almost horizontally, on the wall down the hall."

Rud pointed as he spoke. "The victim bled out of his mouth, so he may have spit or coughed out the blood so that the droplets were sprayed across the wall at an almost horizontal angle. However, it could also be a sign that he was shoved, pushed, or hit while bleeding."

"Surely we can also think about some of the drops originating from the perpetrator himself?" said Schäfer. "If he or she was injured during the killing?"

"It's conceivable," Rud nodded. "We have taken samples of everything and will run it through the system as soon as possible to see if there is DNA from more than one person, and if so, if there is a match in the computer. But you know what it's like. That kind of thing takes time."

The young track technician collected the samples that Rud was talking about and looked at him.

"I'm driving into the lab with these," he said, nodding goodbye. "Have a good weekend!"

"Oh, okay? Well, I . . ." Rud held up a hand to slow him down, but his colleague had already turned his back on him and headed for the stairwell and the white Forensics van sitting in front of the property down on the Esplanade.

Rud let his arm fall with a resigned expression.

"What's the matter?" asked Schäfer.

"Oh, I just wanted to offer my help." Rud looked down at his watch. "But perhaps I should just . . ." He looked up and down the hallway, as if looking for something but couldn't remember what it was. "Yeah, I don't really know . . . maybe we should grab a beer someplace?"

He turned his eyes on Schäfer in cautious invitation.

"What's the matter, Rud?"

Rud's shoulders sank. He took a deep breath and sighed.

"The weekends are not what they used to be," he said.

Schäfer pursed his lips and nodded.

Rud Johannsen had recently confided to Schäfer that his wife of thirty years had left him. On his sixtieth birthday she had announced that she had met someone else: herself! Her reasoning, according to Rud, was that she no longer felt like the person he had married and that she therefore had to explore the new version of herself—alone. Schäfer didn't quite buy the "alone" part of the sales pitch, but Rud didn't seem to question it, and Schäfer didn't think it his place to light the fuse of the bomb that would go off in Rud's head when he realized his wife was out fulfilling herself with nightlife before the sand in her hourglass ran out.

"I don't know what to do now that I only have myself to think about," Rud said, looking lost.

"What about the kids? You still have them."

"Yes, but they're busy with their studies. They shouldn't be saddled with their old father's woes."

"Okay, but you love the job," Schaefer said. "Immerse yourself in that!"

"Yes, I would like to, but Elkjær complains that I take up too much space," Rud said, referring to the head of the National Crime Technology Center. "He says that the new recruits don't have room to grow and learn when I'm out there all the time—that I am a bully with my rigid Stone Age rules. That's how he put it. But I just like things the way I like them, and what's wrong with that?"

Schäfer smiled. "Nothing, Rud. Not a damn thing. The young people should be grateful to have an authority like you within reach."

"Oh, well, I don't know," Rud said, lowering his eyes with a modest smile. "I've been ordered to take some days off. I'm not allowed out there at all if I'm not on the roster. Have you ever heard the like?"

"Welcome to the club," Schäfer said.

"Oh?" Rud lit up at the thought that there were others in the same boat as he was.

Schäfer pointed to the blue-black shadow around his eye and the stitches holding his brow together.

"They tell me to recover."

Rud's face curled up in disbelief.

"Over a tiny scratch? Good Lord!"

Schäfer chuckled.

"Well," he said, giving Rud a friendly clap on the shoulder. "Shall we get that beer?"

33

"WHAT WOULD YOU like? I have Pale Ale? Or would you rather have a regular lager?"

Thomas looked at Heloise from the open American refrigerator.

"Uh, no thanks, but if you have . . ."

He triumphantly brought out a bottle of Nova's Chardonnay from the Casablanca Valley in Chile—Heloise's favorite drink for more years than she was willing to admit.

"What did you expect?" he asked. "That I'd forgotten?"

Heloise looked him up and down and smiled. "How cocky you are!"

"Yes. But am I wrong?"

"No, you're not wrong," smiled Heloise, reaching for the glass he filled for her.

She had put on clean clothes and dabbed Jour d'Hermès on her wrists before leaving home, but she didn't apply makeup or do anything with her hair. Not that she didn't want to make an impression on Thomas. She just knew she didn't have to make an effort with him.

Thomas opened a beer for himself. He stood on the other side of the kitchen island and set about splitting avocados and peapods for the salad.

"Can I look around?" asked Heloise, pointing at the open double door to the living room.

"Yes, of course," he nodded, gesturing with his hand. "Make yourself at home."

Heloise walked into the living room and looked over the furniture. She recognized several of the paintings and old posters from Galerie Maeght, which she had seen so many times before: the blue-glazed clay pots that Thomas's mother had made in her creative phase during the early noughties, and the Poul Henningsen lamp that had hung in his apartment in Christianshavn. Things Heloise had forgotten about and that were now so vivid in her memory.

She glanced over the bookshelf and stopped at one of the books, a copy of Christopher Hitchens's *God Is Not Great*. It was a signed first edition, and Heloise had presented it to Thomas on his thirtieth birthday almost ten years ago. He adored the late Hitchens to a degree that was almost comical for a man who was a declared atheist, and Heloise had spent thousands of kroner on eBay to procure the book for him.

She put down her wine glass and took the book off the shelf. She opened it and smiled when she saw the photograph hidden between the pages. It was an old photo of her and Thomas on their way to a Halloween party at the School of Journalism dressed in a Natural Born Killers version of O'Malley and the Duchess from *The Aristocats*.

Heloise turned the picture over and read what she had written on the back.

Abraham Delacey Giuseppe Casey Thomas O'Malley,
I love you—still, always.
Heloise.

She put the picture back into the book and placed it on the shelf again. She went out to the kitchen and sat down on the bar stool by the kitchen island, where her notes lay on the marble countertop.

"Did you get ahold of the Dalsfort family?" asked Thomas. He had rolled up his sleeves and was filling a fat Label Rouge chicken with lemon, thyme, and rosemary.

"No, I didn't make it over to them today," Heloise said. She collected the notes in a pile and pushed them aside. "I'll do it tomorrow."

"Just explain to me again what it is you need my help with."

Heloise didn't answer. She watched as Thomas poured olive oil over the bird and began rubbing it with salt.

He looked up and met her gaze. Waiting.

"Can't we eat first?" she asked, looking at him with gentle eyes. "Then we can talk about the other thing afterward."

Thomas smiled and nodded. He washed his hands and dried them on a tea towel. Then he lifted his beer and held it out to Heloise's glass.

"It's good to see you," he said.

"You too." She returned the toast and drank from her wine. Thomas stood with the beer bottle raised and his eyes on her.

"You're staring," Heloise said, smiling.

"It's hard not to."

"It's no wonder. You haven't seen me in seven years."

"Well, I . . ." He hesitated. "I *have* seen you."

Heloise frowned and smiled curiously. "What do you mean?"

"Last year," Thomas said. "I was in Copenhagen and had a meeting at that restaurant located at Kongens Nytorv."

"Bistro Royal?"

Thomas nodded.

"I saw you sitting at the bar with that Christiansborg reporter. What is his name? Duvall?"

Thomas said it as if he wasn't sure, but Heloise knew him well enough to know that he had not the slightest doubt.

She also knew what day he was talking about. She and Martin Duvall had been sitting at the bar at Bistro Royal all evening, eating mussels with fries and swilling white wine and kissing so hard and for so long that her lips had been sore for days. The thought that Thomas had seen her like this turned her stomach.

"You looked happy," he said.

"It was an optical illusion," Heloise replied, and meant it.

"Seeing you there . . . for the first time in years. Together with someone else." Thomas shook his head and put a hand to his heart. "I almost died," he smiled.

Heloise met his gaze.

"Yes, well . . . Then you know why I drove away yesterday."

They looked at each other for a long moment, and neither of them said anything. Then Heloise took a deep breath and turned her eyes to the children's pictures hanging on the refrigerator. She nodded toward them.

"How old are they now, your boys? Six?"

Thomas nodded.

"What are their names?"

"Anders and Christian."

Heloise met his look and smiled in amazement. "God, how wonderfully ordinary."

Thomas laughed. "Uh, thank you? I guess."

"No, I really mean that. In Copenhagen, the kids have the wildest, most pretentious names. In my goddaughter's class there are children named Plato, Saxo, Pollux . . . Morpheus! God help me, there's a girl named Oasis. Named after the band."

"At least that's a lot better than being named after Blur."

"Not a lot better!"

Thomas smiled. "What about your goddaughter, what's her name?"

"Lulu."

"Lulu . . ." He tasted the word. "That also sounds kind of like a stripper, doesn't it?"

"Whoa, hey!" Heloise raised both brows and held up a hand. "That's Gerda's daughter you're talking about."

Thomas laughed and crossed his arms. He leaned against the kitchen table.

"Gerda," he said. "It was so damn weird to hear her voice again. How is she?"

"She's fine," Heloise said. "She's kind of in the same place as you. Newly divorced, newly hot . . ."

"Newly hot ?" Thomas raised an eyebrow. "Do you think I'm hot?"

Heloise looked him up and down.

"I've certainly seen you look worse."

She stood up, snatched the plates that were on the kitchen island, and started setting the dining table.

She could feel Thomas's eyes on her.

"What about you and children?" he asked. "Surely your father must have started pestering you to give him some grandchildren?"

Heloise's felt a trembling in her chest. It was the only conversation she didn't want to have with Thomas, and she had hoped to put it off for a little while longer.

"My father is dead," she said, her back to Thomas. She turned around and met his gaze.

He looked at her with wide eyes. "*What*?"

She nodded.

A veil of fog slid across Thomas's face, and he took a couple of steps toward her. He shook his head uncomprehendingly and swallowed the lump in his throat.

"But . . . when?"

"Last year."

"God, Heloise, I'm sorry to hear that." He put his hands on her shoulders.

Heloise nodded. She had known that he would be.

"He was a good man, your father. I was extraordinarily fond of him," Thomas said.

Heloise looked down. She couldn't bring herself to tell him how she herself felt.

"How old was he?"

"Sixty-four."

Thomas shook his head and sighed. "Was he sick?"

I'm sick, Heloise. It's a disease I . . . Oh god, help me!

"Yes," she nodded. "Yes, he was."

"How about Karin?" asked Thomas, referring to Heloise's mother. He knew that she and Heloise had never been close with each other. During the best periods, their relationship had been polite and strangely stiff. At other times, they had had no contact at all.

Heloise shook her head.

"She died a few years after you went to New York. So, to answer your question: No! No one is pestering me about children." Heloise smiled briefly. "Besides, I think that race is over."

"You're only thirty-seven," Thomas said. "There's still time."

"That race is over," Heloise repeated.

She turned away from Thomas and grabbed her glass. She didn't want to talk about her family anymore.

They traversed a long moment in silence. Then Heloise turned her gaze to the garden and smiled.

"To think that you own a flagpole," she said. She watched the pennant hanging limply from the eleven-yard-high flagpole at the far end of the garden.

Thomas smiled at the comment. He turned around and started the oven.

Heloise looked around and continued: "You have a manor house and a double garage and an open-concept kitchen with Italian tiled floors and twins and a . . . a flagpole. And you live in Jutland!" She flung her arms out and laughed. "What the fuck happened?"

"Life," Thomas said, raising his beer. "Life happened!"

"Yes, and I have to admit that it looks like a decent life," she nodded. "Are you happy?"

"Right now I am," he said, meeting her gaze.

"Good," she said, and smiled.

Thomas put the bottle down and put his hands against the edge of the table. "Do you ever think about where we would be today if I hadn't taken that job in the United States? Or if you had gone with me as we had planned?"

"Yes," Heloise nodded. She took a deep breath and shrugged. "Then it would most likely be the two of us who were divorced with two children and a fifty-fifty custody arrangement that we would have to fit into our respective working lives."

He shook his head and smiled slightly. "You know you don't believe that."

The cell phone on the kitchen island lit up, and Thomas looked down at it. His eyebrows drew together over his nose as he read the message that had come in. He picked the phone up and walked over to the living-room window, looking down at the bay.

"What's up?" asked Heloise behind him.

He looked down at the phone again.

"It's my news editor. He writes that a body has washed ashore down on the beach."

"A *body*?" Heloise walked over to him. "Where?"

Thomas pointed out the window. "Down there. A little less than a mile from here."

Heloise peered out over the meadow that sloped down to the bay and could sense faint blue flashes somewhere down there.

"Do they know what happened?" she asked.

"No. We just received the tip from one of our sources in the emergency services. The caller thought it could be a homicide."

Thomas started typing on the phone.

"Shouldn't you sent someone down there to cover it?" asked Heloise.

"Yes," he said, taking her by the hand. "Come on!"

34

THE SUNSET GLOWED low on the horizon like a bonfire about to go out, casting a long, red streak across the bay. The water was blue-black and close to dead calm: with meditative lapping it only beat gently toward the shore. Heloise and Thomas followed the path that ran down the meadow, and when they reached the water's edge, they could see emergency vehicles flashing silently a few hundred yards farther along the deserted beach.

They headed for the blue flashes, walking on an uneven foundation of awkward rocks; yellow and red elongated blocks protruded from the sand with rounded corners that seemed to have been shaped by the water.

"These are old bricks," Thomas explained when Heloise asked. "The area is known for its brickyards, and especially on the beaches you can sense that it has been a big industry down here for many years."

They approached the police car and the ambulance that were parked on the beach and spotted the blue-white body lying on its back at the water's edge.

Heloise's lips parted in dismay, and she reached out for Thomas.

"Good God," he muttered.

The body lying at the water's edge was undressed. The contours of the chest and the musculature of the legs indicated that it was a man between thirty and fifty years old. His chest hair was dark, his stomach and genitals swollen from lying in the water. Both head and hands were missing.

A police photographer was photographing the body, and twenty feet away a couple of officers stood with their backs to the water. They were interrogating an elderly man who Heloise guessed was the one who had reported the find.

She turned her eyes back to the headless man. A fist-sized crab was climbing his left tibia, and she suppressed a rising urge to vomit.

"Hey! You two!" a voice called behind them. The police had noticed that they had guests. "You must leave the area immediately."

Thomas let go of Heloise's hand and walked over to the officers. She stayed where she was, staring at the corpse, at the arms sticking out like pale logs from the torso, at the crab working its way up his leg, and his neck, which was no more than an inch long. Or rather *short.*

"Do you know anything about what happened?" she heard Thomas asking behind her.

"Sorry, you can't be here, Malling."

"But do you have any idea who he is?"

"I have no comment at this time. I must ask you to leave the area immediately."

"You're holding a partially dismembered corpse, Roebel, you damn well have to say something! The citizens have a right to know if there is a murderer running around in Sønderborg and . . ."

"Don't go scaring the whole city with conjecture, okay? We need peace so we can work here, so if you and your friend would be kind enough to go, then . . ."

Heloise turned around and met Carl Roebel's gaze.

"Hello again," she said, and nodded.

He looked at her in amazement for a moment. Then he turned his eyes on Thomas.

"Please leave the area!"

* * *

"Are you still hungry?"

Thomas looked at Heloise, frowning slightly.

She sat down at the kitchen island, looked at the chicken lying in the dish next to the oven, pink and headless, and shook her head.

"Me neither," he said, turning off the oven. He threw the bird in the trash, tied a knot in the bag, and left the kitchen with it in his hand.

Heloise reached for the wine bottle and filled her glass to the rim. She took two large swallows and closed her eyes as she felt the alcohol tingle in her blood.

Thomas came back into the kitchen and took his phone out of his pocket.

He entered a number and put the phone to his ear.

"Who are you calling?" she asked.

"A source I have in the police," he said.

He walked into the living room, and Heloise heard him alternately asking questions and listening. When he came back, he said, "They think they know who it is."

"Who is it?"

"There's a possibility it's a Dutch tourist who has been reported missing for a month and was last seen out in Aabenraa, but they are more inclined to believe that it's a local guy named Glenn Nielsen. Of course, there is also the possibility that it is someone else, but Glenn's wife apparently reported him missing a few hours ago because she hasn't seen or heard from him since yesterday morning, so now we have to wait and see what the police find out. After all, they can't take fingerprints or dental impressions from the corpse, so unless the head or hands show up somewhere . . ." He shrugged.

"Glenn," Heloise repeated. "You sound like it's someone you know?"

"By name only. He's a loser. He hangs out with the wrong crew, so I wouldn't be surprised if it turns out to be him."

"The wrong crew?"

"Yeah, he's connected to a guy named Jes Decker, who's kind of a local Don Corleone down here. He has a whole entourage of psychopaths, and Glenn Nielsen is, as far as I know, one of them."

Heloise opened and closed her mouth, dumbfounded. Thomas looked at her with curiosity. "What?"

"I was in Broager today to talk to him," she said.

"To who?"

"Jes Decker. But only his son was there, and he . . ."

"*You* were with Decker?" Thomas looked at her in astonishment.

Heloise nodded.

"At Club Celeste?"

"Yes."

"Dammit, Heloise, you need to be more careful." Thomas looked at her with wrinkled brows. "They're no joke, those guys out there! Why on earth did you go out to see them?"

Heloise pulled her shoulders up to her ears and turned her palms upward.

"Because I had no idea who they were and because I think they're the key to all this. I think they know what Jan Fischhof has done. And what happened to the missing girls. I'm sure of it."

"Seriously, you have to stay away from those guys." Thomas took her hands in his. "If the Decker family has anything to do with these things, then you should stay far away."

"I can't," said Heloise, shaking her head. "I have to investigate what happened."

Thomas sighed and gave her a look she had seen many times before.

"I gather that you still haven't learned that there's a difference between *can* not and *will* not," he said.

Heloise freed herself from his hands and leaned back in her chair.

"If you don't want to help me, it's okay," she said. "But I could really use someone who knows the rules of the game down here."

Thomas searched her face; his expression was thoughtful and serious.

He got up and left the kitchen.

When he returned, he rolled a large bulletin board in front of Heloise and removed the papers hanging on it. He handed her a box of thumb tacks and pointed his chin at the pile of notes lying next to her.

"Okay," he said. "Let's take a look."

35

HUNGER RETURNED AT eleven PM. Thomas heated a loaf of bread in the oven and emptied the refrigerator of cheese, tomatoes, sausage, and olives. He placed the things on the dining table along with the salad he had made earlier in the evening and opened a new bottle of Chardonnay.

"Okay, so Mia Sark worked for Jes Decker?" he said, topping up the wine in Heloise's glass.

"Yes." She reached across the table and broke off a few pieces of bread. She put one chunk on Thomas' plate and took another herself. "Her mother said that Celeste was a café, but unless the place has changed radically since the late nineties, it is . . ."

"It's a brothel," Thomas said, clasping his hands behind his neck. "Officially it's a strip club, but everyone down here knows it's a whorehouse and has been for many years—even in the nineties."

"If everyone knows, then why don't the police do something about it? Why don't they charge Jes and René Decker with procuring?"

"Why don't they do something about the sale of cannabis in Christiania?" Thomas threw out his arms. "This way, it's gathered in one place, and there are no prostitutes hanging out on the street corners and accosting random passers-by.

Sønderborg is nice and tidy, and everything dirty is housed under one roof outside the city."

Heloise reached for an olive and put it in her mouth. "So it's *both* a strip club and a brothel?"

Thomas nodded. "Yes. Jes Decker owns Celeste, and he owns something called Kingdom. It's a production company."

"What does it produce?"

"Porno movies. They shoot the movies and share them on various sites online, and then people can buy a night out with the girl they've fallen in love with on screen."

Heloise grimaced. "Fuck, how repulsive! How do you know all this?"

"We thought about doing a story about it last year, but management shut it down. Emphatically!"

"Why?"

Thomas shrugged.

"I imagine that they were afraid of suddenly one day washing ashore like Glenn Nielsen—if he's the one the police have fished up down there. I also got the feeling that maybe one or two of the bosses were nervous about what we would discover if we started digging into it."

"You mean about *them*?"

Thomas nodded. "When it comes to people's sex lives—especially those who have fetishes at the dark end of the color scheme—people are almost willing to kill so as not to be uncovered and exposed. Club Celeste is known for rough sex. S&M, bondage . . . Hardcore shit!" He shrugged. "I think a lot of people prefer that this history never see the light of day."

"And Mia Sark worked there." Heloise bit her lower lip while she thought. "Therefore, in theory, all the customers she had are suspects, right?"

Thomas nodded.

"Those sites on the web . . ."

"Yes?"

"What are they called?" asked Heloise.

"Which of them? There are thousands."

She threw up her hand. "What are the names of the most famous ones?"

"YouPorn, Redtube, XVideos, Pornhub."

Heloise raised her eyebrows. "Wow, they were right on the tip of your tongue, huh?"

Thomas gave her a look that said, "What did you expect?"

"But I guess that kind of thing didn't exist back in 1997, when the web was brand new," Heloise said. "I don't even think I had a Hotmail account back then. Google hadn't even been invented yet."

"Yes, there was online porn back then too." Thomas took a bite of bread and chewed while he spoke. "Sometimes I think that's why the Internet was invented—to give the sex industry an easier distribution channel. But, of course, there were not as many sites then as there are today."

He opened his computer and googled, opened some different links, and read.

"According to this article in *The Guardian*, The Hun, Hush-Hush and World Sex were the first sites to offer . . ."

"Wait, *what* did you say?" Heloise straightened up in her chair.

"It says Internet porn really exploded in . . ."

"No, the site you mentioned." She put down her wine glass, walked over to Thomas's side of the table, and looked over his shoulder.

She put a finger on the screen.

"That! Hush-Hush!"

"What about it?" Thomas looked up at her.

"In the box with the Mia Sark case out at the police station there was a VHS tape with her name on it, and it said Hush-Hush."

"Are you sure?"

"Yes. It said "Hush-Hush, December 8."

"Did it have a year too?"

"No, I don't think so. I just noted December 8 because that was the day Lennon was shot."

"Oh, yes, that's right," Thomas nodded. "And the day Pearl Harbor was bombed."

"No, that was December 7."

"Are you sure? I really think it was . . ."

"Pearl Harbor was attacked on the seventh, and the United States declared war on Japan on the eighth."

Thomas smiled, and Heloise knew they were thinking the same thing: that they had fallen back into their old roles and had resumed the ping-pong right where they had left off. Heloise was the sharper of the two on culture and history, while Thomas dominated in politics and business, and since their first meeting at the School of Journalism, they had taken turns correcting each other like an old married couple.

"Do you think the police have a movie with Mia Sark?" he asked. "A porno movie?"

"Well, she did work at the club, so . . ." Heloise shrugged, and thought about what Schäfer had said. That Mia Sark had slapped Jan. Kissed him!

Was Schäfer right in his theory?

Could Jan have sought solace at Club Celeste after Alice's death? Had he found Mia online? At Hush-Hush?

"Does the site still exist?" asked Heloise.

Thomas googled it.

"Yes," he said, nodding.

"So maybe the movie is still there? That is, if there is a movie with her."

"Maybe, but the likelihood of us finding it is not very high. We'd have to plow through thousands of recordings without quite knowing what we were looking for, and we . . ."

"Not when we have a date to go by," Heloise said, pulling out her phone. "Ingeborg Sark told me that Mia worked at Celeste for six months, and she disappeared on May 31, 1997. So it must be December 8, 1996, right?"

"Yes, or the year after. If she has been sold abroad, as the police believe, they may have come across a film that confirms it."

"Well, so it must be December 8, 1996 or 1997."

"Yes, because it can't have been in December ninety-eight, right? By then the search had been put on hold, hadn't it?"

Heloise nodded and looked at the clock.

"I know someone who might be able to help us."

It was Friday night, it was approaching midnight, and she felt sad at the thought that Morten Munk was sure to be at home when he should be out partying, and maybe even meeting a woman who appreciated his gigantic heart and large corpus. Heloise found his number in her contact list and called.

Munk answered the call the second it went through, and she knew he had been holding the phone in his hand.

"You may speak!"

"Hey, it's Heloise," she said. "Am I disturbing you?"

"Not in the slightest." As always, his voice sounded wheezy and strained. "I'm actually just looking at something new I've found about Mázoreck. An old hospital record that might be of interest to you."

"Yeah?"

"Yes, I see that he was hospitalized for a long period of time, and I think it might have something to do with the cases you're investigating." Heloise heard Munk flipping through some papers. He cleared his throat. "From February 14 to March 3, 1994, he was a patient at Sønderborg Hospital. He was hospitalized due to a serious injury of some sort. His left arm was virtually detached at the shoulder, and he went through a ton of surgery and rehabilitation. It does not say whether it was an accident at work or whether it . . ."

"It was a pitbull," Heloise said. "Mázoreck was fighting with its owner, and it attacked him."

"Oh! They're really insane, some of those dogs!"

"Apparently it didn't live that long afterward either."

"Well, so do you need the record?" asked Munk.

"No, but I want to know if you can help me find something else online."

"What do you need?"

"I'm looking for an old recording from a porn site. Can you find something like that?"

"Yuh m'well . . ." He drew it out, and Heloise could hear him munching on something. "It depends a little bit. Are you still working on that story Bøttger can't know about?"

"Yes."

"Hmm, then it's going to be a little tricky."

"Why?"

"Because regular background research is one thing; I can easily camouflage that. But I'll have an explanation problem if I sit there surfing skin flicks during working hours. I can't use the newspaper's servers for that kind of thing."

"But isn't it a weekend now?"

"Yes?"

"Can't you just use your own computer?"

"Oh, you mean *now*?" Munk's voice burst out as if it were about to crack. "You need it here and now?"

"Yes, preferably. If it's not a hassle?" Heloise looked over at Thomas, who was flipping through one of her notebooks.

Munk shuffled some paper.

"Okay, tell me what I'm looking for," he said.

Heloise told him what dates and years to search for and on which site.

"The girl I'm looking for is Mia Sark. I can't imagine her appearing under her own name, but you might be able to find photos of her online to compare with. The film was possibly produced by a production company called Kingdom. They're known for doing S&M and that kind of thing."

"Okay," Munk said. "I'll look at it."

Heloise thanked him for the help and hung up. She turned her eyes to Thomas.

"He's looking at it," she said.

"What is this?" Thomas held up one of her notebooks in front of her.

Heloise narrowed her eyes and focused on the text.

"Those are some notes I took when I stopped by the police in Sønderborg yesterday. Don't you think the investigation was shut down quickly? Fourteen months?"

"Yes, but I'm paying more attention to what you have written about the Palermo Protocol. Where did you get that?"

"It is a UN resolution on the prevention and prosecution of human trafficking."

"Yes, I'm well aware of that, but . . ." Thomas left the kitchen without saying anything more and after a moment came back with a folder in his hand.

"What's that?" asked Heloise.

"It's a case I covered last year—a woman who killed her husband and his mistress out in Augustenborg. This is an excerpt of the murder book from that time."

He put it in front of Heloise and consulted it.

"Every time new information is introduced into an investigation, it is marked with the date and signature of the investigator. It's like a logbook where you can see who did what and when the various clues appeared in the investigation. It is introduced chronologically."

He pointed down the margin of the document.

"Here, for example. You can see that there was a witness interrogation on October 14, a colleague of one of those killed . . . The police suspect that it is a case of jealousy killing . . . They found a letter from suspects saying something about revenge and so on. And then the name is stated, badge number and signature of the investigator who noted it, as well as the date and time."

"Okay?" Heloise looked at him questioningly. "And?"

"Did you see the notes in the case of Mia Sark?"

"Uh, yes, I saw the last one. Why?"

"What date was it?"

"It was August 3, 1998—two days after the accident on Flensburg Fjord in which Tom Mázoreck drowned. It said that the matter was put on hold, but I didn't pay attention to who had written the note. Why?"

"Where was the Palermo Protocol listed?"

"Somewhere early in the investigation. Where Interpol was involved in the case, so it was probably at the beginning of June 1997." Heloise looked at him with furrowed brows. "Why?"

Thomas leaned back in his chair. He ran a flat hand over his mouth and looked at her.

"What is it?" she asked.

"The Palermo Protocol did not exist in 1997."

"What do you mean?"

"It didn't exist. It was only adopted in 2000."

Heloise stared at Thomas as the meaning of what he had said dawned on her.

"Are you saying the police tampered with the documents?"

Thomas shrugged slightly and bit his lower lip. His face was suddenly wide awake.

"But . . ." Heloise shook her head. "Why?"

"As I said before . . ." He looked toward the bulletin board, and his gaze drifted over the notes. "When it comes to people's sex lives . . . their darkest urges . . ." He met Heloise's eyes.

"Someone is trying to hide something."

CHAPTER

36

THE LIGHT SHONE in the hallway behind Thomas, and his silhouette in the doorway to the bedroom was dark, but Heloise could feel his eyes on her.

"Is everything okay in here?" he asked. "Do you need anything?"

"No thanks, everything is fine."

"Good." Thomas nodded hesitantly. "I'll sleep in the boys' room. It's down at the end of the hall if you need me."

"Aren't you staying in here?"

He looked at her for a long moment. "Are you sure?" he asked.

Heloise nodded.

He walked over to the bed and lay down next to her with his clothes on. He rolled onto his side, leaned his elbow on the mattress, resting his head in the palm of his hand.

"Are you okay?" he asked, looking at her.

"Mm-hmm." Heloise turned her gaze to him and smiled, her expression tired. "I was just thinking about Jan."

"What's with you and this guy Jan?" asked Thomas. "Why is this so important to you?"

"I don't know, it just is." She turned her head and looked up at the ceiling. "It's a commitment when you sign up with the Vigil. You feel a responsibility for the person you are assigned to care for."

"I understand," Thomas nodded. "But I know you. It's more than that."

Heloise ran a hand through her hair.

"It's just . . ." She shook her head, searching for the words. "When my mother was dying, I went to Goa with Gerda. At the time, I just felt so bad. I was so unhappy to have lost you, and I think I must have been in a depression, because I couldn't deal with other people's problems at all. So even though I knew she was sick, I left. And while I was at a new-moon party on the beach in Betalbatim, drowning my sorrows in piña coladas, she lay all alone and died in a hospital bed."

Thomas listened and said nothing. He brushed the hair away from her face and looked at her with gentle eyes.

"And my father . . ." Heloise swallowed and paused for a long time before speaking again. "I wasn't there for him either. I knew he needed me to take him by the hand and tell him I loved him so he could leave here with peace of mind, but I . . . I didn't. I couldn't." She shook her head. "I think Jan is trying to make amends for something, and . . . I probably am too." She smiled sadly. "I need to be that person for someone. The one who is there to the end, but now suddenly I no longer know if I can. Whether it's the right thing to do at all."

Heloise sighed, suddenly feeling overcome with fatigue. Weightless. As if she were relaxing for the first time in years.

Thomas put his arm around her and pulled her to him, and she only now noticed that she was a little drunk.

Heloise still didn't know what Jan Fischhof had done or why, and maybe it really didn't even matter, she thought, closing her eyes. Maybe it wasn't his past that she was here to sort out.

She pressed herself against Thomas, lifted her face, and found his mouth in the darkness.

SATURDAY, JULY 13

37

THE ALARM CLOCK rang at nine o'clock, and Thomas reached for it, slapping it hard and causing it to fall to the floor. Heloise blinked in the sun that shone through the master-bedroom window and looked over at him.

"Hey," she smiled with a hoarse morning voice.

"Hey," Thomas replied. He pulled her to him and kissed her.

"Why did the alarm clock go off?" she asked.

"My kids are going to play in the soccer finals, and I've promised to come see them."

"Today?"

"Yes," he nodded. "In half an hour."

"See, that's why I haven't had children," Heloise smiled, pulling the covers up around her. "My Saturdays are sacred. Enjoy the game!"

Thomas smiled as he got out of bed and went out to the bathroom. Heloise heard the shower running, and a few minutes later he was back with water dripping off him. He quickly dried himself with a towel and pulled a T-shirt over his head.

"I would invite you to come, but . . ." He looked at Heloise hesitantly.

"No, no. Of course not," she said, waving the idea away.

"Another time?" he asked, buttoning his jeans.

"Another time!"

Thomas smiled and kissed her.

"I'll be back in a few hours, okay?" He put a hand under the covers and touched her. "Promise me you'll lie right there until I get back."

Heloise ran her fingers through his hair.

"I can't sleep anymore. My body is screaming for coffee," she said. "Besides, I'd like to drive to Egernsund this morning to see if I can persuade Ole or Lisette Dalsfort to talk to me about their daughter. But I can come back at the end of the day?"

"Okay," said Thomas, pulling down the duvet. He kissed her on the stomach. "There's coffee and bread and yogurt and a ton of other stuff downstairs. Take what you want." He pulled the duvet further down.

Heloise smiled and looked down at him. "You'll be late if you don't stop now."

He straightened up and kissed her on the mouth. "Okay, but I'll see you later, right?"

She put her arms around his neck.

"See you later," she nodded.

* * *

Heloise watched the car roll out the driveway, resisting the urge to instantly open all the cupboards and drawers and snoop into the life Thomas had lived during the years they had been apart. Instead, she opened the refrigerator and took out the milk. She threw a Nespresso capsule into the coffee machine and turned it on. While the milk was frothing, she opened her inbox to see if an e-mail from Munk had come in. She found nothing and texted him.

Were there any hits?

He called her up immediately.

"Hi," said Heloise. "Did you find something?"

"Yes, and then some! A total of 118 movies were uploaded on Hush-Hush on December 8, 1996, and December 8, 1997, and I've just watched the last one, so it's been a long night."

"Haven't you *slept* yet?"

"Huh-uh," he yawned.

"Oh, seriously, Morten, you didn't have to spend all night on it."

"Too late," he said. "Only four out of the 118 films were uploaded from Denmark. Two of them are produced by Kingdom, as you mentioned, but Mia Sark is not in any of them. The third is a straight-up gay movie, while the fourth . . . bingo!"

Heloise straightened up. "You found it?"

"Yes, and it's some nasty shit, I can tell you."

"What year was the film posted on the site?"

"It was uploaded in December' ninety-seven, but the date on the recording itself says May 31."

The night she disappeared, thought Heloise.

"I'll e-mail you the link," Munk said.

"Could you also send me the movies from Kingdom?"

Munk was quiet for a moment, and Heloise heard him hitting the keys.

"Done!"

"Thank you, Morten," she said. "I'll treat you to a dinner at Restaurant Frank with all the bells and whistles, okay? Champagne and oysters and the whole mess!"

"You just let me know," he said through a yawn. "To begin with, I'm going to bed now."

Heloise ended the call.

She poured the hot milk into the coffee and sat down in front of her computer. In the e-mail from Munk there were three links, but it was impossible to see on the URL which of them contained what, so she clicked the first.

A dark and amateurish backdrop of a medieval castle appeared on the screen. In front of the gate to the castle stood two watchmen. They were dressed in long, furry coats, the hoods pulled up over their heads so that you could not see their faces, and in their hands they held torches and pointed lances. The film quality was lousy, the production value was zero, and the costumes looked like something they had bought at a Halloween shop. It was almost comical to watch—like overgrown children acting in role-playing games.

A Kingdom Productions logo scrolled across the screen. The film cut to the next scene, and the cast found themselves in a dark, crypt-like room. A young woman Heloise did not recognize was strapped to the top of a large wooden table in a grotesque and unnatural position. She was naked, and her breasts were wrapped in tight leather cords so that they were blue-violet and strangely elongated to look at. Her hands and feet were fixed with ropes, and around the table stood three masked men watching her writhing.

There was nothing comical or playful about the film anymore. It was terrifyingly serious, and Heloise looked away.

She clicked away from the link and pressed the next one. The same logo and intro scrolled across the screen. Same bad backdrop, same hooded guardians. This time it was a man tied to a wide pillar—it looked like he was embracing it. He had a bit in his mouth like a horse, and a young woman clad in patent leather stood behind him with a whip.

Heloise clicked away from the film and pressed the third link.

The screen crackled blankly for several seconds. Then a picture appeared, and Heloise stopped breathing.

The handheld camera was aimed at a black leather sofa, and on it sat Mia Sark. She was dressed in a pair of white cotton panties and a small top and leaning toward the photographer with an uncertain expression. The quality of the movie was like dogma films, and there was no sound.

The camera zoomed in on Mia Sark's face. She smiled playfully with narrowed eyes.

The image shook as someone reached out a hand under the camera lens and grabbed the girl's neck tightly. The image flickered and blurred, and for a moment the lens pointed up at the ceiling. Then the camera was straightened up again and zoomed in on the girl.

Her expression had changed now. She looked scared. Her lips moved as she spoke to the photographer. She shook her head, tried to remove his hand. He released his grip on her neck for a split second. Then his fist hit her hard and Mia

Sark collapsed on the couch. She lifted her face as blood ran out of her nose and down her chin. She trembled, holding up a hand to stop the photographer. Her lips moved and she was crying. Heloise couldn't hear what she was saying, but it looked like a prayer. The man carrying the camera pulled out a knife and pointed it at the girl. Then she started screaming.

Heloise shut the computer screen down hard before she could see more. She got up and walked back and forth in the kitchen, breathing deeply down into her abdomen.

Was that the prelude to a killing she had just seen? Who the hell got turned on by that kind of thing? How sick in the head were you when you did something like that?

She leaned against the kitchen table and stared ahead in shock as the images from the film burned into her retina. The chair legs scraped across the floor as she pulled the chair out from the table again.

She sat down and opened the computer. She backed up the film, paused it, and scrolled through the stills, frame by frame. She scrolled past Mia Sark's playful smile and watched the hand tighten its grip on the girl's neck in choppy slow motion as she went through the pictures.

The camera shook and the lens pointed up at the ceiling, and the next few shots were grainy and blurry.

What was it she had seen?

Heloise scrolled four pictures forward, then one back—and there! She lifted her hands off the keyboard as if she had burned herself on it. She leaned back in her chair and stared at the still image on the screen in front of her.

The wall behind the sofa that Mia Sark sat in was covered with white tiles, one of which was detaching itself in the middle.

It was a fluted tile with a stripe of dark-blue floral patterning.

As if it were Royal Copenhagen porcelain.

38

S CHÄFER BIT INTO a roll spread thickly with butter as his
gaze skated disinterestedly over news of government
infighting, columns about dating challenges for highly edu-
cated women, and warnings of cloudbursts.

He suppressed a yawn and folded the newspaper.

"I'm leaving now," Connie said from the doorway into
the kitchen. She had put shoes on and was standing with keys
in hand.

Schäfer looked up. "Where are you going?"

"Over to Edith's. I think I'll stay there tonight," she said,
referring to the woman she had been watching over the past
few days, a solitary lady of ninety-eight years who lived at
Akaciegården's Nursing Home in Frederiksberg.

"All right," smiled Schäfer.

"I've taken a lasagna out of the freezer for you to heat up
tonight," she said, pointing to the oven.

Schäfer stood up and kissed her.

"Are you okay?" asked Connie. "Are you in pain?" She
looked at him with worried eyes.

"I'm fine." Schäfer put his arms around her waist and felt
the touch make her jump.

He wrinkled his brows and looked at her questioningly.
"Why can't I touch you anymore?"

She looked down, and Schäfer suddenly felt overwhelmed by an unknown anxiety. He thought about Rud Johannsen's wife who, from one day to the next, had had enough. About Bertelsen, who thought he had lost his touch. Just the thought of losing Connie made him want to eat a bullet.

She looked up at him with an ashamed expression.

"I'm afraid you'll think I've gotten too fat," she mumbled.

"*Fat*?" Schäfer looked her up and down, suddenly feeling euphoric relief. "What on earth are you talking about?"

"I've gained fifteen pounds since Christmas."

"So what? They've obviously settled right here," he smiled and put his hands around her breasts.

Connie tilted her head slightly. "Are you sure? You're not thinking about replacing me with a younger model?"

Schäfer pulled her to him and buried his face in her great, frizzy hair. "Never!"

His phone rang on the table next to them and Connie looked down at it.

"Let it ring," he said, grabbing her waist.

"It's Heloise." She picked up the phone and handed it to him. "It may be important."

She kissed Schäfer goodbye and left the kitchen.

He accepted the call and put the phone to his ear. "Y'ello?"

"It was Mázoreck," Heloise said. Her voice sounded geared up and breathless. "I think he killed Mia. Maybe both of them!"

"Hey, hey, take a deep breath!" said Schäfer in a diffusing tone. "Tell me what you're talking about."

"Are you near a computer?" she asked.

"Yes."

"Okay, check your e-mail! I've sent you something."

Schäfer called Heloise back as soon as he had seen the recordings.

"What do you think?" she asked.

"I think you're right," he nodded. "And if it's actually the guesthouse that belongs to the mother's property, as you claim, then we have a crime scene."

"That's it. I'm sure of it."

"Okay, then we need to get hold of Zøllner so he can . . ."

"No, we can't trust him, Schäfer! He's fucking corrupt! Maybe he's even *in* on it?"

"What on earth are you talking about?"

"He fiddled with the file, edited the notes so that the Sark case looks like a trafficking case."

"Fiddled with the file?" Schäfer found it hard to believe his ears.

"Yes, at least someone has. They're trying to sweep all this under the carpet. Zøllner, Carl Roebel . . . It's like they don't want the case to be solved. We can't trust them."

Schäfer was quiet for a moment, thinking about what Heloise had said.

"What about Fischhof?" he asked.

"What do you mean?"

"How does *he* fit into all this?"

"I don't know, but you did see the intro to the Kingdom movies, didn't you?"

"You mean that homemade Game of Thrones setup?"

"Yes," Heloise said. "I've looked into it, and evidently all Kingdom films start with that intro. You know, like all MGM movies start with the lion that roars?"

"Yes?"

"At one point, Jan mentioned something about some men in coats with torches and spears—just like the men in the intro. At the time, I understood it as meaning he was afraid of them, but I don't think so now. Or at least I don't think he has *reason* to be. I was talking to someone from Kingdom Productions yesterday—a guy named René Decker—and it wasn't my impression that he had a problem with Jan. Quite the opposite!"

"Hmm," Schäfer said, scratching his neck.

"The films Kingdom produces are insanely repulsive, but it still seems as if there was some kind of consent among the parties. Like they all *wanted* to do it, right?"

"Yes," Schäfer nodded. "As inconceivable as it sounds, I think you're right that all parties got something out of it."

"But that movie with Mia Sark looks like a snuff film. Or at least the beginning of one."

Schäfer nodded. In the film, the cameraman had thrust out at the girl with the serrated blade of a large hunting knife, and then the tape had stopped.

"I think he killed them both," Heloise said. "Mia, Nina . . . He took them home to that country house, into that guesthouse. And then he killed them! You yourself saw that he threatened Mia with the knife. Do you think he stopped there?"

"No." Schäfer shook his head. "I don't think so. I'd like to ask someone I know to look at the movie. A woman who is an expert in profiling. I want to see what she says about it."

"Why?"

"Because I've been pissing blood since the day before yesterday," Schäfer said. "I don't know if you forgot that a couple of goons showed up here at home the day before yesterday, but I personally would also love to know what the hell is going on!"

39

THE PROPERTIES IN the newly built area near Nordhavn stood like big, shiny dominoes of glass and chrome. They were surrounded by well-groomed green areas and looked out on a white, twelve-story behemoth with a pool and jacuzzi, garlands of lights, and a constantly thumping bass sound from the nightclub on the upper deck.

Schäfer turned his back on the cruise ship and looked down at the text message Michala Friis had sent to make sure he was in front of the right staircase. He pressed his thumb on the bell, and a second later the door made a whirring sound.

He pushed it open and took the elevator up to the sixth floor.

Michala Friis was standing in the open door when he reached it. Her hair was wet, and she was dressed in a pair of loose, worn jeans and a white sweater.

"Hi," she said. "Come inside."

"Thank you," Schäfer nodded. "And thank you for taking the trouble to help."

"Of course, I want to. Are you okay?" she asked, contemplating the stitches over his black eye.

"Yes, it could have been far worse," he nodded. "But now I want to find out what kind of assholes attacked me, so I appreciate your wanting to give me a hand with this."

"What can I do?" she asked, closing the door behind him. "How can I help?"

"I need your take on something," Schaefer said. "Would you feel like composing a profile on someone?"

Michala nodded eagerly. "Do you have any material with you that we can look at?"

Schäfer grabbed his bag. "Yep."

"Do you want coffee?" she asked.

"Yes, please."

Schäfer followed Michala through the apartment. It was open and modern, with bare surfaces, clean lines, high ceilings, and light cascading from every conceivable angle. There were no trinkets on the shelves, only books and art and a single sprig of eucalyptus in a vase on the living-room table.

"How long have you lived here?" he asked.

"Not long. They're still in the process of completing several of the apartments on the property, so it's all new. I'm still trying to settle in."

"Are you happy here?"

"In the apartment?"

"Yes, and happy with the area?"

She nodded. "Yes, for now. Although the ocean view they enticed me with in the sales pitch is mostly blocked by The Majestic, and the Queen of the Sea, and whatever else they're called." She nodded toward the living-room window, where they couldn't see the sky for the big white monstrosity before them. "I meet more Chinese tourists down at the local bakery than I meet neighbors, but . . . Other than that."

"Well, at least the apartment was cheap," Schäfer said, winking.

Michala met his gaze and laughed.

"Exactly," she said. "I got it for a song!"

Schäfer put his bag down on the floor. He felt a shooting pain in his stomach and put his hand to his bladder.

"Can I use your bathroom?" he asked.

"Yes, but you'll have to use the master bathroom because the water in the guest bathroom isn't connected yet." She pointed down the hall. "It's the second door on the right. You have to go through the bedroom."

Schäfer walked down the hall and entered Michala Friis's bedroom. He glanced at the bed and the white double duvet lying unmade on the mattress. There was a black-lace bra on the floor next to the bedside table, and across the dressing screen at the far end of the room hung a dress. There was a sweet smell inside the room—of perfume and sex— and Schäfer felt his body involuntarily react to the aroma.

He shook off the feeling and continued into the adjoining bathroom, locking the door behind him.

He pulled down the zipper of his pants and turned to the toilet, noticing that the seat was already up.

His gaze drifted over things in the bathroom and fell on the razor at the edge of the sink. It wasn't a little pink lady one, but a manly blue three-bladed razor from Gillette. He washed his hands after turning the toilet bowl red and went out to join Michala in the kitchen. He sat down at the kitchen table and opened his bag. A stack of papers and letters sat on the table in front of him, which he pushed aside so he could have space for his computer.

"Cortado? Flat white?" asked Michala. "What are you into?"

"Coffee," Schäfer said.

She smiled and started grinding coffee beans on a behemoth of an espresso machine that sounded like a jigsaw gnawing into metal.

Schäfer's gaze fell on the letterhead of one of the papers he had pushed aside, and he looked up at Michala.

"Don't say it's Sandahl!"

"Sorry?" She turned off the machine to silence the noise and looked at him with wrinkled brows.

Schäfer sucked in his cheeks to hide his smile.

"What?" she asked.

"The toilet seat was up," he said, pointing his thumb over his shoulder in the direction of the bathroom.

Michala shook her head slightly. "So what?"

Schäfer held up the letterhead from the University Hospital of Montpellier in front of her. "Sandahl? The new medical examiner?"

Michala smiled and looked down.

"Well, that was fast, huh?" he grumbled, looking at his watch. "Less than forty-eight hours from the first . . ."

"We've been together for four months." She held out the coffee cup to Schäfer and watched him hesitantly.

Schäfer frowned and tilted his chin down.

"But you greeted each other for the first time the other day when we . . ."

"No, Jakob just doesn't want us to tell anyone yet. It's still so new, so . . ."

Schaefer raised both brows and nodded, surprised.

"Well, it damn well could be true after all, what Bertelsen said." He reached for the coffee without breaking eye contact. "Maybe I *have* lost my touch."

"No, you just haven't registered it because you're not interested in what I do in my spare time." Michala looked down.

"Well, that's not true," Schäfer said, shifting a little in his seat. "But hey, congratulations! Sandahl seems like . . . a nice guy."

"Stop it," Michala said, taking a sip of her cortado. "I know damn well you think he's an idiot."

"No, that I do not!" Schäfer shook his head. "An arrogant asshole maybe, but not an idiot."

Michala smiled.

So did Schäfer.

"By the way, did you hear that he was wrong about Wilkins?" he asked.

"Mm-hmm." Michala nodded. "He wasn't super proud of that."

"No, I can understand that, but hey! You can't get it right every time." Schäfer threw out his arms. He had to get ahold of himself to avoid breaking into song.

"Okay, okay, enough about him!" said Michala, sitting across from Schäfer. "What do I need to look at?"

"A home video," he said, opening his computer. "What do you know about bondage and violent porn in general?"

"Quite a lot, actually. BDSM is taking up more and more space in the industry," Michala said, crossing her arms.

"BDSM?"

"Bondage, restraint. Dominance, submission. Sadism, masochism."

"Christ," Schäfer exclaimed, shaking his head. "What's wrong with regular sex?"

"Nothing," she said. "Regular sex is actually one of the most popular categories. There are hundreds of thousands of amateurs who record themselves on home videos and upload them online. It's a kind of cozy exhibitionism. These are not porno actors with silicone breasts, but somewhat overweight housewives with hair everywhere and men at the less well-endowed end of the scale. In other words: completely ordinary men and women. The lighting on such recordings is rarely good, the camera angle isn't optimal either, and . . ."

"Okay, you make it sound like you've seen quite a few of those movies?"

"By God, so I have," Michala nodded. "You'd be surprised at how much people's porn habits say about them. It is often the slender friendly accountant or the young dedicated schoolteacher who has the most hardcore taste. The ones you would never suspect of having an inner sadist."

Schäfer nodded.

A few years ago, he had helped uncover a ring of pedophiles. Eleven men had been convicted of possession of or participation in the production of pornography with minors. The one who had initially looked most reliable—a puny botanist who was regarded by those closest to him as a bit of a sissy—had been the vilest of them all in the films obtained by the police.

"The one we're going to see here is no altar boy, either," Schäfer said. "So you've been warned."

He opened the link on his computer and pressed Play.

* * *

"What do you think?" asked Schäfer, looking over at Michala. They had seen the recording of Mia Sark three times, and he had told her everything he could think of about the case.

"What type of perpetrator are we dealing with?" he asked. "What's the motive here?"

"I don't know if it boils down to one thing, but I think what matters most to him here is the excitement." Michala put down her coffee cup. "And then the film also makes me ask the eternal question: What is it that drives men to hurt women? Why is there a fundamental animal desire to take women by violence?"

"I guess it's not something that drives normal men," Schäfer interjected.

"Yes, it is. The violence and rhetoric are not limited to the BDSM scene. In almost all porn movies, men are seen treating women violently. Sometimes it's just a slap on the ass, other times they press the woman's face into the mattress, strangle her, spit on her, tear her hair, and so on. The worst is when there are several men around one woman, because then a rush arises, a kind of bloodthirstiness. It gets wilder and wilder, and any idiot with eyes in his head can see that it hurts the woman, but it's as if her pain spurs them on. There is no mercy," Michala said. "You also see it in the way men talk about women. Young guys' jargon when it comes to sex: the woman must be *punished*, she has to be *destroyed*, and so on."

"Hey, hey, now most of us are pretty trustworthy," Schäfer said.

"Yes, of course you are. Don't get me wrong: I love men, men are fantastic! But there is a latent, aggressive drive within you that is all about dominance. Most men use that drive in a positive way—to get ahead in the world, to advance in the job, feed the family so they can survive. But sometimes someone like this guy shows up." She pointed to the screen. "A man who typically can't figure out how to function in a stable relationship and who can't figure out how to have a normal work life—he gets bored quickly if it gets too monotonous. A man who jumps from one woman to another and from one

job to the next—without advancing, without really connect-
ing with anyone."

"And who lives with his mother."

"Did he?"

Schäfer nodded.

"Okay, well then he's almost like someone out of a theoreti-
cal textbook about these kinds of assailants. Adult men who
live with their mother rarely live there because they have a particularly good relationship with her. On the contrary, studies
show that it is this group that hates their mother the most. And
a man who feels anger toward his mother? A mother who may
have ruled his life, dominated, been a source of guilt and
shame?" Michala looked at the paused picture on the screen.
"He needs to vent, but he doesn't dare say no to his mother, so
he finds another victim. This type of perpetrator is typically
enormously charming and usually has a very active sex life, so
there are plenty of victims to choose from. Take someone like
Bundy, for example! The ladies loved him, and he managed to
kill at least thirty of them before he was finally caught."

"Tom Mázoreck allegedly started a relationship with
Mia Sark's mother in the first few months of the investigation," Schäfer said. "What do you think about that?"

"That's what you call post-offense behavior." Michala
stood up and got a book from a shelf in the living room. It
was a technical book: *Forensic Psychology—Behavioral Science*
was written on the front page. She opened the book and ran
her finger down the table of contents.

"Perpetrators are often drawn to the scene of the crime,
you know. They revisit the scene even though the police are
swarming around it—simply because they can't stay away.
They get turned on by the excitement."

Schäfer nodded.

"But in this case, he *lives* at the crime scene, right?"

"Yes," Schäfer said. "I haven't been to the house myself,
but yes. There is some evidence of that."

"Okay, so it takes something else to trigger that tension.
So he participates in the search for the girl, speaks to the

press, gives testimony to the police, as you mentioned." She leafed through the book. "He's playing the worried citizen, right? And we know that the ladies cannot resist him, so he ingratiates himself with the grieving mother . . . Damn, he's good!" said Michala, with what almost sounded like admiration in her voice. She found the page she was looking for and turned the book so Schäfer could see it.

He squinted and read aloud:

"Post-offense behavior might include returning to the scene of the crime, attending the funeral of the victim, befriending family members or friends of the victim . . ."

He lifted his eyes and looked at Michala.

"It almost seems like it was a sport to him," he said. "A game?"

"Exactly," she nodded. "It was all about excitement."

She pointed to the screen where Mia Sark's face was frozen in mid-scream.

"And something tells me that this wasn't the first girl he brought into that house." She met Schäfer's gaze. "Or the last one."

*   *   *

Schäfer pushed through a crowd of Asian tourists boarding the cruise ship in front of Michala Friis's residence and got into his car. He pulled his phone out from his inner pocket and called a number on his contact list.

"Hey Rud!" he said, turning the key in the ignition. "Are you bored?"

"Bitterly so," Rud Johannsen replied. "What can I do for you?"

"Do you want to go for a drive?"

"A drive?"

"Yeah."

"Well, why not? Where are we going?"

"Don't worry, I'll explain that" Schäfer said, putting the car in gear. "Just make sure you pack your equipment and I'll pick you up in half an hour."

CHAPTER

40

THE FACADE OF the large, white villa looked as if it were made of a single massive piece of glass, and Heloise looked into the hall, which was filled with art, designer furniture, and orchids. A half-turn staircase ran up to the second floor, and a giant copper artichoke lamp hung from the ceiling. There was an unobstructed view through the house, and Heloise could see the remains of someone's breakfast—a teapot and half-empty juice glass—standing on the dining table, and the fjord that was on the opposite side of the property.

She pressed her finger against the doorbell and waited, but saw no movement inside the house. She took a few steps backward, leaned her head back, and looked up at the windows on the top floor of the house. She was about to walk around the property when a voice sounded behind her.

"Are you looking for Ole?"

Heloise gaspe, and turned around.

An elderly man wearing a bathrobe and slippers was standing in front of the mailbox belonging to the neighboring property and looking at her with wrinkled nose and narrowed eyes.

"Yes," Heloise said. "Do you know where I can find him?"

"He's in Singapore." The man stuck the newspaper under his arm and locked the mailbox again. "He'll be back on Wednesday."

"What about his wife? Do you know where she is?"

The man glanced at the open garage behind Heloise.

"The Lexus is here, so she must be in there somewhere," he said.

Heloise shook her head.

"I've called, but no one answers."

The man cast his eyes toward the fjord and shaded them with his hand.

"Oh, she's still out there I see. She swims every day." He pointed down at the water. "You can take the stairs at the end of the path. It leads straight down to the jetty."

He pointed to the gravel path that ran between the two houses. Heloise thanked him for the help and went down to the water.

* * *

She stepped out onto the gently rocking pontoons and walked out to the towel and sneakers that lay at the end of the bridge, while following Lisette Dalsfort with her eyes. The woman was gliding through the water a fair distance out in the fjord. She took long, calm crawl strokes and shot forward effortlessly, so expertly that she couldn't be heard breaking the surface of the water. She swam toward a wooden raft that floated like a leaf on the water, and when she'd arrived, she put her arms up on the edge of it and rested her head in her hands for a moment. Then she lifted herself up by the arms, like a freediver taking one last mouthful of air, let go, and disappeared.

Heloise watched for her as the seconds ticked by.

Fifteen. Twenty-five.

Lisette Dalsfort appeared some distance from where she had dived in and treaded water for several minutes before swimming back to the jetty.

She put her hands on the stair railing, and Heloise observed her curiously as she pulled herself out of the water.

An indefinable sense of déjà vu began to tingle in Heloise's mind.

Lisette Dalsfort was wearing a black latex swim cap, a sports swimsuit, and a pair of swim goggles, and her aging body was long and sinewy, with narrow hips and athletic shoulders and a body-fat percentage of what looked like zero.

Had Heloise met her before?

Heloise nodded and smiled politely as she considered how to approach the situation. The recording of Mia Sark still flickered uncomfortably under her eyelids, and now here she was—standing in front of Nina Dalsfort's mother.

Had Nina been exposed to the same thing as Mia?

"How's the water today?" she asked.

"Wonderful."

Lisette Dalsfort's pronunciation was old-fashioned and elegant, but there was no warmth in her voice. It was evasive, as was her body language.

She flicked the water off with her hands and picked up her towel from the jetty.

"I guess I'd better introduce myself," Heloise said, holding out her hand.

"Heloise Kaldan, *Demokratisk Dagblad*. I wanted to know if I could talk to you for a moment?"

Lisette Dalsfort rolled up the towel, put it around her shoulders like a boxer after a fight, and pushed the swim goggles up on her forehead.

"I don't talk to the press," she said, briefly looking down at the outstretched hand before meeting Heloise's gaze.

Heloise's lips parted, and she stared in amazement at the woman in front of her. She had grown older. The face was narrower, the eyes eerily empty, and the screaming green Marc O'Polo blouse had been replaced with swimwear, but Heloise was in no doubt.

It was the woman from the picture in Jan's living room. The photo that Heloise had thought depicted his wife and daughter.

"Sorry, but . . ." Taken aback, Heloise stared at the woman before her. "You *are* Lisette Dalsfort, aren't you?"

The woman straightened her back and focused on Heloise. Her eyes were suddenly clear and hard.

"What do you want?"

"I . . ." Heloise blinked a few times. "I would like to talk to you about the investigation of your daughter's case. I want to talk to you about Nina."

Lisette Dalsfort shook her head, bent down, and picked up her sneakers with one hand. She started walking down the jetty with long, purposeful steps.

Heloise set off after her.

"I understand from the police that you suspected Tom Mázoreck of having something to do with Nina's disappearance?"

Nothing.

"And Jan Fischhof and the other two from the mink farm?" said Heloise. "Why do you think so?"

Still nothing.

"Do you have any idea why Jan Fischhof has a photo of you and Nina in his home?"

Lisette Dalsfort halted. She turned around and gave Heloise a stunned look.

"A photo?"

"Yes." Heloise nodded. "A photo of you and a young girl that I assume is your daughter. She is wearing a suede jacket and blue jeans in the photo. You're wearing a green sweater . . . Does that ring any bells?"

Lisette Dalsfort looked at Heloise without blinking.

"Yes, we . . . we had it taken after her confirmation . . . The police asked for a copy of the photo when she . . ." Her gaze drifted to the side, and she looked out over the water. A nerve was trembling at her right eye.

"Do you have any idea why Jan Fischhof has that photo on his desk?"

The woman did not answer.

"Jan is dying," Heloise said, "and he's started talking about . . ."

"Good!" Lisette Dalsfort suddenly looked awake. She met Heloise's gaze and nodded. "He deserves to die. They all do."

"All of them?"

"Fischhof, Carstensen, Gallagher . . ."

"What makes you say that?"

"Sometimes when I'm out there, I dive in and stay down until my lungs burn. Then I imagine what it must have felt like. Not being able to come up for air . . ." She looked out over the fjord and sounded like she was talking to herself. "The instinct not to breathe underwater is so strong that for a surprisingly long time it trumps the pain of running out of oxygen. Did you know that?"

She turned her gaze to Heloise, who shook her head.

"You only breathe in when you are on the verge of losing consciousness. At that point, there is so much carbon monoxide in the blood that the brain automatically triggers an inhalation because the body can no longer endure the pain of not breathing. And that's not very smart, because the only pain greater than the pain of running out of oxygen is the feeling of saltwater filling your lungs."

She smiled slightly.

"People who are revived after drowning describe the feeling as lava running through the trachea. The pain fills your whole body and you *know* you're about to die . . ." She nodded to herself. "Tom Mázoreck got the death he deserved, and now it's Jan Fischhof's turn, you say. Is he sick?"

Heloise nodded. "What's wrong with him?"

"Cancer."

"Ah!" Lisette Dalsfort's eyes lit up, and she pursed her lips together as if to hide a smile.

"I spoke to Hans Gallagher the other day, and he denies having had anything to do with Nina's disappearance," Heloise said. "The police believe that you have stared yourself blind at the group of men who were present that night, and that you therefore suspect someone who has not . . ."

"My daughter was seventeen years old. Seventeen! They could have made allowances for her. They could have let her go, but they . . ."

"I think you're right," Heloise said.

Lisette Dalsfort looked at her in astonishment.

"I don't necessarily think all four of them played a role, but I think you're right that Tom Mázoreck did. I think you're on to something!"

Lisette Dalsfort's eyes shone damply. "No one else does. Not even my husband."

Heloise took her notebook out of her bag and clicked the pen. "Do you know if Nina knew a girl named Mia Sark? The one who disappeared the year after Nina?"

Lisette Dalsfort shook her head. "No, I don't think she did."

"Could Nina have been associated with a place out in Broager called Club Celeste?"

"No. No!" The glow that had been lit in Lisette Dalsfort's eyes went out again, and she held up her hand to rebuff Heloise. "I know what you're trying to say, but she . . ."

"Maybe you didn't realize it. Ingeborg Sark is also reluctant to acknowledge that her daughter worked in such a place, but perhaps she has . . ."

"Nina wasn't one of those girls out there!" said Lisette Dalsfort furiously. "If that's the angle you're going for, I have nothing to say to you."

She pulled the towel off her shoulders as if to mark the end of the conversation. She started walking.

"Did you know that Mia Sark had a relationship with Jan Fischhof?" Heloise asked, following her. "And that Tom Mázoreck was present the night she disappeared? There are some obvious coincidences between Mia's case and Nina's, and I've found a film that I . . ."

"If you publish a single word that makes it sound like my daughter had something to do with that place out in Broager, then I will personally make sure that you never work as a journalist again. Do you understand what I'm saying to you?" Lisette Dalsfort's voice quivered with anger. "I will *bury* you!"

She turned away from Heloise and headed for the stairs.

41

"HE'S SITTING OUT in the garden. Just a moment, I'll see if he wants to talk to you."

"No, Ruth, it's you I want to talk to." Heloise drove up in front of her rental house and hit the brakes so hard that the dust swirled up around the car.

"Me?"

"Yes." Heloise slammed the car door and locked herself in the house. "Would you please go into the living room to the desk? Where Jan's pictures are."

"In the living room?"

"Yes. You know what pictures I'm talking about, right? They're framed."

"I'm looking at them. What about them?"

"The picture where Alice is wearing a Marc O'Polo blouse . . ."

"With the shoulder pads? Yes, what about it?"

"You were the one who told me it was a photo of Jan's family. Where did you get that from?"

Ruth was quiet on the other end of the line.

"Is Jan the one who told you?" asked Heloise, putting her bag down on the dining table. She pulled out a chair and sat down.

"I don't understand what you're asking."

"Is *he* the one who told you it was a photo of Alice and Elizabeth, or is it just something you assumed?"

"Oh, yeah, well it . . . I can't really remember." Ruth sounded annoyed by the question. "I think maybe it was one of the others who said that."

"One of the other people from the Vigil?"

"Yes, one of the ones he scared away with all his hullaballoo."

"Okay, do me a favor, Ruth. Put down the phone for a moment and go out into the garden to Jan with the picture. Ask him who it is and why he has it on the desk."

Ruth put the phone down, and it was quiet for a few minutes. Then she was back.

"What did he say?" asked Heloise.

"He asked for you."

"But what did he say to that with the picture?"

"That's what he said! I asked what you asked for, and he replied, 'Where is Heloise?' When I showed him the picture once more, he turned his face away from me and wouldn't answer."

Heloise gently bit her lower lip as she considered how to proceed.

"The other pictures on the desk, Ruth. Could I get you to take a photo of them with your cell phone?"

"What do you mean? A photo of the pictures?"

"Yes, take a photo of the desktop where all the pictures are and text it to me."

Heloise hung up and waited until the message came in. She opened it and zoomed in on the image as her breathing stopped.

The picture of Nina and Lisette Dalsfort was in the front row of photos on the desk. In the row just behind, Mia Sark's face lit up.

Heloise's heart pounded in her chest as her gaze roamed over the other photos— across the other faces.

Faces she didn't know.

Photos of young women.

CHAPTER

42

THE GIANT PYLONS of the Great Belt Bridge towered over them, and Rud Johannsen leaned forward in the passenger seat and looked out the windshield.

"It's impressive every time, isn't it?"

Schäfer nodded stiffly. His gaze was fixed on the roadway and his hands locked in a ten-and-two grip on the steering wheel while he stayed in the fast lane as far from the railing as possible.

They passed the first pylon, and the wind pushed the car. It was a police van with civilian plates that Schäfer had borrowed at HQ and they had filled with Rud's Luminol equipment.

Schäfer stepped on the accelerator.

"Who knows how far down it actually is?" said Rud curiously, looking out over the water. "It must be at least . . ."

"Kaldan says the guesthouse is vacant," Schäfer said, overtaking a silver Porsche Cayenne. "Without a doubt, it has been cleaned many times since the film was shot."

"That doesn't necessarily make any difference," Rud said. "She said there was linoleum on the floor, right?"

"Yes."

Rud nodded with satisfaction.

"There are millions and millions of tiny cracks in this type of underlay, and when it comes into contact with blood, the blood seeps into the crevices and stays put—year in and year out. It doesn't matter how much you rinse with soap and water or scrub it. Blood is virtually impossible to remove completely. It seeps under floorboards, into grout between tiles, into crevices and holes and cracks, and it . . ."

Rud was interrupted by Schäfer's telephone. It was connected to the car's intercom, and Heloise's voice filled the cabin as the call came through.

"Jan has photos of Mia Sark and Nina Dalsfort," she said. Her voice sounded uncharacteristically shrill and confused.

"What do you mean?" asked Schäfer.

"He has photos of the missing girls in his living room. What the *hell* is going on, Schäfer? I can't figure out what it is, he has . . ."

"Stop, stop!" said Schäfer. "What photos? Where?"

"In the house in Dragør. Inside the living room! He has a lot of framed photos sitting there. Two of them depict Mia and Nina, and there are photos of seven other young women that I don't know."

Schäfer frowned, staring out at the roadway in front of him as the white stripes flew by.

"Didn't you say that the film had been shot at Tom Mázoreck's house?" he asked. "That Mia Sark was attacked in the guesthouse?"

"Yes, but who says it was Mázoreck who was filming? We saw only one hand! Maybe it was Jan? Or maybe there were more of them," Heloise said. "Lisette Dalsfort believes that both Jan and Mázoreck and the other two from the mink farm were in on it."

"What is she basing that on?"

"I don't know, but I just received an e-mail from my source at TV 2. Do you remember me telling you that Hans Gallagher had recorded the incident on video when they caught Nina Dalsfort and the other three activists at Benniksgaard that night? That it was shown on television?"

"Yes?"

"I just received the recording."

"And?"

"And I haven't seen it yet, but . . ." Heloise was quiet for a moment. "I have a bad feeling, Schäfer. Something is *very* wrong!"

"Okay, listen!" he said. "I'm on my way over to you and I have my best forensic technician with me. We're driving across the bridge now. I reckon we'll be at the guesthouse you told us about by four PM. So let's meet out there and we'll take it from there, okay?"

"Okay, see you out there. Thank you, Schäfer," Heloise said, and hung up.

Schäfer relaxed a bit when he felt Sprogø under the tires, and Rud whistled happily next to him.

"Beautiful day, huh?" Rud looked out over the water and breathed deeply into his lungs. "Beautiful day to go to work!"

43

"HOW DO YOU kill them?"
The young female reporter held out the microphone to the man by her side. He had a gray-rimmed tweed cap on his head, dark shadows of stubble around his cheeks, and a hook of a nose.

"They're being euthanized inside this one," he said, patting the device he pushed in front of him— a brown box device on wheels. Dres Carstensen's name scrolled across the bottom of the screen as he spoke.

The computer was on the dining table in front of Heloise, and she leaned forward in her chair and turned up the volume.

"It's done by carbon monoxide poisoning, and it doesn't take more than half a second from when they go in there until they die." Carstensen snapped his fingers to illustrate. "They don't feel anything."

He turned away from the microphone and opened one of the steel wire cages, stuck a brown glove-clad hand into it, and took out a white mink. He held it out to the camera and stroked its back as it turned its head from side to side and up and down, nostrils quivering, pink eyes widened and watchful. Dres Carstensen opened a hatch in the box in front of him and let the animal slide down a chute that led into the stomach of the device, closed the hatch again, proceeded to the next cage, and repeated the procedure.

Heloise pressed the fast-forward button and watched as the film scrolled forward.

She pressed Play as the camera crew followed Carstensen into the fur house, where he demonstrated how it was done. A dead mink hung by its hind legs from metal clamps, and he made a quick cut between its legs with a scalpel. He stuck his fingers into the cut and peeled off the animal's fur in a quick jerk. What remained was something akin to the anatomy drawings Heloise remembered from public school biology classes—something that looked like a human thigh with red, sinewy muscles that overlapped and were covered with a thin film of fat.

Heloise frowned in disgust and thought of the threatening letters that Gallagher had told her Nina Dalsfort had had on her that night at Benniksgaard. The ones in which the activists had threatened to do to the mink farmers what they did to the animals.

She fast-forwarded further and stopped at the feature on the activists.

"Fur production is an issue that divides opinion both at home and abroad," said the host. "Some call it sabotage, others an act of liberation, when activists from organizations like Greenpeace and PETA break into mink farms around the world and let the animals out. Most recently, Benniksgaard Mink was the target of such action, but then the mink farmers took matters into their own hands. We need to warn viewers about disturbing images."

It was dark, and the handheld camera shook slightly. Heloise could see the Benniksgaard main house in the background, and in the gravel in the courtyard, three young men sat cross-legged with their hands behind their backs. A few yards to their right, a young woman was screaming. She lay on her stomach on the gravel, writhing violently, her hands and feet tied.

It must be Gallagher filming, Heloise thought. Dres Carstensen walked back and forth behind the young men with a rifle in his hands. He looked like he was looking for someone, probably the police.

Tom Mázoreck squatted in front of the girl. His eyes were on her, and his lips moved, but you couldn't hear what he was saying.

Nina Dalsfort's screams drowned out everything.

Behind Mázoreck, Jan Fischhof stood watching the girl as she lay on the ground, fighting to break free. Something white shone in his face, and Heloise felt the hairs on her neck stand up.

It was a smile.

CHAPTER

44

H ELOISE TURNED OFF the computer and leaned back in her chair. What the hell was going on? She stared at the phone next to the computer and considered calling Jan, and it gave her a start when the ringtone sounded.

She picked up the phone and looked at the screen. It didn't give any number.

"Hello?"

"Yes, hello, is this Heloise Kaldan?"

"Yes."

"Hello, my name is Elisabeth Ulvaeus. I understand you've been trying to get ahold of me."

"Elizabeth!" Heloise straightened up in her chair. "Thank you so much for calling back."

"Yes, I'm sorry I didn't get in touch before, but I've been sailing and haven't been online, so I only just now heard your messages."

"That's perfectly fine." Heloise stood up and began to walk back and forth in the living room. "It's great that you called because listen to this: I'm friends with your father, and I'm trying to find out what happened in Rinkenæs before you . . ."

"Yes, that's what I don't quite understand," Elisabeth said. "I think you've gotten things mixed up. Jan is not my father."

Heloise blinked uncomprehendingly. "What do you mean?"

"I'm Alice's daughter."

"I don't understand . . ." Heloise shook her head. "I thought . . . So who is your father?"

"My father's name was Leif. He died when I was little, and my mother met Jan a few years after I left home."

Heloise said nothing.

"When my mother died last year, I inherited the house, and I was supposed to sell it, but Jan was already sick at the time, so . . ."

Heloise stared into the air in confusion.

"I understand you're from the Vigil?" said Elizabeth.

"Yes . . ."

"I'm really sorry that I haven't been there as much as I'd like, but we . . . We live so far from each other and I . . ." She sounded guilt-ridden. "I really appreciate you all being there for him, so he doesn't . . ."

"Sorry, I don't understand . . ." Heloise shook her head. "If *you're* not Jan's daughter, then who is?"

"Then who is what?"

"Jan's daughter? What's her name?"

"I don't know anything about anyone . . ."

"He had a wife who died of cancer," Heloise said. "Back when he lived in Southern Jutland! He had a wife, and he had a daughter that he didn't . . ."

"I don't know anything about that," Elisabeth said. "He has never talked about his life in Southern Jutland."

"Has he never talked about his family?"

"I didn't even know he *had* a family." Elisabeth sounded flabbergasted. "My mother thought that he might have experienced something, because we could always see that something was wrong from his mood swings. But he never wanted to talk about it, so we . . . we just left it alone. But I really had no idea that he . . ."

The connection was severed.

Heloise tried several times to call Elisabeth back, but the call went directly to voicemail. She put her phone down and went up the stairs to the bathroom.

* * *

Heloise put her palms against the tiles, closed her eyes, and let the hot water from the shower head flow down over her face.

She felt exhausted and overwhelmed by the situation. There were so many questions, so few answers.

Why had Jan never told Alice and Elisabeth about his past?

An eye for an eye, Heloise. Tooth for tooth. The same damage he adds to another must be added to himself.

Who were the other girls in the pictures? Why did Jan have them displayed?

Blood . . . There was so much blood!

Heloise turned off the shower and wrung the water out of her hair. She stepped out of the shower and dried herself. She threw the towel on the floor and put on a pair of panties and a T-shirt. The mirror above the sink was fogged up, and she opened the window to let the steam out.

Her eyes moved across the yard, then she stiffened.

There, on the opposite side of the lawn, behind the weeping willows, she could discern the car parked out on the field road. The matte red varnish. The flip lights.

Heloise stood still, holding her breath as she listened. She heard footsteps in the gravel behind the house, and then she started running.

She ran into the bedroom, opened the wardrobe, and grabbed the Aya. Then she hurried down the stairs to the kitchen and emptied the box of cartridges on the kitchen table. They rolled over the countertop; several of them fell to the floor. She frantically picked two of them up, broke the barrel and loaded the gun with shaking hands.

The house was quiet.

She walked through the rooms one by one, the gun raised in front of her, peering out the windows she passed. Her heart pounded in her chest, and she cursed at herself for renting a place so isolated.

Was someone about to force themselves into the house? Had she even locked the front door?

She went out into the hallway to check, and it gave her a start when it was there was a hard knock from the outside.

Heloise raised the gun and aimed at the door. "WHO IS IT?" she shouted.

"My name is Johan Hessel," said the voice on the other side.

Heloise narrowed his eyes. "Who?"

"Johan Hessel. Are you the journalist?"

Heloise ripped open the door and aimed the gun at the man standing in front of the house.

His lips parted.

"Hey, hey!" he said, alarmed, raising his hands. "I just want to talk to you!"

"Who are you?" asked Heloise.

"My name is Johan. I was friends with Mia Sark. You were talking to her mother the other day? With Ingeborg?"

Heloise looked at him through narrowed eyes and recognized him from the picture. The last photo taken of Mia.

"Why the hell are you following me?" she asked.

"Ingeborg said it seemed like you knew something. That maybe you had found out what happened to Mia?" He still had his hands in the air. "If you know anything, I'd like to hear it. The police don't tell us anything."

Heloise looked at him for a long moment as her pulse subsided.

Then she lowered the gun.

45

"How did you know I was here?" asked Heloise.

"Everyone knows you're here," Johan said. He sat on the couch across from her. His gray sweater was blotched with sweat under his arms. His hands were rough, his cuticles black, and his gaze was tense under the shade of the red cap.

"A big-city reporter who rolls into Gråsten and starts investigating old police cases? That's all the town talks about. The Copenhagener who lives at Gerda's Memento."

Heloise smiled.

Big-city reporter . . .

"You were with Mia the night she disappeared," she said. "At the Tin Soldier?"

"Yes," he said. "It was me and Mia and a girl called Malou."

"Ingeborg told me that you still visit her every year."

"Every year on the anniversary," he nodded. "Of course, it's been many years ago now, but it still fills you. It . . . it's still *haunting*."

There was silence between them for a moment.

"I saw you were out at Celeste yesterday," he said carefully.

Heloise nodded.

"Do you think it was some of the people out there who hurt her?" His eyes brightened. "Do you think that's what happened?"

"No, Johan, I don't think so," Heloise said.

"But you think *someone* did? You think someone . . . killed her?"

Heloise took a deep breath. She couldn't bring herself to tell him about the video.

"Ingeborg said you hinted that Mia had been killed, so if you know something you aren't telling me, then . . ."

"No, I didn't say anything about that." Heloise shook her head uncomprehendingly.

"But you asked about Jan Fischhof."

"Yes, I mentioned Jan, and then she got absolutely hysterical and threw me out," Heloise said. "Why?"

"Because hope is the only thing that keeps Ingeborg alive. When you suddenly show up and ask about Fischhof, she naturally thinks it's because you believe there's a connection there." Johan shrugged with an indulgent expression. "She got scared."

Heloise stared at him. "A connection?"

"Yes, to what happened to his daughter."

Heloise stopped breathing. "What happened to her?" she asked.

"I . . . I thought you knew." Johan frowned. "She was murdered."

CHAPTER

46

HELOISE BREATHED A sigh of relief when she clapped eyes on Schäfer. He was leaning up against the hood of a black delivery van parked in the driveway in front of Renata Mázoreck's house, and a small, slender man with wild, white hair was emptying the van of cardboard boxes, tubs, and buckets.

Heloise parked next to the van and got out of the car. She walked straight into Schäfer's arms without saying anything.

"Hey you," he said, pressing her to him. "The cavalry has arrived."

She released her grip on Schäfer and looked over at the forensic technician he had brought with him.

"Heloise, Rud Johannsen—Rud, Heloise Kaldan," said Schäfer.

The little man shook Heloise's hand and bowed. "Enchanté!"

She nodded politely and turned her gaze back to Schäfer.

"Jan had a daughter who was murdered when he lived down here," she said. "Her name was Bianca. Bianca Fischhof."

Schäfer raised his eyebrows and looked at her in amazement.

"She was found killed in her apartment in Sønderborg," Heloise continued. "The police never found out who did it."

They looked at each other for a long moment as some of the pieces slowly fell into place.

"Well," Rud Johannsen said from behind Schäfer's shoulder. "Shall we see if we can find some blood?"

Heloise led them behind the main house and across the large lawn.

"It's in here," she said, walking over to the guesthouse. She pulled the door open and held it for Schäfer and Rud. All three of them went inside and looked around.

Rud Johannsen placed a battery-powered work lamp on the floor of the washroom and immediately began to study the cracking in the linoleum floor, the joints between the tiles, and the broken mirror. He walked around like an exterminator with a large, white spray bottle, spraying a colorless liquid over the ceiling, walls, and floor.

"What's the plan here?" asked Heloise.

"If Mia Sark was killed in here, there may still be traces of blood," Schäfer said. "And if Mázoreck brought other girls in here and seriously hurt them, for example Nina Dalsfort, then maybe there will be traces from her. If so, we can test the blood and see if we can DNA-match it with anyone. Maybe even with victims we don't know about yet."

"Well, folks," Rud Johannsen said, putting down the spray bottle. "If you'll close the door in here, I'll turn off the lamp and we'll see if there's anything to investigate."

Heloise walked over and pulled the door shut.

"The Luminol mixture that Rud sprays with reacts to blood," Schäfer said. "If there are traces of blood in here, they will show up as luminous blue spots and stains."

"Are you ready?" asked Rud.

He turned off the lamp, and the room exploded in a neon-blue firework display. The fluorescent spots lit up everywhere—on the walls, on the ceiling, on the floor.

"Jesus Christ," Schaefer muttered, looking around.

Heloise stared around the room.

"God, it's almost . . . it looks like Kusama's *Gleaming Lights of the Souls*," she said in awe. She had seen the light installation of the Japanese artist at the Louisiana Museum of

Art several times and each time had admired the luminous points as if they were stars in the sky. Now the sight was no longer so romantic.

"Shut the f—g *front door!*" said Rud Johannsen, slapping his thigh excitedly. "There's something to go on here, huh?"

He turned the lights back on and left the room to get more equipment out in the van.

Heloise and Schäfer followed him.

"What happens next?" she asked. "What does this mean?"

Schäfer looked over at the guesthouse. "It's best you ske-daddle," he said.

"Why?"

"Because I have no authority over here. It's outside my jurisdiction, and if someone finds out that Rud and I are sniffing around and investigating criminal cases that fall under the domain of the South Jutland Police, I could lose my job. It's better if you're not here. Too many chefs, you know."

Heloise nodded and pulled out her car keys.

"So what will you do?" asked Schäfer. "Are you flying home?"

"No, I'm going to see an old friend of mine who's the editor of one of the local newspapers down here. I called him on the way here and asked him to find out what he could about the murder of Bianca Fischhof."

"All right," Schaefer nodded. "Call if there is anything, okay?"

Heloise watched Rud Johannsen, who was heading back to the guesthouse with a cardboard box in his arms.

"Are you going back to Copenhagen tonight, or what are you doing?" she asked.

"No, this is going to take time."

"Okay, so take this." Heloise pulled a key out of her bag and handed it to Schäfer. "I'm not going to use the house I've rented, so you can just sleep out there if you want. There is plenty of space. I'll text you the address."

Schäfer accepted the key.

"What about you?" he asked. "Where are you going to sleep?"

"At my friend's house."

Schaefer raised an eyebrow. "Your friend the editor?"

"Yes."

"All right." He smiled slyly and put the key in his pocket. "Enjoy yourself!"

CHAPTER

47

H ELOISE SCROLLED THROUGH the articles on Infomedia.
The killing of Bianca Fischhof had apparently been
covered by all the newspapers in 1998, and the tabloid press
in particular had had a party with detailed descriptions of
The Bloodbath on Brandtsgade, as they had dubbed it.

"Oh no, listen to what it says here," she said, and looked
at Thomas, who had just come through the door. 'The iden-
tity of the woman who was killed in Sønderborg on the night
between April 2 and 3 has now been established, the South
Jutland Police state in a press release to Ritzau. The victim in
the case is Bianca Fischhof, 22 years old. Fischhof was a
second-year student at the nursing school in Sønderborg and
was killed with no less than thirty-seven stab wounds on
Wednesday night when an unknown assailant broke into her
apartment where she was alone. Early in the morning of
Friday, April 5, the slain woman's father found her and rang
the alarm'—oh my God!"

Heloise looked at Thomas.

"I've read it," he nodded. He went over to the table where
Heloise was sitting and hesitated for a moment before placing
a brown-paper envelope in front of her. "Here!"

Heloise looked up at him. "What is it?"

"It's what you're looking for. Details of the killing."
Heloise frowned.

"But how . . .?"

"I have a source in the police." Thomas turned around and opened the bar cabinet. "We need something strong, don't we?"

"Yes, please," Heloise said. "A source, you say?"

"Yes, someone who understands that the chain of command can be usefully restricted in connection with the right of access to documents."

He held two thick crystal glasses in one hand and, with the other, filled them with cognac.

Heloise raised an eyebrow. "Is this someone you're dating?"

"No, we've never *dated*."

"Someone you're banging, then?"

He half-shrugged and turned his palms upward. "Banged. Past tense."

"And you—what? You just asked her to track down the case file for you? Just like that?"

"Yes." Thomas handed Heloise one of the glasses. "But it's only for background. You can't use it in an article, and you can't tell your police friend from Copenhagen how you got access to it, okay?"

"Is it Jessica Rabbit? Are you dating that redhead with the breasts?"

"We're not dating." Thomas sat down across from Heloise and raised his glass to hers. "But it's quite nice to see you get so jealous."

Heloise looked down and smiled.

She reached for the envelope.

"Wait!" said Thomas, placing a hand on top of hers. "Before you open it, I have to say that there are things in that envelope that you won't be able to un-see afterward."

"Whatever it is, I've seen worse," Heloise said, and meant it.

She opened the envelope and poured the contents onto the kitchen table.

Although the images were grainy, the blood was overwhelming. They were police photos, and they had been taken in a living room where Bianca Fischhof—or what was left of her—was lying on the floor. She was wearing a black bra. The rest of her body was naked and smeared in blood. A long rope was wrapped around her neck, and traces of blood ran on the floor behind her, as if she had been dragged around the room.

There were stab wounds all over her body—large, open lacerations. On the face, on the arms. Across the chest and abdomen.

Thomas had been right. Heloise would never be able to erase these images from her mind's eye again.

"Have you ever seen the crime-scene photos of Sharon Tate?" he asked.

"Polanski's wife?" asked Heloise, looking up. "The actress who was killed by the Manson family?"

Thomas nodded.

"You'd almost think it was a deliberate attempt to replicate that murder scene," he said, pointing to the photo. "The rope around the neck, the positioning of the corpse . . . She also looks a bit like her—just with dark hair instead of blonde."

"Yes, except that Sharon Tate was pregnant," Heloise said.

"So was Bianca Fischhof."

She looked up. "She was pregnant?"

Thomas nodded.

Heloise turned her gaze to the slain woman and held a hand up in front of her mouth.

The woman's belly was not distended, but it was not flat either.

"Are you sure?" asked Heloise, without taking her hand away from her mouth. "There is nothing about it in any of the articles."

"It's in the police report," Thomas said. "She was in her fifth month and the child died. The press was never told."

Heloise looked down at the picture again and imagined Jan finding his daughter like this. How did you even continue living after stepping into such a nightmare?

She put the glass to her mouth and emptied it in one gulp.

"Who was the guy?" she asked, setting the glass down on the table. "Who was the father of the child?"

Heloise looked up at Thomas.

She knew the answer before he opened his mouth.

"René Decker," he said.

48

HORSESHOES CLICKED AGAINST asphalt, while hundreds of riders in black event jackets came riding along the harbor with long lances in hand. The Sønderborg Guard set the pace at the front of the field, and the cafés and restaurants along the water were packed with people.

"Sorry, I can barely hear you?" Heloise put a finger to one ear and pressed the phone to the other. "What did you say?"

"He's very far away," Ruth repeated. "I can barely make contact with him."

"But is he okay?"

"Yes, he ate dinner for once, and he doesn't seem to be in pain right now. He's watching TV, but he's just not really there. No one can talk to him."

"Okay, but . . . can you do me a favor, Ruth? Tell him I'll be back soon, and I'll get everything figured out. He won't have to worry anymore."

Heloise hung up the phone and turned to Thomas.

"What's going on?" she asked, pointing toward the horses.

"There's ring riding in town," Thomas said.

"What's that?"

"Yeah, what is that actually?" he said, looking out over the crowd of people. "It's a kind of modern version of the knight tournaments from the Middle Ages. It's an annual event. But instead of smashing the opponent with a lance, it's about getting it into a little ring, and whoever gets the most rings wins. Or something like that. I don't actually fully understand it, but I know that the most important thing about ring riding is not the horses, but the beers and the barbecued sausages and the carousels just over here at the ring-riding site." He pointed in the direction of the large square.

Heloise smiled. "You sound completely native."

"Yes, I've started saying howdy y'all, too."

"You're kidding!"

"No. You say that here!"

Heloise leaned her head back and laughed, and Thomas put his arm around her.

"Come on, let's get something to eat," he said, pointing to a small Italian restaurant, where a table for two had just become available.

* * *

"I feel kinda guilty," Heloise said after the waiter had accepted their order. "I just saw the most horrible pictures of Jan's daughter, and yet I somehow feel relieved."

"Relieved?"

"Yeah."

"Why?"

"Because for the past few days I've been afraid that he would turn out to not be the person I thought he was."

Thomas looked at her with wrinkled brows.

"Why were you so afraid of that? After all, you haven't known him for that long."

Heloise took a deep breath and hesitated. She shook her head.

"I don't know. It's probably just a bunch of nonsense."

She turned her attention to Sønderborg Castle, which was located at the end of the slips in the harbor.

"It sure is beautiful here, huh?"

Thomas's gaze was still on Heloise, his expression searching.

"I seem to remember that it was Valdemar the Great who built the castle," said Heloise. "Right?"

"What are you not telling me?" asked Thomas.

She turned her eyes to him.

"What do you mean?"

"Something has changed since the last time we saw each other, and it's not us. So what is it?"

Heloise looked down and sighed.

"Can't we just stay in the time warp we've been in for the last forty-eight hours?" she asked.

"What kind of time warp are you talking about?" Thomas shook his head questioningly. "We're right here, right now. What are you hiding from me?"

Heloise took a deep breath and exhaled slowly as she peered out over the water.

"I . . . I've been hurt since you last saw me." She turned her head and met Thomas's eyes. "My heart is broken."

Heloise saw him zoom in on her. He was quiet as he regarded her.

"Is it him, the Christiansborg reporter?"

"What? No!" Heloise frowned and shook her head. "No! It . . . he . . . It was never love."

"Then who?"

Heloise swallowed and met his gaze.

"I love that you loved my father."

"He was a good man," Thomas nodded.

"No," Heloise said, shaking her head slightly. "He wasn't." Her gaze moved across Thomas's face, and she smiled sadly. "I envy you that you remember him that way."

Thomas's eyebrows wrinkled and his lips parted in a silent question.

"But as long as you do that, it feels like it was all just a nightmare," Heloise said. "Now I've woken up and you're here and all is well again. If I tell you what happened, then I have to deal with reality again, and that . . ." She shook her head. "I can hardly cope with that, because when I think of my father, I just want to fucking . . . scream! I want to turn my face up to the sky and just *scream*, but . . ." A tear ran down her cheek. "I can't! I have this lump in my throat, this cancerous tumor of anger and sorrow and . . . and I . . ." She shook her head. "I can't get rid of it! When I open my mouth, no sound comes out, and I just . . ."

Thomas leaned forward and pulled her to him.

"Hey, hey, it's okay," he said. He stroked his hand over her hair and kissed her. "We don't have to talk about it until you're ready. We have plenty of time!"

*   *   *

The food came and they ate in silence as they watched the people along the harbor. It was a comfortable, safe silence— the kind you can only have with people who love you completely.

"Shall we go home?" asked Thomas.

Heloise nodded and watched him as he stood up to pay.

He disappeared into the restaurant, and Heloise's gaze slid along the castle and the moored sailboats, and across the old arch bridge that connected Als with the mainland.

Could she be happy here?

It was undeniably beautiful. The pace was calm, the nature wild, and the property prices reasonable. There was an everyone-knows-everyone aspect that she didn't like, but she could say the same about Copenhagen. It was always the same people she saw on the streets at home, the same people she'd kissed on the cheek through twenty consecutive years of city life. A small, intimate group of artists and media types who gossiped and conspired and screwed all over the place. And what exactly did she use the capital for when it came down to it? When was the last time she had been to the Royal Danish Theater or gone out for fun?

She took a deep breath and imagined life as it could be down here.

Maybe she could get a fresh start and finally distance herself from her father's crimes.

Heloise was toying with the idea of calling Bøttger and filing her resignation when a tanned face in the crowd in front of the restaurant tore her back to reality.

She straightened up in her chair and followed René Decker with her eyes. He was dressed in a black undershirt, light linen trousers, and a dark-gray felt fedora with cream-colored silk ribbons, and he was working his way sideways through the assembly.

Heloise looked over her shoulder and searched for Thomas, but couldn't see him.

She turned her gaze back to Decker.

He had slipped through the crowd and picked up speed. He had one hand in his pocket and a cigarette in the other and walked with quick steps past the table where Heloise was sitting, paying no attention to her.

As he turned a corner of a house down the street, she stood up and set out after him.

CHAPTER

49

THE EVENING AIR was warm, and the ring-riding square a
kaleidoscope of neon-colored lights from spinning carousels. The big Ferris wheel twinkled in the twilight to the
sound of tombola sellers calling people in, circus music, and
joyful shrieks.

Heloise followed René Decker as he walked into a huge
tent with tons of long tables and hundreds of people, and
then lost sight of him. People around her danced and bumped
into her. One band played an old song, the stage lights
flashed, and Heloise could feel the bass pounding hard in her
chest.

She was trying to orient herself in the throng of people
when a man stepped in front of her.

"Hey, what's your name?" he asked.

His eyes were half closed, his mouth open, and he stared
at Heloise as if she were naked. He stank of cheap aftershave
and sweat, and from the breast pocket of his open shirt a
bouquet of green test tubes filled with liquor shots stuck out.

Heloise ignored him.

She stretched her neck and spotted René Decker over the
man's shoulder. He was standing at the bar and talking to a
guy who was as big as a house. The guy's head was shaved,
and he had tattoos up his neck and across the crown of his
head; he shook his head and pursed his lips in regret.

Decker's jaw muscles tensed, and even though he was at least a head shorter than the giant in front of him, he grabbed his shirt collar with both hands and pulled him down to him in a quick, angry jerk.

Heloise couldn't hear the words being exchanged, but she saw the giant hanging his head as Decker pushed him back and chucked him away.

René Decker's gaze scanned irritably over the crowd and stopped at Heloise.

He stared at her stiffly for a long moment, then he looked down.

"Why are you so angry?" the man in front of Heloise asked, walking closer to her.

She spotted an opening and began to squeeze through, but the man grabbed her wrist and pulled her back.

"Hey, where are you going?" he asked. He maintained his grip on her arm.

"Let go of me," Heloise said.

"But smile! Why are you so angry, beautiful?"

Heloise pulled her hand away and became aware that she was surrounded. Four of the guy's friends had moved in on her, forming a circle around her.

The air suddenly felt clammy and heavy, as if there weren't enough oxygen inside the tent.

"Would you please move?" she said to the guy in front of her.

"What'll you give me if I do?" He smiled and looked her up and down.

"Move!"

He looked around at his friends and laughed.

Someone's hand brushed against her buttocks, someone else's against one of her breasts. They began moving closer to her.

"I said *move!*" cried Heloise. "Let me out!"

A hand grabbed the neck of the man and pushed him aside so hard that he fell and slid along the floor.

René Decker reached for Heloise and pulled her to him.

The four guys disappeared as if by magic, and the fifth quickly got to his feet, holding his hands up in front of him deprecatingly.

"Hey, sorry man. I'm not trying to make trouble, okay?"

René Decker stared at him coldly.

The man took a few steps backward, then turned around and hurried away.

René grabbed Heloise's arm and pulled her out of the tent.

"What are you doing here?" he asked, releasing her. He peered out beyond the square, avoiding her gaze. "You don't belong here!"

Heloise looked at the man who had pointed a gun at her twenty-four hours ago and thought of the headless corpse that had been washed ashore in Sønderborg Bay. She thought of Jes Decker and Pitbull. Of the pictures of Bianca Fischhof's dead body.

Her heart was pounding.

"I know what happened back then," she said. "With Bianca . . . I know what you lost."

"Have you found anything?" he asked without looking at her. "Did you find out what happened that night?"

Heloise shook his head. "I don't know anything concrete, but I . . . I have a theory. An idea of who did it."

"Mázoreck?"

"Yes."

Decker nodded. "That's what her father said too, but we . . ." He shook his head. "We never worked it out."

"So Jan also thought it was Tom Mázoreck who was behind it?" asked Heloise.

"Yeah."

"And do you think he . . . Do you think he avenged it?"

René Decker met her gaze and smiled. He nodded once. "I hope so."

* * *

Thomas got up from the steps in front of the restaurant and threw out his arms. "Where did you go?"

"I'm sorry," Heloise said, putting the phone back in her bag. "I was over on the square."

"I thought you'd run away again."

Heloise smiled and shook her head. "No, I wouldn't do that."

"Who were you talking to on the phone?" he asked.

"Schäfer."

"Are they still working out there?"

"No, they're done for today. They've taken hundreds of samples, he said, so now we'll see what they find."

"So what happens now?" asked Thomas, regarding her with warm eyes.

"What do you mean?" asked Heloise.

"What's the plan?" There were a thousand questions in his eyes.

Heloise took a deep breath and looked out over the water. Then she turned her gaze on Thomas and smiled.

"Shall we go home?"

50

SCHÄFER PARKED IN front of Restaurant Providence and strolled the last stretch down to the water. He tipped an imaginary hat as he passed a young couple out walking a golden retriever, then proceeded down to the beachfront property.

He checked the name on the mailbox and scouted out the house that was in the first row—an old, gray wooden house. The plot was marked off by a white picket fence, and a large porch ran all the way around the building. Warm light glowed from all windows, and Schäfer could see that there was an old man sitting in a rocking chair on the porch. The man quietly rocked back and forth. His gaze was on the water, and the smoke from his pipe reached Schäfer's nostrils. There were no other sounds but the soft creaking of the chair, the singing of the locusts in the grass, and the water that beat against the beach.

Schäfer knocked on the woodwork, and the old man looked down at him.

"Good evening," Schäfer said.

"Well, good evening," the man said, standing up. He went down to the gate to let Schäfer in. "I was starting to think you wouldn't come after all."

"Yeah, I'm sorry, but there was some work that dragged on."

"It doesn't matter," said the man, opening the garden gate. "Come on in."

Schäfer held out his hand. "Erik Schäfer."

"Kurt," the man said. "Kurt Linnet."

They went up to the porch, and Schäfer looked around. He nodded, impressed.

"You live pretty damn well here, huh?"

"That I do," Kurt said modestly, biting down on the pipe. He put his hands in his pockets and smiled contentedly. "Over forty-four years in this house and counting. "

Schäfer looked out over the fjord and drew the salty air deep into his lungs.

"Can I offer you something?" asked Kurt. "A beer maybe?"

"No, thanks," Schäfer said. "As I said on the phone earlier, I just want to hear what you remember from that night?"

Kurt Linnet signaled for Schäfer to take a seat in a garden chair. He set himself down in the rocking chair.

"It happened right here," he said, pointing out over the fjord. "A few hundred yards out."

"Did you see what happened?"

"Yes, because it was a bright summer evening, and I was looking for Tom's boat when I saw him coming around the point over there." Kurt pointed to the place he was talking about. "There were no other boats on the water, and I was sitting right here." He patted the armrests of the chair.

"I don't understand . . ." Schäfer leaned forward in his seat. "Did you sit and look for Mázoreck's boat before it appeared?"

"Yep."

Schäfer shook his head slightly. "But . . . how did you know he was out sailing?"

"I'd seen him down at the marina. I had a small vessel back then that was in the same place as Tom's Nimbus. I had been on the fjord that day, and on the way back I saw him as I docked. He was standing on the pier, and I could see that he was getting ready to sail out, so—yeah." Kurt shrugged. "He always used to come past here, so I looked for him when I got home after my boat trip."

"So you saw him alive that day just before the accident?"

"Mm-hmm." Kurt rocked back and forth in his chair, puffing on his pipe so the sweet smell of apple tobacco enveloped them.

"How did he seem?" asked Schäfer.

"Well, I don't know. He seemed like he usually did."

"Did you talk to him?"

"No, because I didn't want to disturb them."

"Them?" asked Schäfer.

"Yes, he was standing with another guy, and he was getting the boat ready for the trip. Actually, I thought they were on their way out together, and I also told the police that there were two men, but apparently I was wrong, because they only found Tom when they examined the fjord and the boat. You know, it went down right out here." He pointed with his pipe. "I guess it's still there. Down at the bottom."

"I understand that there was a fire on the boat," Schäfer said. "Was there an explosion?"

"I don't know how the fire started, I didn't hear any explosion," Kurt said. "When Tom came sailing along, I went in to get a beer from the kitchen, and when I came back I saw the smoke, but there was no loud bang." Kurt was silent and looked lost in thought at the memory. "I just saw the fire and then . . ."

"And then what?" asked Schäfer.

"Well, then . . ." Kurt noticed that his pipe had gone out and struck a match. "I called 911, but there was nothing to do when the police arrived." He sucked on the pipe as the flame took hold. "The policeman rowed out in a little dinghy I had lying around and fished Tom up." He blew out the match and shook his head. "It was terrible. Such a young man, and then life was just over? Terrible!"

"I know Zøllner from the old days, and I understand that he was the one who was here?"

"Which one of them?"

"What do you mean?"

"Which Zøllner?" asked Kurt.

"Is there more than one?"

"Yes, there's Steffen, and then there's Peter. They were both here that night."

"I know the policeman," Schäfer said. "The one named Peter. Who's the other?"

"Steffen is a doctor. They're cousins."

"Why was he here?" Schäfer looked questioningly at Kurt Linnet.

"To examine the body, I suppose. I'd called for an ambulance while Peter paddled out to get Tom, but when it arrived, he sent it away and called Steffen instead."

"Why?"

Kurt Linnet pulled his shoulders up to his ears. "I don't know. I was ordered inside when he came back with the body, so I could only follow from the kitchen window." He pointed to the window behind him. "But I guess it was because there was nothing to do. In any case, Peter said that it was easier for Steffen to investigate the matter. Moreover, Steffen is a certified diver, so he was the one who examined the hull to see if there were any other dead bodies; but as I said before, I was wrong. There was no one but Tom on that boat."

"The man who was with him at the marina earlier in the evening," Schäfer said. "Was that someone you knew?"

"Sure," Kurt nodded. He rocked back and forth in his chair. "It was a fella named Fischhof."

51

Schäfer slammed his knuckles hard against the front door and waited. The house was dark and there were no noises from inside.

"Zøllner!" he shouted. "Open up!"

Schäfer waited a moment and listened. A dog began to bay somewhere in the neighborhood. He walked around the house and found Peter Zøllner sitting in the dark in the open patio doorway facing the yard. He had a bottle of vodka in one hand and his service weapon in the other. His face was illuminated only by the moonlight.

"Well, there you are," Zøllner said when he caught sight of Schäfer. He playfully pointed the gun at him. "I wondered when you would show up."

Schäfer pulled his Heckler & Koch and aimed at him. "Put down your weapon, Peter!"

"What weapon?" Zøllner turned the gun on himself. He stared down into the barrel. "Do you mean this here?"

"Put it down!"

Zøllner rested his forehead against the mouth of the gun. He put his thumb on the trigger and closed his eyes.

"Stop!" said Schäfer. "Put down the gun!"

"I wake up every morning and ask myself why I'm here," Zøllner said. His speech was muffled. "Every single fucking morning . . ." He opened his eyes again. "I don't know why

I'm still here, Erik. Do you? Do you know what the point of it all is?"

"Put the gun down, Peter. Now!"

Zøllner threw the gun into the grass in front of Schäfer. He put the bottle to his lips and took a drink.

"Do what you want," he said, running the back of his hand over his mouth. "It doesn't matter anymore."

Schäfer picked up Zøllner's gun and stuck it in his waistband. He secured his own weapon.

"What the hell are you doing, man?" he asked softly, sitting down next to Zøllner. He put a hand on his shoulder.

"Lis is dead," Zøllner said, staring out into the air.

Schäfer pressed his lips together and nodded. "I know."

"And Nicky and Naomi, they . . . they are also gone. All of them are gone."

"I know," Schaefer repeated. "And I'm sorry about that. I really am."

Zøllner met his gaze and snorted slightly. He shook his head.

"Just say what you've come to say."

Schäfer pulled Mázoreck's death certificate out of his pocket and unfolded it.

"Tell me about this," he said.

Zøllner cast a quick look at the document but said nothing.

"Was it a homicide?" asked Schäfer.

Zøllner looked down at his feet and took a deep breath.

"I know everything about the girls," Schäfer said. "About Mia and Nina. About Jes Decker and his sex club out in Broager."

Still nothing.

"I just visited Kurt Linnet down in Stranderød, who says that he testified to you that he saw Fischhof with Mázoreck at the marina that night," Schäfer continued. "And I can see that it's your cousin who is a signatory on the death certificate. As an experienced doctor, he must be able to tell the difference between a homicide and a drowning—or at least know that such a body must always be sent for an autopsy.

How do you explain that there were no proper investigations into the case?"

Peter Zøllner stood up and walked over to the railing that separated the porch from the yard. He put his hands on the handrail.

"I was the one called out that morning," he said, his back to Schäfer.

"What are you talking about?" asked Schäfer. "What morning?"

"I got the case in Brandtsgade. Bianca, the poor girl, she . . . Her body was one open wound, and she . . ." He shook his head. "A witness had seen a car similar to Mázoreck's drive away that night, and I *knew* he had a grudge against Jes Decker. The girl was pregnant with Decker's grandchild, and I . . . I couldn't prove it, but I knew it was Mázoreck who had killed her." Zøllner's shoulders lifted for a moment as he took a deep breath. "So I . . . I contacted Jan. I told him that I suspected Mázoreck, and that Bianca was not the only one I suspected him of killing."

"Mia Sark and Nina Dalsfort?"

Zøllner nodded. "Mia and Nina, yes, and several others. Other young women who disappeared from the region in those years. I asked Jan to keep an eye on him. To record his actions. They both worked on the mink farm, so Jan had daily access to him."

"How did Fischhof react?"

"He got sick with rage. Said he was going to kill him! I told him to simmer down and use his anger to lure Mázoreck into a trap so we could gather evidence against him, and I thought I had talked him to his senses, but when I had Mázoreck pulled out of the water that night, I knew right away that it was a killing."

"How?"

"The fire had taken a good hold of him, but you could still make out stab wounds on his neck, and when Kurt told me that he had seen Mázoreck with Jan earlier that night, I knew what Jan had done and I . . . I let him get away with it."

"You didn't confront him?"

Zøllner shook his head. "He had already left. He had left a letter on the kitchen table in one of the official residences at Benniksgaard, where he lived."

"A letter?"

Zøllner nodded. He took a deep breath, his hands tightening their grip on the railing.

"It said he couldn't go on like this. At first, I thought it was a suicide note, but when I checked the apartment, I found that he had taken his passport with him. His wallet was also gone, so I thought he had cleared out and gone abroad. It's not until now that I find out he's lived in Zealand all these years."

"But you knew that a murder had been committed and you put a lid on the case?"

Peter Zøllner nodded.

Schäfer shook his head. "What the hell were you thinking?"

"A man should have that right." Peter Zøllner turned toward Schäfer. "His daughter had been murdered, Erik. She had been tortured. A pregnant woman! Twenty-two years old, for God's sake." His voice cracked. "It's possible that you see this kind of shit all the time and therefore have become immune, but what that young girl was subjected to . . ." He squeezed his eyes shut and shook his head. "I'll never forget it."

"But you're talking about vigilantism, Peter. About revenge! Shit, this is goddamn Southern Jutland. Not the Wild West."

"Lis was pregnant with Nicky when Bianca was killed. She was *pregnant*."

Schäfer said nothing, and Zøllner shook his head.

"You wouldn't understand," he said. "You don't have kids."

"It doesn't matter if I have children or not," Schäfer said angrily. "The law is the same for everyone! You can't just choose who should be allowed to break it. That's not how it works."

"I don't care. It worked! Mázoreck got what he deserved." Zøllner met Schäfer's gaze with his chin raised.

"And what about the parents of the other girls? Don't you think they deserved to know what had become of their children?"

"It wouldn't have brought them back."

"So instead of doing your job, you've let these parents live in uncertainty for twenty years? Twenty years during which Ingeborg Sark has been waiting for her daughter to come home. Twenty years in which the Dalsfort family has fallen apart because the mother has been obsessed with finding answers?"

Peter Zøllner looked down at the ground.

Schäfer shook his head.

"What about the other girls you were talking about?" he asked. "Were their bodies ever found?"

Zøllner shook his head. "I had the feed machine they used on the mink farm tested and there were traces of blood in it. DNA from three different people, bone fragments, tooth splinters. It wasn't a match for Mia or Nina, and I never found out who they were."

Schäfer was quiet for a moment as the meaning of what Zøllner had just said sank in, and he frowned in disgust.

"Are you telling me that he fed his victims to the minks?"

Zøllner nodded absentmindedly.

"At least some of them. I started looking at the jobs Mázoreck had had, and I found out that he had been working nights at The Brickworks in Egernsund for a number of years. I examined the ovens they had out there: temperatures of over a thousand degrees. Throw a corpse in there and it's dust and ashes in seconds."

Zøllner took a swig from the bottle.

"On the mink farm, containers with mink carcasses were transported to Germany for bioprocessing every Friday, and Mázoreck worked part-time at a slaughterhouse out in Blans and was responsible for the production of the feed they used at Benniksgaard. Can't you see it?" asked Zøllner. "He arranged his life to get rid of his victims. Bianca's case was the only one where we found a body. The only one where he changed his behavior."

"Why did he do that?" asked Schäfer.

"Because he wanted her to be found. It was classic over-kill: thirty-seven stab wounds, her head was practically chopped off. I think Mázoreck wanted the Decker family to know what she had been subjected to. It was a kind of fuck you all!"

Schäfer was quiet as he pondered what Zøllner had said. He pulled out a cigarette from his shirt pocket and stuck it in his mouth.

"Did you make a fake file on Mia Sark?" he asked, lighting the cigarette.

Zøllner narrowed his eyes. "What do you mean?"

"Did you fiddle with the papers?" He took a long drag and pulled the smoke into his lungs. "Did you make it look like a trafficking case?"

Zøllner looked down and nodded.

"Why?"

"Because the Decker family kept asking questions about the investigation of Bianca's case. They sought me out for years, sent one henchman after another and threatened my life because I had no answers for them. I didn't want anyone to know what Jan had done, so I thought it was best if the cases didn't seem to be related. I have a colleague that I've always suspected of working for Decker, so . . . At some point, I changed some of the information in the file."

Schäfer ran a finger over the stitching above his eye and nodded. "Who else but you and your cousin knows what happened that night on the fjord?"

"Can't we keep Steffen out of this?" asked Zøllner. "He was just trying to do the right thing."

"He clearly didn't succeed," Schäfer said pointedly. "Things need to be cleaned up down here, Peter. The cases and your police district, both."

Zøllner hung his head.

"Now you reopen those cases tomorrow morning and invite me officially into the investigation, and then you send an urgent request for a warrant so we can dig up Tom Mázoreck's body," Schäfer said.

"Dig him up? Why?"

"Because the guesthouse where he lived is completely covered in traces of blood. We need to match it with the girls so that families can know what happened, and we need DNA from Mázoreck for exclusion. Moreover, his death must be investigated as a homicide."

"What are you going to do about Fischhof?" asked Zøllner.

"If he lives long enough, he must answer for what he's done."

Zøllner met Schäfer's eyes.

"What are you going to do to me?"

Schäfer took a pull on his cigarette and looked at the man in front of him. He felt sympathy for him and understood the dilemma he had faced.

But the law was the same for everyone.

"It's going to cost you your job, Peter."

SUNDAY, JULY 14

52

S CHÄFER CAUGHT SIGHT of Heloise as he drove up in front of the church, quietly cursing to himself. She stood in the parking lot with her back to him, looking out over Rinkenæs Cemetery, which lay in front of them and sloped down toward Flensburg Fjord.

He parked next to her car and got out.

"What are you doing here?" he asked, trying to keep the irritation out of his voice. He had called her an hour earlier and told her what he had found out—what Zøllner had told him about the killing of Mázoreck and the missing girls. He felt he owed it to Heloise to keep her updated, but he had explicitly asked her to stay away from the exhumation.

"The local authorities are here, and I can't justify to them having a journalist in tow."

Heloise turned around.

"This is my case, Schäfer. If anyone has to follow it through, it's me."

"It's a police matter now," he said. "It's no longer about your friendship with Fischhof."

"It is for me!" Heloise met his gaze with a stubborn expression.

They stared at each other for a long moment.

Then Schäfer reluctantly nodded.

"Okay, but you don't say a word to anyone but me when we get there, is that understood? You are an observer—nothing else. Not a word!" He pointed a warning finger at her.

Heloise nodded in agreement.

They entered the cemetery and saw the grave diggers preparing to raise Mázoreck's coffin.

"Where is Zøllner?" asked Heloise, looking around.

"He's sleeping it off," Schäfer said. "I was with him all night while we went through all the cases and reopened them one by one, and then this morning the warrant came."

His phone hummed in his inner pocket. He pulled it out and looked at the screen.

"I have to take this one," he said, and pointed to the grass in front of him. "Wait here!"

He answered the call and walked a few steps away from Heloise.

"Yo! What's up?"

"Hey, how is the eye doing?" asked Bertelsen.

"It's still working," Schäfer said, looking out over the water. "Is there something new?"

"No, I just ran into Augustine; she says "hi," and there is still no breakthrough in the case of the assholes who beat up on you."

"That's okay," Schäfer said. "I think I have an idea of who's behind it."

He thought about what Zøllner had told him about Jes Decker's henchmen: that they had been demanding answers from him for years. It could well be that they'd been sent to Copenhagen to find out if Schäfer had new information about the killing of Bianca Fischhof.

"What about Wilkins?" he asked. "Has there been progress there?"

"Yes, we have a suspect," Bertelsen said.

"Who?"

"The neighbor's eighteen-year-old son. We have a surveillance camera that caught him and Wilkins fighting down on the Esplanade that night."

"Is he under arrest?"

"Yes. A patrol car has just picked him up at Herlufsholm boarding school where he's a student. He was at a party in Østerbro on the night of the killing, and he didn't show up for classes the next day. They're coming back with him now."

"All right," Schäfer said, nodding in satisfaction. "I'd like to be at the interrogation, so can you guys wait to talk to him until I get back? I'm not in Sjælland right now, but I expect I'll be there in the early evening."

"Okay, we'll wait," Bertelsen said. "We'll throw him in the cell and let him shit his pants until you come."

Schäfer ended the call and walked back to Heloise. He looked over at the crane that was raising the coffin with Tom Mázoreck's body from the hole in the ground.

"Is this the first time you've seen a corpse dug up?" he asked, sticking a cigarette between his lips.

Heloise waved a fly away from her face and nodded.

Schäfer fished his lighter out of his pocket. "It's no joke, ll tell you that."

"COME ON, COME on!" Heloise pressed the button feverishly as the elevator doors slowly slid closed, and she watched the floor numbers that lit up the board, one by one, as the elevator was pulled rapidly upward. It had been three hours since she received the call from the Vigil as she stood in the cemetery in Rinkenæs with Schäfer. Three hours in which Fischhof had drifted further and further away from her. Although the flight home to Copenhagen had lasted the same thirty-five minutes as the trip out, it had felt infinitely long. She had sat above the clouds, squeezing her fingers white against the armrest, praying to a god she didn't know if she believed in. Asking to arrive in time—to be allowed to say a few last words. When she had landed in Copenhagen, she had received a text message from Ruth telling her to go directly from the airport to the State Hospital instead of driving out to Dragør.

Was she too late?

The elevator doors opened, and Heloise hurried out and looked around. She found the department she was looking for and quickly moved down the long hallway. At the opposite end stood a lab-coat-clad woman and a young man. They both looked up at the sound of her soles beating against the floor.

"Kaldan?" the man asked as she reached them.

Heloise could see from the room number that they were standing in front of Jan Fischhof's room.

"Is he dead?" she asked, feeling the muscles in her throat contract.

"Markus Senger," he said, extending his hand. "We spoke on the phone earlier today."

Heloise shook his hand without taking her eyes off the door.

"Is he dead?" she repeated.

"No, but we've given him painkillers to the extent possible, so you need to be prepared for him to be very far away." It was the woman in the white coat who spoke. "He's breathing on his own, but he's no longer conscious, so it's a matter of hours, or maybe minutes, before he . . ."

Heloise didn't wait for the woman to finish. She walked over and opened the door to the hospital room.

* * *

The afternoon sun shone through the window of the small room. Jan Fischhof was lying in a bed in the middle of the room, looking more peaceful than Heloise had dared to hope for. In her mind, she had seen him writhing in pain, entangled in rubber tubes with invasive needles in his body, scared and alone. But apart from the ECG machine beeping softly next to the headboard, the hospital room almost looked like a bedroom. Even the oxygen apparatus that used to follow him everywhere was gone. He lay as if sleeping a deep, comfortable sleep, with his hands on his chest and his lips slightly parted.

By his side sat Ruth. Her eyes shone wetly, and she let out a relieved sob as Heloise walked through the door.

"Oh, thank God. I was afraid you wouldn't make it. He kept asking for you last night."

"I came as fast as I could," Heloise said, walking to the bed.

Ruth stood up and put her arms around her. Heloise could feel the woman's chest quiver and her stomach surge in hiccupping thrusts.

"All right, then," Ruth said, letting go of Heloise. She wiped her eyes with her palms. "Sit down now. Then I'll leave you in peace to say goodbye."

"Can he hear me?" asked Heloise.

Ruth looked down at Jan Fischhof and shrugged.

"I don't know. I have sat and sung some hymns to him because the doctor said it could be calming. It certainly can't hurt to try."

Ruth walked over and put her hand on Fischhof's arm and stayed like that for a long moment before turning around and leaving the room.

Heloise pulled the chair Ruth had been sitting on closer to the bed and sat down on the body-warm seat. She looked at Fischhof's face and the vein throbbing slowly in his temple.

Heloise leaned close to him and put his hand in hers. She took a deep breath.

"It's me. Heloise," she began. "I'm sorry I'm only getting here now. I . . . I promised you that I would send you off, so I hope you can hear me."

She was silent as she waited for a reaction—a sign that he was still in there somewhere.

There was no trace of change in his face.

"I hope you know I'm your friend," Heloise continued, squeezing his hand. "I know what you've done and I'm still your friend. I'm not a priest, but if it's absolution you're looking for, know that *I* don't blame you for what you've done. Do you hear what I'm saying? I don't blame you!"

There was a muted moan from Jan Fischhof, which Heloise chose to interpret as a sigh of relief. An indefinable expression flickered across his face, pulling lightly at one corner of his mouth.

"Just let go," Heloise said, stroking the back of his hand. "You have nothing to be afraid of."

She put his hand to her cheek, and that's how she stayed. Waiting.

She had lost track of time when the alarm from the ECG machine sounded, but the light from the window shone orange-red and the sun had sunk below the horizon.

She knew it was over.

54

T HE DOOR TO the hospital room opened, and the doctor whom Heloise had spoken to in the hallway entered the room. Her movements were calm and methodical, and the quick look she gave Heloise underscored an expected priority: the patient first, then the relative.

She pressed a button on the monitor, where a flat, neon-green line rolled dead across the screen, and the alarm immediately fell silent.

There was no panic. No shouting for assistance or red lights flashing and howling. No charging of cardiac defibrillators needed to bring Jan Fischhof back to life.

It was just past.

The doctor put two fingers on his neck and stood still for a moment. "Did you get to say goodbye?" she asked, without taking her eyes off Fischhof.

Heloise's mouth felt as if it were full of dust, and the word came out like a whisper.

"Yes." She cleared her throat and swallowed a couple of times. "But I don't know if he heard me."

The doctor put the stethoscope in her ears, pulled the collar of Fischhof's hospital shirt down a little, and put the shiny chest piece against his skin. She listened for a moment, shifted the stethoscope a little, and listened again. She hung the stethoscope back around her neck and turned to Heloise.

"Hearing is one of the last senses to disappear. Although dying patients or people in a coma do not respond to voices, studies of brain activity in this group of patients show that in many cases they register the sounds around them."

"I think at one point he looked like he was trying to smile."

"He probably did," said the doctor, looking at Heloise with furrowed brows. "How are you?"

Heloise shrugged. "Okay, I guess."

"Is there anyone we should notify? Family members or something?"

"No, there is only a stepdaughter, and she lives abroad. I'll call her."

"How about a pastor? There's a hospital chaplain on the ward if you think there's a need for it."

Heloise shook her head.

The doctor put her hands into her coat pockets. "When you're done here, we'll take him down to what we call the six-hour room and later down to the hospital mortuary."

Heloise nodded.

"There are many who sing their loved ones out. I don't know if it's something you're interested in?"

"Sing them out?" asked Heloise.

"Yes, a hymn or something. While the dead is carried out."

Heloise shook her head. "It's only me here, so . . ."

"What about the woman who was with him earlier? She's waiting in the day room."

"Ruth?"

"Yes, I think she's waiting for you."

* * *

Ruth rose from her chair in the living room and hugged Heloise as a mother would embrace her child. The gesture touched Heloise, and it struck her that Ruth might have no one to care for but those she met on their way through the Vigil's domino trail of dying. Heloise took her hand and let it go only when they stood next to the hospital bed together, looking at the man they had both come to care about.

"I'm so glad you made it," Ruth said. "He was only waiting for you, I'm sure."

"I'm glad too," Heloise said.

There was a black garment bag hanging on the door of the bathroom. Ruth unzipped the bag and took out a dark suit, a white shirt, and a tie patterned in blue. She placed the clothes on the foot of the bed at Fischhof's feet and smoothed them carefully with her hands.

"What is that?" asked Heloise.

"These are the clothes he asked to be dressed in when we reached this moment. It was several months ago that I had it cleaned so it could be ready for him, because he got quite upset at the thought of being seen in this hospital get-up." Ruth smiled at the memory of Fischhof's overdramatized outbursts.

Heloise laughed and wiped away a tear at the same time. "I can imagine."

"The old grumbler!" smiled Ruth. "But, deep down, he was all right."

"The doctor asked if we wanted to sing him out. What do you say to that?"

"Yes, that's a nice gesture. We can sing *Always Cheerful When You Go*? Or *Look, Now the Sun Rises from the Lap of the Sea*? It's so beautiful," said Ruth. "Could you give me a hand getting him dressed?"

Heloise helped get Fischhof into a sitting position so they could get the white terry-cloth shirt off him.

"Can you get the shirt?" asked Ruth, pointing with her chin to the foot of the bed.

Heloise let go of Fischhof and went to get it, while Ruth continued to maneuver the hospital shirt off him.

"After he's been to the six-hour room, they'll take him down to the mortuary," Heloise said, turning to Ruth again. "The doctor asked if a pastor should come by to say a few words, but I don't think Jan would . . ."

Heloise stiffened.

Her breathing stopped as she stared at the man lying in the bed in front of her, and she let the shirt fall to the floor.

Her gaze slid over the scars running in parallel streaks over his left shoulder—red, thickened lacerations where pit-bull teeth had once ripped the skin.

Horror rose into her body, squeezing the air out of her lungs.

"No," she murmured.

She bumped against the bedside table as she took a step backward and a vase of flowers hit the floor.

Ruth looked up with a start.

"Heloise, you're white as a ghost?" she exclaimed. "Are you okay?"

Heloise shook her head.

She turned around and yanked the door open.

*   *   *

"Glad you called!" Schäfer's voice chattered good-humoredly on the phone. "I'm over at forensics, and Oppermann is about to open Mázoreck, or whatever is left of him, up as we speak. He's badly burned in the face and on most of his torso, so it's a little trickier than I expected, but I think we'll know something within the next few . . ."

"It's not him," Heloise said. She stepped through the sliding doors and headed for the park across the street. She didn't know where she was going—she just had to leave.

"Pardon me?" The connection crackled. "What did you say?"

As if in a nightmare, Heloise's voice lost its strength, and the words came out in a whisper.

"The body from the coffin . . . It's not him. It's not Mázoreck."

"You have to speak a little louder. I can't hear what you . . ."

"He fooled me. He . . . he fooled all of us." Heloise released her grip on the phone.

She walked a few steps, fell to her knees, and sank her fingers into the grass beneath her.

She breathed in quick, shallow jolts, as images of young women flashed past her mind's eye.

She had been holding his hand. She had given him absolution.

Heloise turned her eyes to the sky.

Then came the scream.

SATURDAY, AUGUST 10

Epilogue

THE RAIN FELL heavily for the third week in a row and whipped the petals off the flowers in Gråsten Cemetery. The pea gravel shone wet in the footpaths, and the birdbath by the neighboring grave was filled to the brim.

Heloise stared down into the open grave in front of her. The coffin that had been lowered down rested on the muddy bottom, and the rain drummed hard on the lid. It shone like a freshly polished sports car and had cost almost as much. Heloise had swiped the credit card at the funeral home without blinking and now felt that neither the coffin nor the opulent creation of white lilies lying on top made inroads into the feelings of guilt burning in her chest.

"I know this sounds weird when I've never met him," she said, "but . . . It feels like I'm burying a friend."

Schäfer nodded.

"It's a nice headstone you got for him," he said.

Heloise looked at the granite block that lay next to the tomb, ready to be raised.

Jan Fischhof, it said. * January 18, 1951—† August 1, 1998.

"I couldn't get a plot next to Bianca, but at least now they are closer to each other than they were before, and he lies under his own name . . ."

Heloise nodded to herself. Her hair was soaked, and the rain ran down over her face and into her mouth.

Schäfer looked intently at her as a bullet train roared past on the tracks that ran along the cemetery.

"It is not your responsibility to remedy what Mázoreck did. You know that, right?"

Heloise said nothing.

"You can't atone on his behalf, nor should you. You haven't done anything wrong!"

Heloise stared down at the hole. "Haven't I?"

"No," said Schäfer. "You haven't."

Heloise said nothing.

She squatted down in front of the grave and reached for a handful of wet soil. She held her hand over the hole and took a deep breath. Then she let the soil fall.

*   *   *

"Thank you for driving all the way down here once again," Heloise said as they approached Schäfer's car.

"You're welcome," he said. "I didn't think it was something you should go through alone."

He pointed the car key at his black Honda, and there was a loud double beep.

"I'm just sorry I have to go back home already, but I have an important date."

"A date?"

"Yes. Connie and I are having our silver wedding anniversary."

Heloise smiled in surprise. "It's you guys' silver wedding anniversary today?"

Schäfer nodded. "Twenty-five long ones."

Heloise hugged him hard.

"You're a lucky man," she whispered in his ear.

"I am indeed."

He gave her a kiss on the cheek. Then he directed his gaze to the black Range Rover that was driving up in front of the chapel.

"I'll have to greet your editor-in-chief another time, okay?"

Heloise nodded and watched as Schäfer got into his car and drove away. Then she walked over to Thomas and hopped into the passenger seat.

"Thank you for coming," she said, closing the door behind her.

"Of course," he said. "I would have come earlier if I'd known you were here."

"Yes, I know, but . . . it just seemed like something I had to finish with Schäfer."

Thomas nodded.

"What would you like to do?" he asked, turning the key in the ignition. He looked at her expectantly. "Where do you want to go?"

Heloise glanced at her watch.

"We can't really do very much," she said. "My flight is in a few hours."

Thomas nodded.

The car sat still, and for a moment neither of them said anything.

Heloise stared at the windshield wipers whipping across the front of the windshield.

"I don't want to go home," she said.

"You don't have to," Thomas said.

Heloise met his gaze. "Don't I?"

He shook his head. "You can stay here with me."

"For how long?" she asked.

"As long as you want."